Praise for Am

'Her character-driven books, which feature trolls, hobgoblins and mystic elements, and keep the pages turning, have generated an excitement not felt in the industry since Stephenie Meyer or perhaps even J. K. Rowling' *New York Times*

'A fast-paced romance . . . addictive' *Guardian*

'In terms of page-turning immediacy, they are unrivalled'
Daily Telegraph

'Drew me in and kept me hooked . . . cracking pace' *Sunday Express*

'Well-told . . . You can have fun and get lost in a world'
Irish Independent

'Amanda Hocking is one of the most experienced and successful first-time novelists around' *SFX*

'There is no denying that Amanda Hocking knows how to tell a good story and keep readers coming back for more. More is exactly what they will be looking for once they've turned the last page'
Kirkus Reviews

'Hocking's novel effectively melds myth and contemporary teen life. High school, family, young love, and mythology all combine to create an easy-to-read paranormal suspense story that will have fans eagerly awaiting new instalments' *Booklist*

'Amanda Hocking has a gift for storytelling that will grip readers and keep them wanting more . . . Entrancing' *LibraryThing*

'I ate this book up. I could barely put it down before bed, and was also trying to sneak time in my busy morning to read some extra sentences. This was an awesome first book in a series' *Midnight Glance*

'I started reading *Switched* in the evening one night and stayed up until 3 a.m. because I didn't want to put it down . . . Yes, it's *that* good' *A Tale of Many Reviews*

'I read these three books back-to-back-to-back on my Kindle. The story had me so engaged that I could not put it down. I was reading in the car, at school, on my bed, at the dinner table and in the media room. You could call it an obsession' *Reading Vacation*

'This series has a bit of everything – magic, myth, action, romance . . . ah, the romance! There is something so appealing about forbidden love . . . Of course, I won't give spoilers, but the ending was perfect' *Diary of a Bibliophile*

'I absolutely looooveeed *Switched*. From the first pages I found myself totally caught up, stealing moments to read this book. Visually I "saw" this book so well in my head. Just an awesome read that makes you feel for the characters' *Novels on the Run*

'Full of adventure, tense moments – the sort of "what is going to happen next" moments, a romance and a great plot . . . I will definitely be looking out for the next book in the series!' *It's Time to Read*

Ice Kissed

AMANDA HOCKING lives in Minnesota, had never sold a book before April 2010 and has now sold over a million. According to the *Observer,* she is now 'the most spectacular example of an author striking gold through ebooks.' Amanda is a self-confessed 'Obsessive Tweeter. John Hughes mourner. Batman devotee. Muppets activist. Unicorn enthusiast.' Please see more at www.worldofamandahocking.com

The Trylle Trilogy

Switched
Torn
Ascend

Trylle: The Complete Trilogy

The Watersong series

Wake
Lullaby
Tidal
Elegy

The Kanin Chronicles

Frostfire
Ice Kissed

Ice Kissed

Amanda Hocking

TOR

First published 2015 by St Martin's Press

First published in the UK 2015 by Tor
an imprint of Pan Macmillan, a division of Macmillan Publishers Limited
Pan Macmillan, 20 New Wharf Road, London N1 9RR
Basingstoke and Oxford
Associated companies throughout the world
www.panmacmillan.com

ISBN 978-1-4472-5682-3

1 3 5 7 9 8 6 4 2

A CIP catalogue record for this book is available from the British Library.

Printed and bound by CPI Group (UK) Ltd, Croydon, CR0 4YY

Ice Kissed

ONE

retention

Fresh snowflakes stung my face, so I closed my eyes and lowered my head and urged Bloom to run faster. For being one of the largest Tralla horses in Doldastam, Bloom was surprisingly quick, and his heavy hooves plowed through the snow as he raced beside the stone walls that surrounded the town.

My head had begun throbbing again—a dull pain that radiated out from the gash just under my hairline along my right temple, held together with six stitches. I tried to ignore it, the same way I had any time the pain had flared up over the last two days, and gripped Bloom's reins tighter.

Late last night, Ridley Dresden and I had arrived back home from our job in the Skojare capital of Storvatten. Though we'd been released from our duties since the mission was declared complete, I would hardly call it over. Konstantin Black had escaped, and the Queen we'd gone to find was still unaccounted for.

All the royals were resigned to the fact that Queen Linnea Biâelse was probably dead, most likely killed before Ridley and I had even arrived in Storvatten, so none of them held her persistent absence against us. In fact, the missing Queen's brother-in-law, Prince Kennet Biâelse, had seen us out, and he seemed concerned that we didn't judge ourselves too harshly.

In the majestic hall of the Storvatten palace, with its frosty glass walls shaped to look like waves encircling us, Kennet had stood with Ridley and me by the door.

"I'm very sorry we weren't able to do more," I apologized once more before we departed.

"You did all you could." Kennet stared down at me, his aquamarine eyes sparkling like jewels, and sighed heavily, making the nearly translucent gills just below his jaw flutter.

Then he took one of my hands, holding it warmly in both of his. While I was surprised by the heat and strength of his large hands encircling mine, I felt too numb to really register it. The failure of the mission left me distraught and defeated, and after the previous night's attack my head was still in a painful fog.

"Don't be too hard on yourself, Bryn," Kennet said in a voice like rolling thunder. "You're better than you give yourself credit for."

"We should get going," Ridley interjected, "if we want to make it back to Doldastam by nightfall."

"Yes, of course." Kennet smiled wanly and seemed reluctant to let my hand go. I tried to smile back at him, but I couldn't muster it in my current state.

Ridley had the front door open for me. As we stepped out

of the palace of glass, Kennet called after us, "I hope to see you again. You're both always welcome here."

I said nothing in reply, because I had no intention of ever returning to Storvatten or to that palace. With no sign of Linnea or Konstantin, there would be no reason for me to ever come back.

When we'd left Storvatten, my memory of Konstantin Black's escape from the prison was still a bit of a blur. My head injury made it difficult for me to think clearly or recall the incidents surrounding my skull being smashed into the stone wall of the dungeon.

Ridley had scoured Konstantin's cell before we left Storvatten, hoping to find a few hairs or a bit of cloth that he could use to track him. But Konstantin was smart—long before he'd become a traitor to the Kanin, he'd been a tracker. He knew how our world worked, so he hadn't left a trace of himself behind for Ridley to get a read on, making it impossible for us to know where he had gone.

On the long ride back home, Ridley drove, and I lay with my head pressed against the cold window of the SUV, trying to force my mind into clarity.

I told Ridley the truth about Konstantin's escape—that I had gone down to the dungeon to reason with him and find out what happened to the missing Queen Linnea, and that Konstantin had already gotten out of his cell. I'd been overpowered, and he'd escaped. But I had left out one glaring detail—it wasn't Konstantin who had smashed my head into the wall until I was unconscious.

That had been Viktor Dålig.

Fifteen years ago, Viktor had tried to overthrow the Kanin King Evert, and in the process, he'd killed Ridley's father. Since that attempted coup, no one had seen or heard from him.

Then, out of the shadows, he'd appeared in the Storvatten dungeon to help Konstantin Black escape.

I knew I needed to tell Ridley, but I was terrified that my memory was playing tricks on me. The attack still felt jumbled and hazy. What if the head trauma made me recall Viktor's face when he'd never been there?

But now as I rode Bloom through the falling snow, pushing him hard as though I could somehow escape the truth, I realized I was more afraid that my memories were right. That Viktor Dålig had been there, and I hadn't stopped him. I'd let the two greatest enemies of our kingdom get away.

TWO

concession

The King stood with his back to us, warming his hands over the crackling fireplace. A cold snap had descended on the kingdom, and even in the palace we could hear the icy wind beating against the stone walls.

None of us said anything as we waited for King Evert Strinne to take his seat at the head of his table next to his wife, Queen Mina. The Queen sat rigidly in her seat, and Ridley and I sat across from her at the other end of the long table. Though she looked in our direction, her gaze seemed to go right through us.

Normally she had a softness to her—in the way her body leaned toward you, as if she really cared about what you were saying—and her gray eyes had a warmth in them. But it was as though the cold had somehow gotten deep inside her, and she sat frozen in her chair with a white fur cape draped over her slender shoulders.

In her lap sat a small, white Gotland rabbit, Vita. It was the Queen's personal pet, and she sometimes brought her with her to meetings, although I hadn't seen Vita much lately. As we spoke, Mina pet the rabbit absently.

"So." Evert finally turned away from the fireplace. His dark blazer had a bit of a shimmer to it, making the light from the flames dance across it as he walked over to his high-backed chair. "I take it from Bryn's injury that things did not go well in Storvatten."

I lowered my head, hoping my blond hair would fall forward enough to cover the bruise on my temple, but it was an awful dark purple and extended to my eyebrow. It was hard to hide. Fortunately, my worst injury was behind my hairline. Stitches mended the nasty gash, and my waves of hair helped to mask the swelling and discoloration.

"It could've gone better," Ridley admitted. "But overall, it wasn't terrible."

"Evert spoke with Prince Kennet on the phone yesterday before you arrived back in Doldastam," Mina said, and her voice lilted with the subtle British accent she used on occasion, usually to impress visiting dignitaries or other royals. "We know *exactly* how everything went in Storvatten."

I stiffened in my chair, instinctively pulling my shoulders back, but I kept my expression even. While I was disappointed in my own performance, I also knew that the failings in Storvatten weren't entirely my fault. The Skojare had inadequate guards and security, not to mention a weakly protected prison.

King Evert held up his hand, the gaudy diamonds on his

platinum rings catching the light, and silenced his wife. "I want to hear how you think it went in your own words."

"Well." Ridley shifted his weight in his seat and cleared his throat. "We were tasked with locating the missing Skojare Queen, but all our efforts for gathering information were stonewalled. The Prince refused to tell us anything or let us speak to any possible witnesses."

Mina raised her chin haughtily, and her eyes were hard. "I didn't realize the Prince had that much power."

"He got his orders from the King, but we were almost solely in contact with the Prince. He was the one who directed us," Ridley elaborated. "We went out to search the area for possible clues as to what happened to the Queen, and that's when Bryn and a Trylle ambassador managed to apprehend Konstantin Black and Bent Stum."

"You overpowered Konstantin?" Evert appraised me, appearing impressed for a moment.

"Yes," I said. "I subdued him and brought him back to the palace, where he was placed in the dungeon, along with Bent Stum."

"It's my understanding that Bent killed himself?" Evert asked.

"Yes, we believe he took his life shortly after being placed in the cell," Ridley answered. "Later, Bryn went down to question Konstantin further, and he'd gotten free from his cell. He assaulted her and knocked her unconscious, and then he fled."

"That . . ." I took a deep breath, steeling myself for their reactions. "That's not entirely accurate."

From the corner of my eye, I could see Ridley turn to look at me, but I refused to look back. I kept my gaze fixed on the King.

"Oh?" Evert sat up straighter. "What did happen then?"

"I went down to question Konstantin, and he was already out of his cell—that part was true," I said. "But what I didn't realize initially was that he wasn't alone. It wasn't until it was too late that I saw that Viktor Dålig was also there."

Mina breathed in sharply, and Ridley swore softly next to me. King Evert's expression faltered, but only for a second, and then he narrowed his eyes at me.

"Viktor Dålig?" Evert asked. "You're sure it was him?"

"I've been training as a tracker since I was twelve," I said. "I've seen his Wanted poster hundreds of times. I'm sure it was him."

Evert turned away, toying with his rings as he stared into the distance thoughtfully. The Queen looked like she had been punched in the stomach. Ridley's hands were on the table, balled up into fists, and his breath came out in angry bursts through his nose.

"Why didn't you say anything sooner?" Evert asked finally, still looking away.

"Viktor slammed my head repeatedly into the stone wall of the dungeon," I explained. "I couldn't remember things very well at first, and I wanted to be absolutely certain before I said anything."

Evert turned to look at me, his dark eyes on mine. "And you're certain now?"

"Yes, I am," I told him honestly.

"Did he say anything?" Evert asked.

"He just told Konstantin to kill me, and when Konstantin didn't act fast enough, Viktor grabbed me and attacked me."

"This changes everything," Evert said with a heavy sigh. "We must prepare for war."

"Based on the word of a tracker with brain damage?" Mina nearly shouted in disbelief, and I bristled.

"Viktor Dålig has already tried to kill me once," said King Evert, "and he's been on the run for well over a decade. I have no idea what he's been up to in that time, but if he's been working with Konstantin Black I must assume he's grown even more dangerous. I will not let him make an attempt on my life again."

"These are all assumptions." Mina shook her head. "You can't prepare for war on assumptions, especially when we don't know what we're up against or where our enemy might be."

"Mina, I value your counsel, but on this matter, my decision has already been made," Evert told her firmly. "We will find him, and we will destroy him, and that's final."

Mina lowered her eyes, holding Vita more closely to her, and she said nothing more after that. Evert stood up, saying he needed to meet with advisors, but he'd be calling on Ridley soon. If we were preparing for war, Ridley would have to gather the trackers and start readying them to be soldiers.

As soon as we were dismissed, Ridley stood up and stormed out of the meeting room. I followed quickly, but his strides were long and angry and it took me a moment to catch up with him.

"Ridley," I called after him as we walked down the palace hallway, empty apart from a few maids with their hands full of cleaning supplies. "Wait."

He whirled on me then, his dark eyes blazing, his lips pressed together. I couldn't help but think back to when his eyes had blazed in an entirely different way a few days ago, when he'd pulled me into his arms and pressed his lips passionately against mine.

But whatever desire he'd held for me was gone, replaced by barely restrained anger. "You should've told me, Bryn."

"I wasn't sure—"

"That's bullshit!" he roared, and I flinched. The maids were at the other end of the hallway, and they glanced back at us before hurrying on. "That may be why you didn't tell the King right away, but you should've told *me.*"

"I'm sorry," I said, since there was nothing else I could say.

He ran his hand through his dark hair and looked away from me, his jaw set hard. "I know things have been . . . complicated between us lately, but that's no excuse not to tell me this."

"That's not why." I hurried to reason with him. "I just had to be sure. I couldn't tell you something this big without being absolutely certain."

He smirked darkly at me. "So you thought it would be better to blindside me in a meeting with the King and Queen?"

"No, I . . . I wasn't thinking." And that was the truth. Everything had been such a mess lately, and I hadn't been able to think clearly—especially when it came to Ridley. "I screwed up. I'm sorry."

"No." Ridley waved his hands and took a step back from me. "I don't need your apologies, Bryn. And I think for right now it'd probably be best if we stayed away from each other as much as we can."

"Ridley," I said lamely, but I didn't argue with him.

Then he turned and walked away, his footsteps echoing heavily in the empty hall, and as my head began to ache again I felt more alone than I had in a long time.

THREE

militia

When I stepped into the gymnasium, the noise from training fell to a dull murmur, and I could feel eyes turning toward me as the door groaned shut behind me. Thanks to my Skojare-esque appearance, I was used to being stared at in Doldastam—my blond hair and pale skin had always stood out in stark contrast to the tan skin and dark hair of the rest of the Kanin. But this was way beyond normal.

Since the King had officially declared war on Viktor Dålig, Konstantin Black, and all of their associates yesterday afternoon, the tracker school had been turned into an army training camp.

The changes had fallen over the city swiftly and quietly. As I'd walked to the tracker school in the blowing snow, I'd noticed Högdragen standing guard in front of houses—two in front of the more important Markis and Marksinna homes, while one was enough for the less notable families. In the least prominent neighborhoods, one guard would be enough for a whole block.

Even this room full of trackers seemed different: some stood in rows listening to an instructor, while others ran laps and still others did combat drills. Yesterday they had been merely trackers, but now they were soldiers, preparing for a war with an enemy that they might never encounter.

All these changes had taken place because of me, because of what I'd told the King, and because I'd let Viktor Dålig and Konstantin Black slip through my fingers once again. That's why everyone looked at me, their expressions ranging from respect to skepticism to annoyance.

Ember Holmes broke through the trackers practicing combat drills. Her dark hair bounced in a ponytail behind her, but her bangs were damp with sweat, making them stick to her olive skin.

Boxing tape bound her hands, but her knuckles were still red and one of them was bleeding. To make up for her petite size, she fought twice as hard as anybody else, and I'm sure she'd given her training opponent a run for his money today.

"Haven't any of you ever seen another tracker before?" Ember asked over her shoulder, casting an irritated glare at everyone in the gym as she walked toward me.

The teacher instructing the trackers barked an order, and that seemed to get everyone back in motion. The volume in the room returned to normal, and I could feel eyes shift away from me.

"You're late," Ember pointed out, as if I weren't aware. "I thought you might be taking the day off to recuperate."

"I had considered it," I told her, but that was a lie. The headaches still flared up intermittently, and occasionally the vision in my right eye blurred for a few minutes. But I didn't need any more time to rest. I was ready to get back to work.

I just hadn't wanted to come here and deal with all this. Especially when I didn't know what the point of the heightened security was. Viktor Dålig and Konstantin Black were dangerous, but we didn't know where there were, and there were only two of them. It wasn't like we were planning to invade another tribe or country. An army felt unnecessary.

"Bryn Aven." Tilda Moller smirked down at me, but there was a playful gleam in her smoky eyes. "Nice of you to join us."

Unlike the other trackers who were dressed in workout clothes, Tilda had on a tailored black linen jacket with epaulets on the shoulders and matching trousers—our army uniform. The jacket hung open, revealing a white shirt and the subtle curve of her belly. Her hair was pulled back into a smooth ponytail, and with a clipboard and papers in hand Tilda looked every bit the part of an officer.

"I didn't expect to see you here." I smiled up at her. "I was afraid you were on leave."

"Modified duty," she corrected me. "I won't be fighting, but I can help organize and make assignments."

"Where do you want me then?" It didn't really matter where Tilda put me, as long I was doing something. I had plenty of frustration I needed to get out.

As Tilda ran her finger down the clipboard, I caught sight

of a shiny new silver band wrapped around the ring finger on her left hand.

"Whoa, what's that?" Ember asked, noticing the same thing I had.

"Oh, this old thing?" Tilda laughed, and her cheeks reddened as she held up her hand for us to get a better look. "Kasper actually proposed to me at the beginning of the month, but I've been waiting to tell anyone until after I'd told you about the baby. Since you guys know, I thought I ought to start wearing the ring."

"Oh my gosh, Tilda! Congratulations!" Ember squealed and threw her arms around Tilda, giving her an awkward bear hug.

I smiled. "Yeah, congrats. That's great news."

"I'm glad you're both so excited," Tilda said, carefully prying herself out of Ember's hug. "Because I was going to see if you two wanted to be my bridesmaids?"

"Are you kidding me?" Ember asked, and she was so excited I feared she might actually explode.

"Yeah, of course," I said. "It would be an honor."

"When is it? What do you want me to wear?" Ember asked in one quick breath.

"Well, that's another thing," Tilda said, appearing sheepish. "We were originally thinking we'd get married in a couple months, before the baby was born. But with everything that's going on right now, we decided we want to do it sooner rather than later. So we're thinking the third of May."

"That's only a little over a week away," I said in surprise.

"I know, I know, but we're all here, and you and Ember could get sent off on a mission at any moment," Tilda explained. "We just wanted something small and intimate anyway, and we love each other, so why not do it now?"

She looked at me hopefully, almost asking for my approval. After the way I'd botched the news about her pregnancy, I knew I had to handle things much more maturely this time.

I smiled. "You're right, and that sounds really great, Tilda. I'll be happy to help you celebrate your day whenever you want me to."

"Thanks." She looked relieved then waved her hand. "Anyway. We can talk about all the wedding stuff later. Right now, we should all get to work."

"Right. So what should I be doing now?" I asked again and cast a glance around the room to see what my options were.

"If you're up to it, you could work on combat training with Ember," Tilda suggested, apparently deciding to go with her gut instead of the clipboard.

"Good. The guy I've been going against could use a break anyway," Ember added with a laugh.

That did sound like the best possibility, but my attention was elsewhere so I didn't immediately reply. While I was scanning the room, I'd spotted Ridley in the far corner, nearly hidden behind the boxing ring. A group of maybe twenty trackers sat on the floor around him, staring up with rapt interest as he paced in front of them.

I was too far away to hear him over the noise of the gym, but his arms were clasped behind his back and he spoke with a kind of intensity. He wore the same uniform as Tilda, though his jacket was buttoned up and he had a large silver rabbit pinned to his jacket—the sign that he was the Överste.

In times of war, the Rektor took on the role of the head officer overseeing the army. The head of the Högdragen, the Chancellor, and the King all ranked above him. The Överste made no decisions in terms of battle, but the position still had great responsibility in commanding the trackers/soldiers and preparing them for their orders.

"Bryn?" Ember was saying my name, but I didn't look back at her.

"What's going on over there?" I asked and motioned toward Ridley.

"Ridley's training the scouts," Tilda answered.

I turned back to her. "Scouts?"

"They're going to go out and find Viktor Dålig and Konstantin Black," Tilda explained. "They're supposed to find the base camp, get a rough idea of how large Viktor's operation is, and then report back to us. Based on the scouts' information, we'll send out troops to find Viktor and everyone that works for him, and destroy them.

"The Högdragen will stay behind, so Doldastam's not left unprotected while all the trackers—sorry, troops—are off to war," Tilda finished, and I remembered the guards I'd seen stationed at doorsteps.

Until—and *if*—scouts found Viktor Dålig, we had no idea when or where he would strike again. That meant everyone here would be on high alert as a precaution, especially since we still didn't understand what he or Konstantin wanted.

"And before you ask, no, you can't join the scouts," Tilda said, her eyes apologetic. "Ridley told me to tell you."

"It's probably just because you're injured," Ember said. "Just like how I didn't go on the last mission, because I'd broken my arm." She swung her arm around now, fully healed by medics since Bent Stum had broken it.

Tilda looked down at me, her full lips pressed together and her eyes grim, and she didn't say anything. Like me, she knew my injury wasn't the reason I was being held back. I'd already let Viktor Dålig get away once. They weren't about to let me make that mistake again.

"We should get training," I said, because I was tired of talking.

Tilda nodded then walked away, checking over the papers as she did. Ember led me to a spot on the mats where she'd been practicing. Her partner had moved on to work with someone else, and when he saw that Ember would be training with me and not him, he appeared relieved.

I wrapped my hands with boxing tape while Ember explained what specific moves she'd been instructed to focus on today. When I finished, I tossed the tape aside and glanced over at Ridley. He happened to look up at the same time, and his eyes met mine.

Even across the room, I could see the anger still burning in them. He hadn't forgiven me yet, and I wasn't sure if he ever would.

Then Ember's fist collided painfully with my jaw, and I swung at her instinctively. She blocked her face, so I went for her stomach—connecting solidly with the firm muscles of her abdomen.

She gasped in pain, but smiled broadly at me. "Now that's more like it."

FOUR

compunction

The wind had calmed down some, so I left my jacket open, letting the air freeze the sweat that still stuck to me. After we'd finished training for the day, Ember had insisted that I join her for a treat at the bakery in the town square, saying we'd earned it. Tilda had to finish up some paperwork, and then she planned to meet us so we could talk more in depth about her wedding plans.

My muscles already ached and my right wrist cracked loudly every time I moved it, but I wasn't sure I felt like I'd earned anything. The day left me feeling more like a failure than I already had.

Several inches of snow had piled up while we'd been working. Although there were still tracks from people and animals braving the weather, the streets were mostly deserted. The Kanin could handle whatever the weather threw at them, but that didn't mean they were masochists. Most of us knew when it was worth it to stay in by the fire.

But Ember didn't seem to mind. She just pulled her hat down over her ears and trudged through the snow banks.

"You were awfully quiet today," Ember commented as we made our way down to the bakery.

I shrugged. "I was just training."

"It's more than that." She paused before adding, "You know no one blames you."

"Some people do."

Ember scoffed. "Those people are stupid. Everyone who knows you knows that you did everything you could to stop Viktor Dålig and Konstantin."

We'd been outside long enough that the cold had started to get to me, but I didn't zip up my jacket. I just clenched my jaw, refusing to let my teeth chatter.

An oversized white husky was digging through the garbage outside the butcher shop. Large snowflakes clung to his thick fur. He looked at me as we passed by, his bright blue eyes seeming to look straight through me, and a chill ran down my spine. I quickly looked away.

"What if I didn't do everything I could?" I asked.

Ember was so startled that she halted. "What? What are you talking about?"

"I mean, I did." I turned back to face her, since I had walked a few steps after she'd stopped, and behind her I saw the husky had returned to rooting through the trash buried beneath the snow.

Ember narrowed her eyes. "Then what are you saying?"

"I don't know." I let out a deep breath, and it was shaky from the cold. I turned my head toward the sky, blinking back the snowflakes that hit my lashes. "I did everything I could, but it wasn't good enough. So then . . . what does it matter?"

There was something more to it than that, though. Something I couldn't explain to Ember.

Viktor Dålig had beaten me, that was true. The sight of him had been like encountering a ghost, and I'd been in shock, so he'd been able to get the best of me. That didn't mean I hadn't wanted to stop him, but it had been my fault for letting myself be caught off guard, even for a moment.

But Viktor had wanted to kill me. When he'd smashed my head into the stone, he'd been trying to execute me—I knew that with absolute certainty. But he hadn't succeeded, and I had a feeling that I had Konstantin Black to thank for being alive.

Run, white rabbit, as fast and far as you can, he'd whispered when I came upon him in the dungeon. Even though he'd been escaping, he'd looked so defeated then—his gray eyes soft and mournful, his entire body sagging, his olive skin going pale beneath the shadow of his beard. Konstantin hadn't wanted me to get hurt.

I'd been convinced that Konstantin had been working for someone, that his attack on my father and his plots to go after changelings weren't his idea. In Storvatten, he'd even said as much to me, telling me that he'd done it all for love. Whatever that meant.

"What happened in Storvatten?" Ember stepped closer to

me. "You never even told me about Viktor Dålig. I've had to hear everything through other people," she added, trying not to sound hurt that I hadn't confided in her more.

"What have you heard?" I tilted my head, curious to know what people were saying.

"That he surprised you and overpowered you, and then he escaped with Konstantin," she explained with a weak shrug. "Is there anything more to it than that? Did Viktor say anything to you?"

The butcher leaned out the back door of his shop and banged loudly on a metal pan, scaring the husky. The dog gave one hungry glance in my direction before running off and disappearing into the snow.

"No. He didn't say anything." I shook my head. "But . . ."

"But what?"

The wind came up a bit, blowing my blond waves of hair in front of my face, and I brushed them back absently. Ember pulled her jacket tighter around her, but she kept her dark eyes locked on me.

"I can't help but feel like if I'd found the Queen, I'd have some answers," I said finally, deciding that part of the truth was better than admitting that I didn't think Konstantin was as evil as I once had.

"The Skojare Queen?" Her brow pinched, not understanding. "I thought she was dead."

"That's the theory," I said. "I wanted to look for her more, but the Skojare King called off the search, and Ridley said there wasn't anything left for us to do."

"If the Skojare King doesn't want you looking anymore, then Ridley's right," Ember said.

"I know, but . . ." I chewed my lip. "If I could find Linnea, I think I could find out what Konstantin is up to."

"*If* you find her, and that's assuming she's even alive," Ember pointed out. I lowered my eyes but didn't say anything. "And you have direct orders to stay here and prepare for war. You can't go off on some kind of wild-goose chase at a time like this."

"I know." I let out a reluctant sigh. "I just hate feeling so useless."

"Everything that's happened lately has to have been rough on you." Ember looped her arm through mine and started leading me away, toward the bakery. "But that doesn't mean you're useless. You're strong and you're smart. You're a great soldier, and that's important too."

We rounded the corner, and the sweet scent of pastries wafted through the air. My stomach rumbled, and I realized I'd skipped lunch that day. I'd been so focused on my training that I'd completely forgotten about it.

I began fantasizing about a delicious blackberry tart—a wonderful combination of sweet and bitter, with an emphasis on the bitter. But my momentary good mood immediately soured when the door to the bakery opened, and Juni Sköld stepped out into the snow.

It wasn't exactly the sight of her that made me freeze in my tracks. Juni worked at the bakery, so I shouldn't have been that surprised to see her here. She had to be one of the nicest people in all of Doldastam, and her luminescent skin literally radiated with happiness and kindness.

It was who she was with, and what she meant to him, that made me stop cold. Following right behind her was Ridley Dresden. He still wore his uniform, so he'd come here right from work to walk his girlfriend home.

"What's wrong?" Ember asked. Since her arm was looped with mine, she'd been forced to stop alongside me.

Juni was laughing at something Ridley had said, but then she turned, and as soon as she spotted us her smile widened. Ridley, on the other hand, looked stricken at the sight of me.

I'm certain that part of it was because he was still angry at me. But another part was probably because he'd kissed me—*twice*—since he'd been dating Juni. The first time was only a few short blocks from here, and it had been so passionate and so intense that even thinking about it now made my pulse race and my stomach swirl with butterflies.

"Bryn!" Juni exclaimed, walking over to me while Ridley trailed several slow steps behind her. "It's so good to see you! How are you holding up?"

"I'm . . ." I couldn't even muster a fake smile.

Seeing her sheer delight and genuine concern for my well-being made me recognize that I had to be one of the worst beings who ever lived. And that was combined with the way Ridley was acting right then—shoving his hands in his pockets, avoiding looking at me at all costs. When his eyes finally did manage to land on me, his gaze was so harsh I felt about two inches tall.

"We've had a long day," Ember supplied, since it seemed that I would stand there forever without saying anything.

"I'm just cold," I said suddenly. "I think I should get inside."

"Well, you stay warm," Juni said, but she looked puzzled. "And take care."

"Thanks, you too." I ducked my head down and hurried toward the bakery as fast as I could.

"Why didn't you say anything to her?" I heard Juni ask Ridley as I pulled open the door. "Are you two fighting?"

I practically ran inside the bakery so I wouldn't have to hear his answer.

FIVE

archives

The day started rough, and it ended with me falling asleep among stacks of books in the palace library. It began with a five a.m. run around the outside of the school, shoving through the massive drifts of snow with all the other trackers. Ridley walked alongside us, barking orders and demanding that we push ourselves harder.

And I did. I pushed myself all day, through every workout and obstacle course and combat training session. The hope was that eventually I would be too exhausted to think. If I drove my body to the very brink, all my concerns about Konstantin and everything that had happened in Skojare would finally die out. Not because I wasn't still worried, but because I no longer had the strength to worry.

It didn't matter, though. My entire body ached from the strain, but the thought wouldn't stop gnawing at the back of my mind—I had left unfinished business in Storvatten. I'd been sent to find Queen Linnea, and I hadn't. And with all the signs pointing to the fact that Konstantin Black had to have had some part in her disappearance, Linnea had to know *something*. She might even be able to shed light on his connection to Viktor Dålig.

But since I had no idea where she was or if she was even alive, I had to move on to other sources. After training had finished up, Ember invited me to go out with her and a few other trackers to the wine bar in the town square. I declined, telling her that I needed to get some rest, but that was a white lie. Ember would offer to join me if I explained what I was up to, but she'd worked hard all day. She deserved to have fun instead of helping me to try to work off my guilt.

The library in the palace was always open to the public, but by the looks of it it had been at least a day or two since anyone had visited. It was an immense room with bookshelves lining the walls from floor to ceiling, nearly two stories above.

The room was dark and freezing, so the first thing I did was get a fire going in the hearth. A large window lined one wall, and all the panes had been frosted over. When I walked past it on my way to search for books, a cold draft blew in through the cracks.

The Kanin took their history very, very seriously. There were shelves upon shelves of tomes on lineage, public records, and accounts of events dating back hundreds of years. Fortunately, the ones I wanted were more recent, so they were located on the lower shelves, which meant I didn't have to use the precarious ladders to reach them.

In trying to find a connection between Konstantin Black and Viktor Dålig, I decided to go to the most obvious place—family lineage. Before he had been condemned as a traitor and stripped of his title, Viktor had been a Markis, so his bloodlines were recorded in great detail in a fine, black leather-bound volume with gold lettering on the spine and cover.

Although Viktor had been a fairly high-ranking Markis, his wife had actually been higher—a Kanin Princess, with both her father and her brother holding the crown. Had she not died in childbirth twenty-two years ago, she would've most certainly been Queen after her brother King Elliot Strinne's death, which meant Viktor would've been King.

But that was not how things had gone.

I went back several generations, trying to see if there had been overlap with any nonroyal Kanin, but Viktor's bloodline remained unsoiled. He shared ancestors with my father, but that wasn't a surprise to me. If I went back far enough, every Markis and Marksinna in Doldastam shared an ancestor.

While tracker lineage is important—the purity of all bloodlines is important to the Kanin—it's valued less than that of the royalty. The book detailing Konstantin's lineage wasn't as well made, so it was more worn, with the older pages in the front coming loose.

Konstantin's family records were just as detailed as Viktor's, but his family was much smaller. He'd been an only child orphaned at an early age, and his parents had come from small families of trackers. Especially in the past, when medical treatment had been harder to come by, the infant mortality rate had been very high for trackers, and it showed in Konstantin's family tree.

But he had come from a long line of trackers who had survived against the odds, which probably explained his determination and strength. He was the very best many generations had to offer.

Nowhere in Konstantin's past did the records show any familial mingling with Viktor Dålig. The two were of no relation, classes apart. They should have no connection to each other.

When the bloodlines proved fruitless, I moved on to the records of recent history—most notably Viktor's attempts at overthrowing the King. Much had been written about them, and I'd had to read about them often while I'd been in school, but I needed a refresher.

King Elliot Strinne had become very ill, very fast. It started with a severe headache, and within a few days he was dead. His death was eventually attributed to complications due to meningitis, and that winter there were three more cases of meningitis in Doldastam—including Chancellor Berit Abbott—although thankfully, no one else died from the disease.

The panic of the illness was also quickly overshadowed by the controversy surrounding the King's death and the appointment of his heir. The most direct heir to the throne at the time was been his niece, but she was only ten.

There also hadn't been a Queen in power without a King by her side in well over two hundred years, and while I would have liked to believe the patriarchal nature of Kanin society hadn't affected the decision to pass over the King's niece, that was most likely wishful thinking.

Chancellor Berit—along with a board of advisors—had decided to appoint Elliot's cousin Evert Strinne as King, despite Viktor Dålig's protests that his daughter should be next in line. On January 15, 1999—two weeks after Elliot's death—Evert was crowned as the King of the Kanin.

It was then, while I was reading the passage about Evert being sworn in, that my heart froze.

At 1:08 p.m. on the fifteenth of January in the year nineteen-hundred-ninety-nine, Evert Henrik Strinne took the oath of the King, with the acting-Chancellor Iver Aven officiating.

In the late 1990s, my father, Iver Aven, had been working his way up the political ladder, and eventually he worked underneath the Chancellor. When Berit Abbott had become ill with symptoms of meningitis, he'd had to take a step back from his duties to focus on his recuperation. That left my father to fill in as the Chancellor.

When King Evert had been sworn in, I had just turned four, so I have only vague memories of the time—mostly the dark colors of the funeral and the bright colors of the banners and flowers at the coronation. I had known that my father worked for his predecessor, Chancellor Berit, and I had heard that Dad had sworn in the King, but that fact had never seemed important.

In history class, that bit had always been glossed over—the King was sworn in by the Chancellor, blah blah blah, and since my father was acting under the umbrella of Berit Abbott's authority, it was Berit who had signed the official document. My dad acting in the Chancellor's absence was perhaps the most benign part of how Evert had become King, but now I realized it might hold extreme weight: it was the connection between Konstantin Black and Viktor Dålig.

Two days after Evert was crowned, Viktor Dålig had led a coup trying to overthrow Evert in an effort to get the "rightful" monarch—his daughter—on the throne. He'd killed four members of the Högdragen before being captured. Over the next week, a brief trial was held, with the King presiding. Viktor was convicted of treason, stripped of his title, and sentenced to be executed the following day.

In a move that many believed extreme, King Evert also stripped Viktor Dålig's three young daughters of their titles and inheritance, and banished them from Doldastam and Kanin society. This enraged Viktor, leading him to swear vengeance on anyone who had anything to do with the verdict.

At the time, Evert had laughed it off, but during the night Viktor Dålig managed to escape from his cell, and he had been on the run for the past fifteen years.

My father had nothing to do with Viktor's conviction, since it was King Evert's decision and his alone. But Viktor had been in attendance at the coronation, as had everyone in Doldastam, when Evert was crowned. He had to have seen my father swearing him in, and with Berit Abbott's illness, it was easy to believe that my dad had helped the council decide that Evert should be crowned over Viktor's daughter.

This could finally be the explanation for Konstantin Black's attempt on my dad's life four years ago. It was just an extension of Viktor's revenge.

The actual Chancellor at the time of Evert's ascension to the throne, Berit Abbott, had succumbed to the damages of his disease, forcing him to step down in 2001 when my dad took over his job. Berit died not much longer after that. Time had already gotten its vengeance on Berit, so Konstantin had moved on to the next guilty party—my dad.

But why would Konstantin care? He'd been seventeen at the time of that whole mess, a tracker with aspirations of becoming a member of the Högdragen, but no affiliations with the royalty. By all accounts, he was a loyal servant of the kingdom, with no hints of rebellion or mutiny.

How would Viktor have recruited Konstantin to join him for his vengeance? And why wait so long to get started on it? When Konstantin had attempted to kill my dad, it was eleven years since Viktor declared vengeance on the King.

And what did any of this have to do with Konstantin going after the changelings? Perhaps he was attempting to be some kind of Pied Piper—taking all the children until he received his payment, which in this scenario I could only imagine would be the King's head.

But that didn't explain Viktor's interest in the Skojare. They had nothing to do with the perceived slight against Viktor or his family, so they did nothing for his for retribution.

I could see connections that hadn't been clear before, but there were still pieces missing, leaving me feeling more frustrated than ever. Surrounded by books and all the information of my people, I could find no answers.

The fire was now only embers, but I preferred the cold, hoping it would help keep me awake as I sat hunched over the old books. Eventually, though, my body collapsed with exhaustion. I don't even remember falling asleep.

One moment I was reading, the lines of text blurring in the dim light, and the next I was dreaming nothing but white. Then, slowly, I saw a face begin to take shape, and eyelids fluttered open, revealing startling sapphire eyes.

Somehow, I knew it was Linnea, the missing Skojare Queen.

Her lips appeared, bright red from the lipstick she wore, and her face was fully visible, surrounded by a halo of platinum blond curls and backlit by a bright white light. And then, as if she were whispering right in my ear, I heard her.

Come find me.

SIX

tonåren

As I approached the house where I'd grown up, I could see my mom shoveling snow off the front walk.

Her long blond waves of hair were falling free from their loose bun, and the cold had left a bit of rose on her fair cheeks. Mom was on the tall side, and while her beauty and lithe figure appeared deceptively delicate, she was athletic and strong, able to toss away shovels full of heavy, wet snow with ease.

"Bryn!" Mom smiled broadly at me. "I wasn't expecting you today. I would've thought you had training today."

"It's Saturday, so we have a break," I lied.

While preparing for war, there were no breaks. On Sundays, our training would be slightly more relaxed, but we never had a day off. I was skipping today—and probably tomorrow, and the day after that—but I didn't plan on telling my mom that. At least not yet.

After I'd woken up in the library with a horrible crick in my neck, my dream had haunted me. It felt ethereal but all too real. I was positive it was a lysa, even though I'd never had one before. While lysas were more common among the Trylle, who had the strongest gift of psychokinesis, they weren't unheard of in the Kanin, the Skojare, and even the Vittra.

A lysa is something between shared dreaming and astral projection. It's the ability to psychically enter someone else's thoughts through a vision, usually a dream. Unless the troll giving the lysa is very powerful, it's usually brief, and in tribes like the Skojare who aren't known for their psychic abilities, it only works in an emergency. Necessity and fear tend to strengthen telekinesis enough to enable a lysa.

I didn't know why Linnea had picked me to receive her lysa, but now that I had proof she was alive, I knew one thing for certain—I had to find her.

I'd wanted to rush out and talk to my mom immediately, but if I was unkempt and unshowered, that would alarm her. So I'd hurried back to my apartment and gotten cleaned up before trekking to my parents' house. I had to be as careful and discreet as possible, since I was supposed to be working today. If someone saw me—especially Ember or Tilda or Ridley—things would get unnecessarily complicated, and I didn't have time for that.

"Is something wrong?" Mom asked, narrowing her eyes in concern. She reached out, gently touching a gloved hand to the fading bruise on my temple. It had been worse the day I'd returned home after the attack, and when she had seen it then, she'd been frantic.

"I'm fine," I tried to assure her with a smile. "I was hoping we could talk for a minute, though."

"Yeah, of course." She dropped her hand and motioned to the house. "Let's go inside."

I waited until after we'd both peeled off our winter jackets and heavy boots, and I even waited until after my mom made us cups of hot blackberry tea. All I wanted to do was rush through, asking my questions, but I did the best I could to make this seem like a normal visit.

"Your dad's at a meeting in the palace," Mom said as she set a cup of tea in front of me at the kitchen table, and then she sat down across from me, sipping her own tea.

"It has to be so hectic for him, with everything's that's going on," I said.

She nodded. "I'm sure things are just as crazy for you."

"Yeah, things are busy," I said before lapsing into an awkward silence.

"Just spit it out." Mom leaned back in her chair, appraising me with a bemused smile. "You came over here to talk about something, and there's no point in dancing around it."

I took a deep breath before launching into it. "Konstantin Black went to Storvatten to take Queen Linnea, but he didn't. He swore on his life that he had no idea where she was, and it didn't appear that anyone in Storvatten knew where she was either. At least not the people who cared the most about her."

Mom considered this for a moment. "And you believe Konstantin?"

"I do," I told her, and she inhaled sharply but said nothing.

"There are three options—Konstantin took her and killed her, someone in Storvatten killed her and tried to frame Konstantin, or she ran off. In the first two scenarios, she's dead, so the only one that's really worth following up on is the third option."

"You think she ran away?" Mom asked, her interest piqued. "Why would she run off?"

I pursed my lips, wishing there was another way to say it. My mom was not a particularly hateful or vengeful person, but I couldn't blame her for the anger and distrust she still felt toward Konstantin. After all, he had nearly killed both her husband and her daughter.

"I think Konstantin warned her," I said finally. Mom lowered her eyes and shifted her weight in her chair, growing irritated, but I pressed on. "After what happened with Emma Costar in Calgary, when Bent Stum killed her, I think Konstantin didn't want anybody else to get hurt."

"Bryn." She raised her eyes so she could stare harshly at me. "You can't possibly believe that."

"There's something really weird going on in Storvatten," I said, ignoring my mom's challenge. I couldn't win that argument, so I didn't engage it. "It doesn't fit Konstantin's pattern—he had been targeting Kanin changelings still living with humans. Linnea was a Skojare Queen in her palace, and she'd never even been a changeling."

Mom fidgeted with her tea cup, twisting it on the table and staring down at it. Her shoulders were rigid, her entire body held at nervous attention.

"Let's say I believe you," she said, almost reluctantly. "Why are you here? What light do you hope I can shed on any of this?"

"If I'm right, and somebody warned Linnea that she had better get out of Storvatten, where would she go?" I asked.

Like my mother, Linnea had been born and raised in Storvatten. She had probably never met a human and hardly stepped out of the palace, except to go for a swim or visit other royalty. Thanks to her Skojare gills, she would never be able to blend with human society.

The Skojare didn't have that much money anymore, and most of what they did have of value were jewels locked up in safes. None of it had been reported missing when Linnea had disappeared, so if she was on the run, she had no money with her.

Her options as a penniless, sheltered, beautiful but mutated teenager were extremely limited.

"When I was growing up in Storvatten, locked up in that frozen palace while my parents tried to sell me off to a suitor for the highest price, I often dreamed of running away," Mom admitted quietly. "I finally did when I ran off with your father, but I hardly imagine that Linnea is hiding among us in Doldastam. We Skojare tend to stand out here."

She offered me a weak smile then, and I knew how painfully true her statement was. Thanks to the unique fair skin of the Skojare, Linnea would be unable to blend in with any of the other tribes of trolls.

"There's nowhere?" I pressed. "Didn't you tell me once

about how you and some of your friends took off somewhere for a week when you were a teenager?"

A look of wistful surprise passed across her face, and the corner of her mouth curled up slightly. "The tonåren. I'd nearly forgotten about that."

"Yeah, the tonåren," I said, trying to remember what she'd told me about it.

"It wasn't an official thing," Mom explained. "That's just the word we used for when the royal teenagers grew restless and didn't want to stay cooped up anymore. Those without gills would sometimes try to make a break for the human world, heading out to cities for a week or two before coming back.

"But my best friend had gills, and I didn't want to leave her behind, so we had to choose another option." Mom took a long drink of her tea. "Lake Isolera."

"Lake Isolera?" I asked. "You never told me about that."

"I'd nearly forgotten, and it feels like a half-remembered dream." She shook her head. "It was a story we'd heard from our childhood. A magical place that an ancient powerful Queen had a put spell on, so it would always be warm and private. An oasis to swim in when the harsh Canadian winters bore down on us.

"But it had an enchantment on it, to keep humans or unwanted trolls from stumbling upon it," Mom went on. "Everyone who says they've been there is never entirely sure if they really went or if they only imagined it."

"So, is it real?" I asked her directly.

"I . . ." She furrowed her brow in concentration and sighed.

"Honestly, I can't say for certain. But if Linnea was running from someone, and she believed Lake Isolera was real, the same way I believed it was real when I was her age, then that's where she would head."

"Where is it?" I asked, stifling my excitement.

"Swim one day along the shore, and then walk half a day due north, and you'll find it under the brightest star if you've followed the right course," Mom said, sounding as though she were reciting an old nursery rhyme.

"You don't have more accurate directions than that?" I asked hopefully.

She raised an eyebrow at me. "For a magical place that probably doesn't really exist? No, I'm sorry, I don't. It's like asking for specific directions to Narnia."

"You just go through the wardrobe to get to Narnia. That's pretty specific."

Mom rolled her eyes, but she pushed her chair back and stood up. "Let's go to your dad's study. If we look at a map, I might be able to figure it out better."

I followed her back to my dad's cluttered office, and she pulled down his heavy, worn atlas from a shelf and spread it out on his desk. Unlike the atlases humans might find in their world, this one was marked for troll territories, major cities, and places of importance, all overlaid atop the human landmarks so we could find the troll locations when we ventured out into the human world.

As Mom bent over the atlas, she mumbled to herself. I stood beside her. I didn't catch every word she said, but from what I gathered she was trying to remember how fast she could swim.

Then finally, after some deliberation, she took a pen off my dad's desk and circled a blank spot on the map in Ontario.

"There. That's Lake Isolera," she proclaimed rather proudly.

I leaned forward, squinting at the map. There were plenty of blue splotches covering the area, indicating all of the lakes. But the spot Mom had circled was completely devoid of water, an odd dry patch in an otherwise watery land.

"Are you sure that's the right place?" I asked. "There's nothing there, but there are tons of lakes around it."

"Well, either it isn't real or it's hidden under a magic spell, so of course there wouldn't be anything on the map." She straightened up and folded her arms over her chest. "But if it does exist, that's where it is."

"If Linnea ran away, you think that's where she would be?" I looked up at her.

"Either at the lake, or trying to find it." Mom nodded, her lips pressed into a grim line. "Assuming she isn't dead, of course."

SEVEN

abscond

"You have to talk to Ridley," Tilda told me firmly, and I groaned and slumped back against the wall.

After talking with my mom, I'd snuck into the school, barely managing not to be seen, and then lay in wait in the locker room that doubled as a women's restroom. Thanks to her pregnancy, Tilda had to use the bathroom rather frequently—as she had lamented several times—so I knew it wouldn't be too long before she came in.

In fact, I'd only hidden in a stall for fifteen minutes before she entered. I waited until she'd finished, and when she came out of the stall she nearly screamed at the sight of me. Once she calmed herself, she gave me a hard look—one that could cut twice as deep as any lecture.

I hurriedly explained my absence from training today, and my plan to find Linnea and why I thought it was so important.

As she listened, the steel in her gray eyes began to soften, but she didn't exactly look at me with approval either.

"But you're my commanding officer," I insisted. "You should be able to give me the go-ahead."

Tilda shook her head. "You know I have no authority to release you from your duties. Even if I did, it would mean nothing. Unless you get Ridley's approval, you'll be considered AWOL."

I leaned my head back against the wall and stared up at the ceiling, weighing my options. On one hand, if I left without permission, not only would I lose any hope of being on the Högdragen, but I'd most likely be fired as a tracker. I'd still have to stay in the army until after this "war" was over, but as soon as it was, I'd be out of work.

And on the other hand, getting permission meant I'd have to talk to Ridley.

"If you think this is the right thing to do, and it seems that you really do, then you need to talk to him," Tilda said, her voice low and comforting. "Whatever is going on between the two of you, he'll still be fair and hear you out."

I looked up at her hopefully. "Will you get him for me?" She started to scoff, so I quickly explained. "If I go out there now, it'll be a big spectacle because I've already skipped half a day. I just wanna get this over with and get out of here."

Tilda sighed but smiled crookedly at me. "Fine. Wait here."

While she went to retrieve Ridley, I sat down on one of the benches by the lockers. It may have seemed strange talking to the Överste in the girls' locker room, but with so few female trackers, odds were that no one would use it. In fact, it was probably the least used area in the whole school.

Ridley pushed open the door hard enough to make it bang against the wall, and I hopped to my feet. He didn't look at me when he came in, instead preferring to stare off at some point directly to the right of me, but finally, he forced his dark eyes to rest coldly on me.

His uniform looked good on him; like always, he'd left the top button undone, revealing just a hint of his chest. If the King or members of the Högdragen came around, he could get in trouble for that, but by the hard look on his face, I didn't think he gave a damn.

"What the hell is so damn important that you think you can just blow off your job?" Ridley demanded.

"Queen Linnea."

"We already went over that—"

"I think I know where she is," I cut him off, and that got his attention.

For a brief second, he looked at me the way he always had—his mask of anger momentarily displaced. A wave of heat flushed over me, reminding me of the way I felt about him, but I pushed it away. I didn't have time for that, even if he didn't hate me right now.

"What are you talking about?" Ridley asked.

"She came to me in a lysa," I said, and skepticism flashed in his eyes. "I know how rare they are, especially coming from a Skojare. But I also know that it was real. Linnea is alive, and she told me to come find her."

He arched his eyebrow and folded his arms across his chest. "Did she happen to tell you where she was?"

"No, not exactly," I admitted.

"If this was a true lysa, and Linnea really wanted you to come find her, why wouldn't she tell you *exactly* where she was?"

"I don't know." I shook my head "The Skojare don't have a ton of psychic powers, so it most likely took all she had to get out that one quick message, like an SOS."

Ridley narrowed his eyes slightly. "That leads to another question—why you?"

I let out a frustrated sigh. "I don't know. When I find her, I'll ask."

"How do you plan to find her if you don't know where she is?" Ridley asked, and I hurried to explain my conversation with my mom about Lake Isolera.

When I finished telling him my plan to find Linnea, reiterating why it was so important, Ridley didn't say anything. He stared down at the floor, breathing in deeply through his nose, and then he closed his eyes and rubbed his forehead.

"How far away is it?" he asked finally.

"Based on the point on the map, I'd guess around a hundred to a hundred and fifty miles from Storvatten. So that puts us at about a day's journey from here."

He considered it, then nodded once. "Okay." For a second I was so relieved that I almost hugged him, and then he added, "But I'm going with you."

"What?" I asked, and I'm sure I sounded as shocked as I felt. "You—you . . . you're running the army."

I'd stumbled because I wanted to say, *you hate me.* But I couldn't say that, so I pointed out the next logical reason why he wouldn't be able to go.

"Tomorrow is Sunday, and that's a light day. If we head out now, taking shifts driving, we should find the place and be back by Tuesday," Ridley reasoned. "The scouts left this morning to search for Viktor Dålig and Konstantin Black. We'll just be doing basic drills back here. Tilda can handle it until we get back."

I opened my mouth, trying to think of protests, but I merely ended up gaping at him.

"You don't need to come with," I finally said.

"If Linnea knows *anything* about Viktor, I want to be there when you find her," he said, and by the resolve in his eyes I knew he wouldn't back down. Not that I blamed him.

I swallowed hard, as if my guilt had taken physical form as a painful lump in my throat. "Understood."

"Go pack and get the things you need," Ridley instructed me. "I'll talk to Tilda and the King and get everything arranged. When I'm finished, I'll meet you at your place, and we'll head out."

EIGHT

skirmish

What had started as light snow an hour ago had switched to an icy sleet that sounded like pebbles hitting the windshield. To Ridley's credit, he slept through it—his head lolled to one side, bouncing along with the Land Rover as it navigated the worsening terrain of the back roads.

It was over twenty hours into our journey to the mythical and possibly nonexistent Lake Isolera, which had begun with an awkward train ride during which we both struggled to fill the silence by inspecting maps of Ontario.

Before we left, I'd borrowed a Skojare book from my mom. She kept a few artifacts from her past life in Storvatten, and this was a book of fairy tales that her beloved grandmother had read to her. It had a few poems and stories that mentioned Lake Isolera, and since that was the only thing we had to go on, I took it.

On the train, Ridley had read the stories about the lake

aloud. They had a tendency to switch between English and Swedish mid-sentence, and his pronunciation was much better than mine. Out of the five tribes, the Skojare were the most isolated, and therefore, most attached to the ways of the old world—including the original language of all the troll tribes.

"Through the trees and past the *slinggrande flod*, in the depths of snow that no human would trod," Ridley read aloud. "There is a land of *trolleri* and beauty, the most wonderful place that ever you'll see."

I closed my eyes, listening to the comforting baritone of Ridley's voice. When he was reading from the book, he spoke like he normally did—no hint of anger or unease. My chest ached with regret and longing. He was so close to me. Our arms brushed up against each other on the armrest. But he was still so far away.

If I looked up at him, I would see an icy wall in his mahogany eyes where once there had only been warmth.

All I wanted was to take back everything that had happened—not telling him about Viktor right away and even kissing him. I just wanted things to go back to the way they used to be between us, but I didn't have the words to erase what had happened. So I just closed my eyes and listened to him read.

Once we'd picked up a rental car at the train station, things had actually gotten easier. We needed to take turns driving, and Ridley had offered to take the first shift. I hadn't slept well, but at least it wasn't tense or weird that we weren't speaking.

I'd taken my shift a few hours back, and Ridley had been sleeping soundly the whole time. Most of the drive had been easy and relatively uneventful, but gradually the clouds had moved in, growing darker and blotting out the sun. Then the snow had begun, which wasn't bad when compared to its icy counterpart that pounded down now.

The windshield wipers could barely keep up at this point. The SUV slid on a slick patch. I managed to catch it before we went off the road, but it jerked hard when it hit a dip on the pavement.

"What's going on?" Ridley asked, waking up with a start.

"Everything's okay."

He sat up straighter, blinking back sleep, and looking out the window at the mess the sky was pouring down on us.

"Do you want me to take over?" he asked, eyeing my hands gripped tightly on the wheel.

I shook my head. "No, I've got it. You just woke up."

And at that moment, the Land Rover decided to skid again. It wasn't bad, and I recovered easily, but it hadn't eased Ridley's concerns.

"Are you sure?" he asked. "Because I got plenty of sleep, and I'm feeling alert now."

"Yeah, I'm sure," I insisted. "Besides, I think we're getting close."

He waited a beat before adding, "Because sometimes you say you're sure, and you're not."

"What are you talking about?" I gave him a sidelong glance, since I didn't want to take my eyes completely off the road. "I never say I'm sure unless I am."

He laughed dryly. "Whatever you say."

"What's *that* supposed to mean?" I asked.

"It means . . ." He ran a hand through his wavy, sleep-tousled hair. "Nothing. I shouldn't have said anything."

"But you did."

Ridley let out a long breath. "It's just . . . you sure kissed me like you meant it, and then you told me that you didn't."

At first I was too stunned to say anything. I couldn't believe he was even bringing it up. Finally, I managed a plaintive "That's not fair."

"Life isn't fair, Bryn," he muttered dryly, and for some reason that set me off.

"You kissed me like you meant it too," I shot back. "And you have a girlfriend!"

"Juni's not my girlfriend," he nearly shouted, shifting in his seat. "We've gone on a few dates is all."

I scoffed. "That's bullshit, Ridley."

"And it doesn't matter," he said, instead of arguing my point. "You've made it perfectly and repeatedly clear that you have no interest in dating anyone ever, so I don't know why it bothers you if I'm seeing someone or not."

"It doesn't bother me. Do whatever you want."

He mumbled something, but I didn't ask what. I just let him lapse into silence and stare out the window, not that there was much to see. The sleet was coming down so heavily that visibility was completely shot.

That's how the tree appeared out of nowhere. It had been

uprooted by the excessive weight of the snow-sleet mixture, and it tipped across the road, angling upward with branches sticking out haphazardly.

I jerked the wheel, attempting to swerve around the tree, but there was nowhere to swerve to. This was a narrow road, barely wider than a lane, and the tree had it blocked entirely. The tires slipped on the icy mixture, and we careened off the road.

NINE

collision

Ridley cried out in surprise as the SUV spun ninety degrees, and bounced down the shallow embankment next to the road before slamming into a tree and coming to a hard stop.

We both sat there panting, neither of us saying anything. The dashboard console began to beep angrily, letting us know that we'd collided with something—as if we couldn't figure that out already.

"You okay?" Ridley asked.

"Yeah. You?"

He nodded. "You should've let me drive."

"There was a tree in the road!" I gestured back toward the road several yards behind us. "That wasn't my fault."

"Right." Ridley rolled his eyes. "Of course. *Nothing* is ever your fault."

I didn't want to argue with him, so I got out of the SUV under the ruse of inspecting it for damage. Fortunately, the Land

Rover had hit a massive pine tree, and its long branches covered with thick needles helped to keep back the sting of the sleet.

We'd been going relatively slowly when I swerved on the road, so thankfully the SUV hadn't been going that fast when it hit the tree. Other than some minor bumper damage, it didn't seem like the Land Rover was any worse for wear.

Ridley got out of the vehicle and walked over to where I was standing near the tree. The branches mostly sheltered us, but it was warm enough that when the sleet rested on the pine needles they eventually began to melt, dripping through the branches in a light shower that sprinkled down on me.

"I've never said nothing is my fault," I said. The adrenaline from the accident left me feeling sharper, pricklier, and I know that my words came out harsher than I meant them, but I didn't care. "I've never even thought that."

"You sure as hell act like that," Ridley snapped back, matching my intensity, and I turned to glare up at him.

"If you think I don't constantly blame myself for letting Viktor get away—"

"I don't blame you!" he shouted, then he stopped. As quickly as that, the fight had gone out of him, and his whole frame seemed to sag. The icy mask he'd been wearing melted away, and he just looked hurt and a little lost. "Why can't you just tell me things?"

"I'm sorry I didn't tell you about him." I was surprised that my voice quivered with my sincerity, and I hastily steadied it. "I just had to be certain about what I saw. After all you've been through with Viktor, I didn't want to get you upset for nothing. But now I realize it would've been better if I had told you sooner, and I'm sorry. I can never tell you how sorry I am."

"I don't need your apologies." He shook his head. "And I'm not even really mad at you."

"You're not?"

He shrugged. "I mean, you should've gotten me before you went down to talk to Konstantin."

"I thought he would be more likely to open up if it was just me." I tried to explain my reasoning, and I couldn't tell if he accepted it or not.

Hesitantly, Ridley said, "I know that makes sense."

"But?" I prompted, since he'd left that statement hanging in the air.

"But Viktor almost killed you, Bryn." He looked at me for the first time since he'd gotten out of the SUV, and the heat had returned to his eyes, burning darkly within him. "I was asleep a few floors above you, and the man who killed my father came back after being gone for years and nearly killed the person . . ."

Ridley trailed off, and I didn't push him to finish. Whatever he was going to say, I didn't think I wanted to know. The pounding of my heart would argue with that, but I knew logically it was better for us if he didn't finish that sentence, if I don't know what I really meant to him.

"I don't know what's going on between us," he said finally. "But I do know that I don't want to lose you."

I swallowed hard. "I don't want to lose you either."

"Then you need to confide in me, okay?" Ridley asked. "You can't go running off without letting me know. I told you before that we're in this together, and with Viktor back, I mean that now more than ever."

"I can do that," I agreed. "And I promise not to keep secrets from you anymore."

"Friends again?" he asked with a hopeful smile, holding out his hand to me.

"Friends."

He'd had his hands shoved in his pockets, but mine were cold and damp from touching the vehicle to check for damage. When I took his hand to shake it, the warmth that enveloped me was astonishing. Instantly, I knew this was a bad idea, but I didn't let go of him.

The air smelled of snow, water, and fresh pine needles. The dripping water had dampened our hair, making his a bit wavier than normal, and for some reason it made his mahogany eyes appear brighter. I was cold and wet, and I imagined how much warmer it would be in his arms.

And then I wasn't imagining it. We'd both moved forward, filling in the gap between us, and he let go of my hand.

"We should, um, probably get going," he said in a low voice.

"Right," I agreed, forcing a smile when I stepped back from him. "We should check the GPS and find out how close we are."

Pushing down all the conflicting emotions I had swirling inside me, I turned to the job at hand and got back in the car.

The coordinates for the lake weren't exact, so we'd made our best guess with longitude and latitude on the GPS app on Ridley's tablet. I grabbed the tablet off the dashboard, but it was updating slowly. Service could be sketchy out here, blinking in and out. At least it was working now.

"What's it say?" Ridley asked when he got in the SUV. He shook the water from his hair then peered over at the tablet in my hands.

"According to the GPS we're not that far anyway, and there isn't a road going directly to Lake Isolera. Want to try walking it?"

"Sure. Why not?"

I started the Land Rover and carefully drove it back up to the road, parking it near the tree that had diverted our course. It ran normally, which was a bit of a relief, and parking it along the road would make it easier to find when we came back.

We added ponchos over our winter gear, then grabbed our packs and locked up the vehicle before making the trek out into the wilderness. Ridley had a waterproof case for his tablet, which was good because the weather showed no signs of letting up.

The first hour we wandered through the trees was the worst. We went where the GPS directed us, and when we found nothing, we began circling out further. Every time I had the chance, I broke branches and tied red string to trees, trying to leave some signs so we wouldn't get lost, and we'd be able to find our way back to the SUV.

Though we had put on boots, hats, and gloves, it had all soaked through. We were used to the cold, but it seemed to permeate everything, making my bones ache. Every step had become painful, but neither Ridley nor I were willing to give up so easily.

Just when I was getting to the point where I wasn't sure I could take the cold much longer, I saw an odd shimmer through a patch of pine trees. A subtle change in the snow falling down, like it was bowing around the side of a snow globe, but it only lasted a moment. When I tilted my head, though, I was almost certain I could see rays of light spilling out through it.

I started walking forward, moving more quickly than I had before, with Ridley following.

"What's going on?" Ridley called from behind me.

I stopped long enough for him to catch up, and I pointed at the trees in front of us. "I think I see something." I tilted my head again, and for a split second, I saw it—a shimmer across the air. "When I look just right, I can see it."

Ridley squinted and brushed back the snow that clung to his eyebrows. "I can't see anything."

I knew that I might be crazy, that this might be some cold-induced insanity causing me to see a mirage, but deep down, it just didn't feel that way. The closer we got, the more certain I became. Ridley continued to echo his inability to see what I was chasing, but he never suggested we turn back.

Maybe it was my Skojare heritage. My mom had said that the lake had been cloaked in enchantment so that even other tribes wouldn't be able to find it. I must've had just enough Skojare blood in me that I could see the faintest hint of it.

The pine trees were growing closer together, so I had to bow my head and physically push branches out of the way to get through them.

When I finally made it through and lifted my head, the sun was shining so brightly I had to squint. I held up my arm to block the light, and it was a few seconds before my eyes adjusted enough to really see anything.

The first thing I saw, sparkling like a massive sapphire, was a lake spanning several miles. It sat in the center of a clearing surrounded by a thick barrier of pine trees, and it had to be the most beautiful body of water I'd ever seen.

"Lake Isolera," Ridley whispered behind me, sounding in awe. "It does exist."

TEN

isolera

In the bright light, the grass that framed the lake appeared almost lime green, sprinkled with brightly colored wildflowers in shades of pink and purple. The grass gave way to fine white sand that sparkled as if it were mixed with diamond dust, and the water lapped gently against it.

It was so warm that all my winter gear felt unbearable. I shed my hat and poncho first, then I kept going until I was left in the black leggings and tank top I'd worn underneath my sweater and jeans.

"How is this even possible?" Ridley asked.

I glanced back at him, pulling my eyes away from the lake with some difficulty. He'd taken off his boots and jacket but apparently moved much slower than I did. A bright blue butterfly fluttered past him, and his eyes followed it, transfixed for a moment.

"The Skojare must've had power unlike anything we've ever

seen if they could cast a spell like this and keep it going for years," I said, then turned back to the water. "Hundreds of years, if my mom's book is to be believed."

In Doldastam, it took half a dozen gardeners working in special "greenhouses" to keep the garden up and running. Growing grapes and tomatoes couldn't be anywhere near as difficult as this oasis, even if the gardeners' psychokinetic abilities were working against subarctic temperatures to keep fruits and vegetables alive. On top of that, we'd had to poach several of the workers from the Trylle, since their powers were stronger than ours.

"Our ancestors used to be more powerful," Ridley reminded me, but he sounded as if he was in a bit of a daze. "We've lost our abilities over the centuries. I mean, we've heard that our whole lives, but if another tribe could do this, then we've lost so much more than I ever imagined."

The grass felt like soft downy carpet under my feet as I walked toward the lake. I expected the sand to be scorching hot, the way beaches always seemed to be under the glaring sun, but instead it felt perfect—silky and warm against my frozen toes.

"Have you ever seen anything like this?" I asked Ridley.

"No." When he spoke again he sounded closer to me, so he must've been walking up behind me, but I didn't look back. "I sorta feel like I'm in a dream."

I nodded slowly. "I know exactly what you mean."

While my mom literally felt the water calling to her when she'd been away from it too long, thanks to her Skojare blood,

I'd never felt such a strong pull. I enjoyed the water a little more than the average Kanin, but it wasn't exactly a *need*.

But now I felt it. Tugging at something inside me, like I was connected to the lake by an invisible thread wrapped around the very core of my being, and now the thread had pulled taut. I stepped close enough that the water lapped against my toes. A delicious wave of relief rolled over me, and I hadn't even noticed how apprehensive I'd been feeling.

I crouched down and cupped the water in my hand. At first, I just watched it drip through my fingers, running clearer than any river or lake I'd seen. Then I held my cupped hands to my mouth, taking a long sip, and it tasted crisp and pure and luscious. Almost instantly, I felt refreshed in a way I never had before, even after the deepest night's sleep.

"Bryn?" Ridley said in a way that made me realize he'd been calling my name, and I looked back over my shoulder at him. He stood at the edge of the beach behind me, and his expression had a lax, dreamy quality to it, but anxiety had edged into his eyes.

"Yeah?"

"We still have a mission," he reminded me. "We need to find Linnea, and I'm not even sure if she's here."

I turned away from him for a moment to stare out at the lake before me. I wanted nothing more than to submerge myself in Lake Isolera, letting it wash over me, warm and cool all at once. But Ridley was right. We had a job to do.

I stood up and stepped back, so the water wasn't lapping at my toes any longer.

"Where should we look?" I asked, but my eyes were already scanning the clearing.

Other than the thick evergreens that walled out the cold reality beyond the magic of Lake Isolera, there were no trees. There wasn't even much land in the clearing. It was mostly the lake. If I didn't see Linnea now, I had no idea where she could be hiding.

"If she's here, she's in the lake," Ridley decided. "We should swim."

And I didn't need any more convincing than that. I knew I couldn't let the water enchant me the way it had a few moments before, but I would still be more than happy to swim in it. I just had to keep my wits about me.

Ridley stripped down to his boxers, and while part of me wanted to appreciate the taut muscles of his chest and abdomen, I deliberately did my best not to look at him. Not only because we had a job to complete, but because we'd just agreed to be friends, and I didn't want to muck that up by fantasizing about what it would feel like to run my fingers down the hard contours of his chest and stomach until . . .

I shook my head and waded out into the water, hoping that it would wash away my thoughts. As soon as I was out far enough, I dove under, letting the lake completely cover me, and I honestly can't remember a time when I ever felt better. It was like enveloping myself in unadulterated bliss.

For a few moments, I did let myself just swim and relish the feeling. But then my lungs began to demand oxygen, and I surfaced. I breathed in deeply, staring up at the blue sky above me, until Ridley came up a minute later, gasping for breath.

"Are you okay?" I asked, swimming closer to where he'd emerged a couple yards from me.

"I'm fine," he insisted and wiped the water from his eyes. "How long can you hold your breath?"

I shrugged. "I don't know. Maybe five minutes."

During grade school, I had frequently shown off my ability to hold my breath for extended periods of time. I thought it would make the kids think I was cool, but it turned out I was nothing more than a circus sideshow. The average Kanin could hold their breath for roughly thirty seconds, so my feat seemed quite impressive and a little freaky. But by comparison, my mom could hold her breath under water for nearly a half hour.

"Yeah, I can't do anywhere close to that." Ridley shook his head. "I tried to go down to the bottom of the lake, but it's way too far for me. If Linnea has gills, she could be hanging out in the depths of it."

"That makes sense," I agreed. "I'll see how far down I can go and look for her. You wanna stick to the shallower areas?"

"Works for me."

I took a deep breath, then plunged under the water. I went straight down, thinking that I would find the bottom and search along there. If this was a hidden paradise built for gilled trolls, it wasn't a stretch to guess that there might be something at the bottom.

Ridley wasn't kidding about how deep it went. Even with the water being totally clear, it soon became too dark for me to see well. When a small silver fish swam by, I caught just a glimmer of light on its scales.

Even as a dull ache in my head and chest began to build, the delirium of the water overtook me. It seemed to flow through me, filling me with pure elation, and I swam deeper. I'd like to say I was more determined than ever to find Linnea, but really, that came in second to the way the lake made me feel.

But slowly that was beginning to give away to pain and panic as my body struggled with a buildup of carbon dioxide. My lungs started to burn. I looked up toward the rays of light barely breaking the water, and it occurred to me too late that I had gone down too far.

I had swum down for almost five minutes, which meant that it would take me almost five minutes to surface. That was twice as long as I could hold my breath. I was in trouble.

With my eyes fixed on the sun above me, I kicked my legs as fast as I could, racing against the clock. My lungs felt like they were going to explode, and the muscles in my abdomen began to painfully spasm.

But the light above was growing brighter, and if I pushed myself, I could just make it. The pressure aggravated my head injury, making the vision in my right eye blur and my head throb. A fog was descending on my brain. Then everything faded to blackness, and my legs went limp underneath me, despite my demands that they swim on.

ELEVEN

delusion

The good news was I was breathing. I could feel it—oxygen filled my lungs with ease. Beyond that, my stomach ached as if I'd been punched, and my head throbbed dully. But all that pain meant I was alive.

"I think she's coming to," a female voice was saying softly.

"Bryn!" Ridley shouted in a panic, slapping me on the cheek.

"Stop hitting me," I mumbled and weakly pushed his arm back. The ground felt soft beneath me, so I assumed I was lying on the grass, safely out of the dark clutches of drowning.

He exhaled roughly. "You scared the crap out of me, Bryn."

"Sorry." I opened my eyes to see Ridley and the missing Queen Linnea bent over me. "Hey, I found her."

Linnea smiled—there was no lipstick out here, so her lips were a pale pink, in line with the porcelain tones of her skin.

Strangely, without the makeup she actually looked older than when I'd seen her before.

She was sixteen but a young sixteen, with an innocence about her. The too-bright red lipstick had reminded me of a little girl playing dress-up, whereas now she simply appeared to be her age. It probably didn't help that with her ringlet curls and wide blue eyes, she bore a remarkable resemblance to Shirley Temple.

"Actually, I found you," Linnea correct me. "You were about to drown when I spotted you and pulled you to the shore."

"Thank you."

I sat up, and a wave of dizziness nearly knocked me back, but I fought it off. It didn't help waking up in this place, where everything felt like a dream. Everything had a shimmery edge to it, like it wasn't quite real.

"You okay?" Ridley put a hand on my shoulder to steady me, and his strength reassured me the way it always did.

For a moment, with the sun backlighting him and the water dripping down his bare chest, Ridley appeared absolutely dazzling. He'd leaned over when he touched me, and the very nearness of him took my breath away. That only made his chestnut eyes darken in concern, and I hurried to shake off the feeling and pull my attention away from him.

"Are y-you okay?" I asked Linnea, stuttering a bit as I composed myself.

She nodded. Other than the lack of makeup, she looked the

same as she had when I saw her last—no signs of injury. She wore a blue bikini, revealing her slender figure, so any bumps or bruises would have been visible.

"What are you doing here?" I asked, deciding to cut to the chase. "Why did you leave Storvatten?"

"I couldn't stay there anymore." She shook her head, and her translucent gills flared beneath her jaw. "Something is going on there."

"What do you mean?" Ridley asked.

"The guards at the palace have been acting strangely," she explained. "They were normally aloof and careless, but lately I've felt like they were watching me too closely. I don't know how to explain it, but everywhere I went, I felt like I had eyes on me."

"Did you tell anyone about it?" I asked.

"Not right away," Linnea went on. "At first I thought I was only being paranoid, so I waited a few weeks before bringing it to my husband. Mikko wasn't overly concerned, but he tried to ease my fears by saying he would talk to the guards."

"Did anything change after that?" Ridley pressed her, and I could tell he was doing his best not to sound accusatory.

We'd long suspected that Linnea's husband, the Skojare King Mikko, had had some involvement in her disappearance. Even with Konstantin Black's presence, there still seemed to be something odd about Mikko and the guards in Storvatten. They had blocked our attempts at gathering information and doing a proper investigation, not to mention that Mikko had shifted from indifferent about his wife's disappearance to devastated rather quickly.

There was also the matter of his marriage to Linnea. It had been arranged by their families, as most royal mergers were, and Mikko was twice her age. They'd been married for less than a year, and I had to wonder what exactly those kind of nuptials were like.

"Things didn't really have a chance to change," Linnea elaborated. "I told Mikko about my suspicions, and two days later the dark man was telling me that I had to get out of there."

"Wait." I waved my hand. "What man?"

"He never said his name, but he had a darker complexion, like you." Linnea pointed to Ridley, referring to his dark olive skin. "Black wavy hair, a beard, and gray eyes."

I hadn't really needed her to describe him, but I wanted to be absolutely sure. It was Konstantin Black.

"What were you doing when he approached you?" Ridley asked.

"I'd gone to bed with Mikko, the way I always did, but I couldn't sleep." Linnea sat back and pulled her knees up to her chest, wrapping her arms around them. "I've been a bit on edge lately, since I've been getting this weird vibe from everyone at the palace. So I went down to the pool to swim, hoping to burn off some of my anxiety.

"I actually snuck down to the pool," she went on. "With the guards acting so strangely, I didn't want any of them following me. But as soon as I got there and slipped off my robe, that man emerged from nowhere.

"It was almost like Mystique from the *X-Men*," Linnea continued with wide eyes.

With the Skojare spending most of their lives locked inside the palace, hidden away from humans and the rest of the world, they spent a great deal of time watching movies and reading books. It was a way to make the time go by faster.

Konstantin appearing out of thin air had to be an amazing thing for her to see. Even though Linnea had been exposed to some of the magic of our world, she had limited interactions with other tribes. Like many Kanin, Konstantin's skin could change color, so he could blend into the background. It was disorienting to witness in real life.

"Did he hurt you?" Ridley asked, since he was more fixated on the idea that Konstantin was a villain. I hadn't completely ruled him out as one yet, but my certainty was wavering. "Did he threaten you at all?"

"No. I mean, I don't think so." Her brow furrowed, and she pursed her lips. "He didn't hurt me, but he said, 'You must leave. If you want to live, you must get as far away from the palace as you can, and never come back. And you must tell no one.'"

"Did he say why?" I asked.

"No." Linnea shook her head, making water spray lightly from the wet curls that framed her face. "I tried to ask him why I had to leave and who he was, but he just became more insistent and said there wasn't any time."

"And you listened to him?" Ridley asked, unable to hide the incredulity in his voice. "Why?"

"Because he voiced what I'd already been feeling," Linnea

explained with a half-shrug. "I didn't feel safe in the palace, and he'd confirmed my fears."

"And you told no one?" I asked.

"No." She frowned. "I didn't think I had time. I wanted to tell Mikko and my grandma. They must be worried sick." She perked up then. "Have you talked to either of them? How are they doing?"

"We were in Storvatten helping the search for you, and we saw them both. They're doing fine." I glossed over it. I didn't want to share my concerns about her husband, at least not until I heard everything she had to say.

"How did you escape from the palace without being seen?" Ridley returned to the subject at hand.

"The palace has a freshwater pool that connects to Lake Superior by a tunnel, so I just swam out that way. Since no one had spotted me coming out of my chambers, it was fairly easy," Linnea said. "Once I was out in the lake, I had no idea where to go, so I just kept swimming. Then I remembered the stories my grandma had told me about Lake Isolera, so I decided to try to find it."

"So you've been out here for . . ." I paused, trying to remember when Linnea had gone missing. "Ten days? How have you survived? What have you eaten?"

"I don't know." That seemed to puzzle her too. "I haven't been hungry. I didn't even realize it had been ten days. I thought maybe two or three."

I glanced out at the lake behind her and remembered a line

that Ridley had read from the fairy tale book on the train. *The water of Isolera will sustain all who dream of it.* There was some serious magic here. Maybe it was the near drowning, but its power had begun to unnerve me.

"Did you call for me?" I asked Linnea, pulling my gaze from the lake back to her. "In the lysa?"

"Yes!" Linnea beamed. "And I am *so* happy it worked! My grandma had trained me to use it in case of an emergency, but I'd never been very good. It uses so much energy, but I think the magic of this place helped strengthen me."

"But why me?" I shook my head. "Why not your grandma or your husband?"

"I was afraid that if I got to Mikko or Nana, they would mistakenly alert the guards to search for me, and I don't trust the guards," Linnea explained. "I wasn't sure if anyone without Skojare blood would be able to find Lake Isolera, and you were the only Skojare I knew who wasn't connected with Storvatten."

"So what do you want to do now?" Ridley asked. "Do you plan to go back to Storvatten?"

Linnea let out a heavy sigh, and for a moment she looked much older. "I don't know. I know that I can't stay here forever, and I miss Mikko desperately."

She was staring down at the sand beneath her toes, which allowed Ridley and me to exchange a look. We were both surprised to hear that she missed Mikko. So far, our impression had been that she was in a marriage of obligation.

"Why don't you come back with us to Doldastam?" Ridley suggested. "Once we get there, we can contact your family and decide what to do."

I was eager to get going, so as soon as Linnea agreed, I went over to gather our winter clothes. They had completely dried, and when I looked up, I realized the sun had moved all the way across the sky. It felt like we'd been here for maybe 15 minutes, but it must've been much, much longer than that.

Linnea had swum here from Storvatten, so she had only her swimsuit. Fortunately, when she'd made the trek across land a week and a half ago, the weather had been a bit warmer, but I still wasn't sure how she had made it.

I supposed she was like my mother—much tougher than she appeared. Skojare like my mom and Linnea had to be in order handle the harsh temperatures of swimming in a freezing lake during the winter.

Ridley gave her his jacket, and I gave her my jeans. That meant I'd be venturing out in only my leggings, which wasn't ideal, but I would make due.

When we pushed through the branches the way we had come in, it was the strangest feeling. It was almost like a dream within a dream, where even after you awake, you're still dreaming. It was totally dark when we emerged from Lake Isolera, which was very disorienting since the sun had somehow still been up there.

Fortunately, the snow had stopped. The moon was only a sliver, but the fresh snow reflected it, making it appear brighter.

Thanks to the strings and broken branches I'd left behind on our trail, we were able to make it back to the SUV with relative ease.

But by the time we reached it, I could barely remember what Lake Isolera had looked like.

TWELVE

repatriation

It was very late on Monday night when Ridley pulled the SUV in front of the palace in Doldastam. Ridley and I had taken shifts driving on the way back, the same way we had on the way there, but we were both tired and sore from the long journey. Linnea, on the other hand, sat up in the backseat, wide eyed and excited the whole time.

She'd hardly seen any of the world outside of Storvatten, and even though most of our trip involved empty roads and wide open spaces, Linnea still watched out the window with rapt interest. For what little interaction she had with the human world—when we'd stopped at gas stations and boarded the train—she almost exploded with delight.

We'd disguised her gills as best we could by giving her a scarf to wrap around her neck, and she'd worn one of my hoodies and a pair of jeans. My clothes were a bit big on her, but that worked in the case of the sweatshirt. It gave the hood ample room to cover her curls and drape over her gills.

Two Högdragen stood guard just outside the front door of the palace—a new feature since the whole "war" had started—and they stopped us, as if Viktor Dålig would knock politely on the front door if he came to assassinate the King.

One of the Högdragen was Kasper Abbott, Tilda's boyfriend—well, fiancé now. The streetlamps made the silver flourishes on his black uniform shimmer. His black curls were gelled perfectly into place, and his beard was immaculately groomed. He stood at attention, but he gave me a quizzical look as Ridley, Linnea, and I approached them.

"The palace is closed for the night," the first guard informed us.

"We have business with the King," Ridley replied.

"What business do you have with the King?" Kasper asked, and he glanced away from me over to Linnea, who was still hidden in the oversized hooded sweatshirt.

The other guard glared at Kasper, and then before Ridley could answer, the guard told us, "The King and Queen have retired for the night. Come back in the morning."

"Elliot, this is Ridley Dresden, the Rektor and the Överste," Kasper said, doing his best not to chastise his comrade in front of us. "If he wants to see the King, it must be important."

"I have orders from the King not to disturb him." Elliot kept his head high and his shoulders back.

I could see this was going to get us nowhere, so I turned to Linnea, who had been staring up at the massive stained-glass window above the front door to the palace. When she looked back down at me, I nodded, encouraging her. Linnea pushed back her hood and pulled the scarf from around her neck, then smiled up at the guards.

"You may recognize Linnea Biâelse, the missing Queen of the Skojare," Ridley explained with a hint of snark. "I think that King Evert will make an exception for us now."

"Elliot," Kasper said in a voice just above a whisper. "Get the King. I'll take them to the meeting room to wait for him."

"Yes, of course." Elliot quickly bowed before Linnea. "Sorry, Your Highness." He took a step back, stumbling on the cobblestones, and then hurried inside to get the King.

"I'm sorry about that." Kasper relaxed his demeanor after Elliot left. "He's a good guard. He can just be overzealous sometimes."

Kasper led us inside the palace and down the hall to the room where I usually met with the King. Since nobody had been expecting us, the hearth was dark, and it was rather chilly. The cold front that had descended upon Doldastam last week showed no signs of letting up.

Linnea shivered involuntarily, but I wasn't sure if it was because of the cold or something else. When Kasper rushed over to start a fire for us, she smiled as she thanked him, but it didn't quite meet her eyes.

"Are you okay?" I asked her, and she nodded and met me with the same smile she'd given him—thin, forced. There was a hardness to her expression, making her appear like a china doll.

While Ridley brought more logs over to the fireplace to help Kasper get it going faster, I walked over to Linnea. She stood at the edge of the room, her arms wrapped around herself, and when I put my hand on her shoulder, she jumped a little.

"What's wrong?" I asked softly.

"I'm just nervous." Linnea tried to force a smile at me, but she gave up and let out a panicked breath. "There's no going back now, is there?"

"What do you mean?" I asked.

But before she could answer, King Evert threw open the doors to the meeting room with Queen Mina following right behind. His black hair was disheveled from sleep, and he wore a silver satin robe lined with fur, while his wife wore a matching feminine version. Her hair hung down her back in a thick braid, and though both of them appeared to have just been roused from sleep, Mina had managed to put on her crown and a necklace before coming down here.

I walked over to the end of the table with Ridley to greet them, while Kasper took his post next to the fireplace, presumably leaving Elliot to guard the front gate by himself.

"What's this I hear about the Skojare Queen?" Evert asked and put his hands on his hips, managing to sound both concerned and irritated.

Mina had already spotted Linnea, gasping when she did. "It's true."

While the King demanded to know what was going on, his wife strode over to Linnea. Mina put her hands on Linnea's shoulders in a gesture of reassurance, and when she spoke in her faux-British accent the way she did whenever she was around royalty, her words were filled with soft comfort.

"How are you doing?" Mina asked her. "I can't imagine the ordeal you've been through."

"I'm all right," Linnea said, but her voice cracked a little.

Mina put her hand on Linnea's cheek and bent down to look her right in the eyes. "You're safe now. And that's what matters."

Linnea smiled gratefully at her and wiped at her eyes before a tear spilled over.

Ridley had been filling the King in on our adventures in finding Linnea, but I'd only been half-listening since I wanted to keep an eye on her. Mina looped her arm around Linnea's waist, and they turned their attention to Ridley and King Evert, so I did the same.

"Once we found Queen Linnea, we drove back here," Ridley said, finishing up the story.

Evert sat in his high-backed chair, and he scratched his head for a moment, taking in everything Ridley had said. Ridley and I stood across the table from him, waiting for his response.

"This is all well and good, and I am glad the Skojare Queen is safe"—he paused to look over at her—"I truly am. But Ridley, if I recall correctly, you asked to be relieved from your post for a few days to help the scouts track Viktor Dålig. You made no mention of the Skojare Queen."

Ridley cleared his throat and shifted his weight. I'd wondered what exactly he'd told the King so that both Ridley and

I had been able to get out of our duty here in Doldastam. Since we were on lockdown, I knew it couldn't have been easy.

"I believed that Queen Linnea may have had some information on the whereabouts of Viktor Dålig," Ridley explained.

Evert arched an eyebrow at Linnea. "Do you?"

"I don't—don't know who Viktor Dålig is." Linnea shook her head. "Should I?"

"No, you haven't had a reason to before." Evert held up his hand to her and turned his hardened gaze back to Ridley.

"It is unfortunate that she doesn't know anything, but it was a risk I thought was worth taking." Ridley stood firm. "Besides, she is the Skojare Queen. Her whereabouts are important to our people as a whole."

"My King, he's right," Mina chimed in. "Ridley and Bryn found Queen Linnea safe and sound. They did a commendable thing. You should not be yelling at them for it."

He let out a sigh, then nodded. "I'm sorry. My sleep-deprived brain is not functioning properly. This should be a time for celebration." Evert straightened up and smiled. "We'll call the Skojare King to retrieve his young bride, and when he does, we'll have a party in Queen Linnea's honor."

"Must I go back?" Linnea blurted out suddenly, and everyone turned to look at her.

"Don't you want to go home?" King Evert asked her.

"I miss my husband terribly, and my grandmother," Linnea hurried to explain. "But there is something going on in Storvatten. I don't feel safe there."

Evert shifted uneasily in his chair, unsure of how to deal

with a frightened teenage queen. "You have guards, and you have your husband. Talk to them, and I'm sure you'll sort it out."

"I don't trust the guards there." Linnea shook her head.

"Speaking from experience, I would say the guards in Storvatten are rather inept," I added. When we'd been at the palace right after Linnea had gone missing, I'd found the guards to be lazy, incompetent, and entirely unfit.

"That may be." Evert cleared his throat. "But this is something you must talk about with King Mikko. We have no control over the happenings in your kingdom."

Linnea lowered her head and nodded once. The last thing I wanted to do was send Linnea someplace where she was unsafe, but I couldn't think of a way to disagree with the King. He couldn't control the guards in another kingdom. That was up to Linnea and her husband.

"What if we send a couple guards with her, to help keep her safe?" Mina suggested. "At least until she and her husband get the situation sorted out in Storvatten."

Evert shook his head. "My Queen, you know we can't spare anyone right now."

"Surely we can spare one or two," Mina insisted, and I was aware that this was the exact opposite position she had held the last time I went to Storvatten. Then, she'd been fighting the King who wanted to send aid to the Skojare, saying we couldn't spare anyone.

It was also surprising how kind Mina seemed to be tonight. When I'd returned a few days ago, she'd been cold bordering on mean, which really wasn't like her. But now she seemed to have returned to her normal self.

I wondered if something had happened, or maybe her current disposition was simply because Linnea was here. I couldn't tell if Mina was genuinely concerned for her, or if our queen just wanted to save face in front of foreign royalty.

"What about Bryn?" Mina gestured to me. "She's familiar with the Skojare, and she's already proven herself to be a great help to Queen Linnea."

King Evert considered it for a moment, then nodded with some reluctance. "Bryn can go to Storvatten, if it's as Queen Linnea wishes, but we cannot spare Ridley. He's too important here."

"What about him?" Linnea asked, pointing to where Kasper stood next to the fireplace, and he appeared as startled as the rest of us. "I'd feel better going with someone I've already met, even if it's only briefly, than someone chosen at random."

"A member of the Högdragen would be good," Mina decided. "He can help retrain the guard in Storvatten."

"It's settled then," King Evert declared, probably before either Mina or Linnea suggested that anyone else tag along. "Bryn Aven and Kasper Abbott will accompany Queen Linnea back to Storvatten." He stood up. "Now, I will call her husband to let him know she's safe, and then I will return to bed since it's very late."

THIRTEEN

tutoring

"If you're going to represent the Högdragen, then you need to act like one."

Kasper stood in the center of the Högdragen training hall. Since he'd taken time out of his busy schedule specifically to work with me this morning, I knew that I should be paying attention to him, but I couldn't help but look around in awe.

The Högdragen area was located off the back of the palace, so I'd only ever caught glimpses inside it when I'd been in school, touring the palace. Attached to the training hall was a gym fully loaded with all kinds of equipment and a small dormitory, where the unmarried guards lived.

The training hall itself had less square footage than the tracker gymnasium at the school, but the ceilings seemed to go on forever, with iron lighting fixtures hanging from exposed beams and skylights above them. Tapestries of silver and black—the colors of the Högdragen uniform—adorned the walls. The floors were a glossy black walnut hardwood.

A few black wrestling mats were spread out in the center of the room, and Kasper stood on one. His dark tank top revealed the thick muscles of his arms, which were crossed over his chest. He was tall and broad-shouldered, especially for a Kanin, who tended to be on the slight side.

"I have had training before, you know," I reminded him as I walked out to meet him. We were the only two in the room, and my footfalls echoed through the cavernous space.

He smirked. "Not like this."

Since I would be going to Storvatten to help guard Linnea and I'd be accompanying Kasper, I'd technically be working as a liaison for the Högdragen. King Evert hadn't sorted out all the details before he'd gone to bed last night, but we'd gotten enough of them for Kasper to feel that some Högdragen training would be good for me.

For as long as I could remember, it's been my dream to be a member of the Högdragen, so I was doing my best to hold in my excitement and act professional. Ridley said it wasn't absolutely necessary, but I wasn't one to turn down doing anything that might help me join the Högdragen someday.

So I'd helped get Linnea settled in last night—along with Queen Mina, who insisted on personally seeing her to the guest chambers—and then I'd gone home, gotten a few hours of sleep, and woken up bright and early to meet Kasper for training.

"So what are we working on?" I asked.

"Since I probably only have about a day to get you ready, it's gonna be a crash course," he said grimly. "I wanna see where you're at, and we'll take it from there. And I want to work on how you carry yourself."

"How I carry myself?" I bristled. "There's nothing wrong with that."

One thing I took pride in was how I carried myself. Trackers had to learn to stand tall, shoulders back, chin up, feet together. We were slightly more relaxed than the Högdragen, who tended to stand and march like toy soldiers, but because of my aspirations, I mimicked the Högdragen the best I could.

"We'll talk about it when we get to it." Kasper held up his hand, silencing my argument. "But we should get started." He lowered his arms and stood with his feet shoulder length apart. "Show me what you've got."

I shook my head, not understanding, and my ponytail swayed behind me. "What do you mean?"

"I wanna see how you handle yourself in a fight. If we're going to protect the Skojare Queen from possible attempts on her life, I need to see how well you can do that."

For a moment, I hesitated out of a strange sense of intimidation. I'd fought guys as big as Kasper before, and Bent Stum had actually been much stronger than him. So that wasn't the issue. It was reverence for his title, and my fear that I wouldn't live up to the expectations of a proper Högdragen.

But Kasper had decided that it was time to start, so when I didn't move, he did. He came at me, and I quickly slipped out of the way. I was stocky and strong, but not as strong as him, so I knew that I'd have to use my agility and smaller stature to my advantage.

I swooped around him and crouched on the ground, preparing to kick out his legs from under him. As soon as I crouched, he grabbed my leg and flipped me back, so I landed on my back on the mat with a painful *thwock* that echoed through the hall.

The vision in my right eye blurred again for a moment, and I was beginning to wonder how long I'd have to deal with the aftermath of my injury. But within a second, I had jumped to my feet.

"The true testament of a good fighter isn't the ability to not get knocked down, but in how fast they can get back up," Kasper commented as I dusted myself off, then he grinned. "Though I've found it never hurts to avoid getting knocked down in the first place."

"Want me to go again?" I asked.

He nodded, and that was all the incentive I needed this time. I ran at him, and when he grabbed for me, I dodged around his side. This time, I jumped on his back and wrapped my arm around his neck, hoping that either my weight would throw him off balance or I could put him in a kind of sleeper hold.

But neither of those things happened. Instead, he threw himself back with all his might, crushing me against the floor before he hopped to his feet.

I got up again, just as quickly as I had before, even though that fall had hurt twice as badly, and it took longer for the vision in my eye to correct itself. As soon as I did, Kasper commanded, "Again."

So I went at him again. And again. And again. Sometimes our skirmishes went for longer, while others were over in a matter of seconds. I got the best of him a few times, knocking him down or pinning him.

By the time Kasper had knocked me on my back for the twentieth time that morning, I was not getting up so fast anymore. I lay on my back, staring up at the overcast sky through the skylights, and catching my breath.

I expected Kasper to tell me to go again, but instead he sat down on the mat next to me. Sweat glistened on his brow, and he appeared a little winded himself. I might not have beaten him as often as I'd have liked, but he was on the Högdragen. He was supposed to be a much better fighter than me, and the fact that he was tired at all showed I was doing something right.

"What do you think?" I asked.

His hair was cropped rather short, and he usually kept it back with gel, but the sweat had loosened a few curls so they fell forward. Kasper leaned back, propping himself on his arm, and absently pushed back the locks from his forehead.

"You're good for a tracker," he said with a light laugh. "We'll take five, and then I'll show you a few moves that I think can help you out where you're getting stuck."

The door at the end of the hall opened, and I craned my neck to see who was disturbing our practice. If it was somebody important, like another member of the Högdragen or the King,

I'd have forced myself to my feet, but it was only Tilda, carrying two bottles of water, so I could keep relaxing.

"I thought you two could probably use a bit of a break by now," Tilda told us with a smile and she sat down cross-legged on the mat.

"Thank you." I sat up so I could take the water from her and quickly guzzled it down, while Kasper gave her an appreciative peck on the mouth.

"Aren't you working this morning?" Kasper asked, motioning to her uniform.

"I am, but they're just running drills, so I snuck out for a few minutes." She smiled when she looked up at him, but it was bittersweet. "If you're leaving soon, I want to get in as much time with you as I can."

Kasper slid across the mat, moving closer to her. He wrapped an arm around her waist and leaned in even closer. "I'm sorry. You know I wouldn't leave if I didn't have to."

"I know." Tilda let out a heavy sigh and stared down at her lap. "I'll miss you, but I understand. I just wish that this didn't mean we'd have to postpone our wedding."

As a member of the Högdragen, Kasper really had no choice. King Evert hadn't consulted with him last night about whether he'd be willing or able to go, and he hadn't needed to. Being on the Högdragen was essentially like being property of the kingdom. Everyone in Doldastam had to follow the King's orders, but none so strictly as the Högdragen. If the King said jump, they didn't ask how high—they just jumped.

"I shouldn't be gone for very long," Kasper assured her.

"We just have to make sure the Queen is safe and help set up a more functional guard, and then we'll be home. And as soon as I get back, we'll be married."

He put his hand on her stomach, rubbing the bump where their child grew, and Tilda smiled at him. They kissed again, more deeply than the last time, and while it wasn't a crazy makeout session, it was enough that I began to feel uncomfortable.

And not just because I felt like a creepy voyeur. They were so clearly in love—evident in the way they looked at each other and touched one another. For a fleeting second, it made me think of Ridley and wonder if I had made the wrong choice pushing him away.

But then I remembered why they were kissing in the first place. Kasper was comforting Tilda because he was leaving her, because he wasn't in control of his own life. He'd given himself to the Högdragen, and no matter how much he loved her, she'd have to come second to the job.

I didn't want to do that to anyone else, and I never wanted to be forced to choose between love and duty. So it was best if I just avoided love altogether.

"I can give you two a minute alone, if you want," I offered.

"No, we're fine." Tilda laughed and blushed before putting some distance between her and Kasper. "I should probably get back soon anyway."

"And we should get back to training," Kasper agreed.

"How is that going?" Tilda asked me. "He's not being too rough on you, is he?"

"No. He's not dishing out anything I can't take."

"I'll have to try harder then," Kasper said, and Tilda laughed.

"You two just better not hurt each other," she warned us. "Or you'll have me to deal with."

"Yes, ma'am." I saluted her, and she rolled her eyes.

"I really should get back," she said, and she kissed Kasper before getting to her feet. "I'll see you tonight?"

"As soon as I'm done working the dinner for the Skojare King and Queen," he said. "Then I'll be over."

"I love you." Tilda looked between the two of us. "Both of you. So play nice."

As soon as she was gone, Kasper and I got up, and he told me to come at him again like I had before—only this time, he would teach me how not to end up flat on my back.

FOURTEEN

beholden

Even though there were only eight of us attending the celebratory dinner, we still waited in a line to be announced by King Evert's personal guard, Reid Kasten. It was a meeting of royalty, which called for formality. King Mikko Biâelse of the Skojare, and Linnea's grandmother, Marksinna Lisbet Ahlstrom, had arrived to retrieve Linnea.

They were so grateful that Ridley and I had found her that we were invited to attend the dinner as honored guests, which felt a bit odd for us. I would always have rather been working than making awkward dinner conversation, but I would be lying if I said that I didn't enjoy a reason to put on the new dress I'd gotten from the town square.

As much as I loved working out and showing my strength—the way I had been all day with Kasper—I loved getting dressed up almost as much. For most of my life, I'd been pigeonholed as purely a tomboy, but that wasn't accurate. I could hold my own wrestling in the mud with boys, and I could hold my own in a gown in the ballroom.

The dress I wore today was silvery white with a damask design in pale blue velvet over it. The front hem of the dress fell just above my knees, on the off chance I'd need to fight or run, and the back flowed out much longer behind me, trailing on the ground.

As strange as I felt waiting beside Ridley in line to enter the dining hall, Kasper seemed even more awkward. He'd only planned on working the party—standing at attention by the door. Instead, Markisinna Lisbet had insisted he join as a guest, and he stood behind us, fidgeting with his uniform and muttering anxiously.

Reid loudly announced King Mikko and Queen Linnea, and they entered the dining hall to formally greet Evert and Mina before taking their seats at the long table. Since Lisbet was of a lower rank than them—a Markisinna is a step below Princess—she would be introduced after them. While waiting, she took a moment to turn to Ridley and me.

Her golden hair was carefully coiffed on her head, and her elegant gown easily surpassed mine in loveliness. Large diamonds and sapphires adorned heavy rings on her fingers. Even though she had to be in her sixties, she still had an incredible, refined beauty.

"I am so sorry about the way things went in Storvatten when you were there before," Lisbet said, her brilliant blue eyes moist with tears.

"There is no need to be," Ridley assured her.

I wasn't completely sure what she was apologizing for, other than when Victor Dålig had slammed my head into the wall. But that wasn't her fault. That was mine.

She smiled and took my hand and Ridley's in each of hers—her skin soft and warm like thin velvet. "I cannot thank you enough for bringing my granddaughter safely back to me. Anything—*anything*—either of you ever need, let me know."

"Marksinna Lisbet Ahlstrom of the Skojare," Reid announced.

Lisbet squeezed our hands and mouthed the words *thank you* again before letting go. She gathered up the length of her dress, then entered the dining hall.

Since Kasper was a member of the Högdragen, it meant he outranked us, so he was called next, leaving Ridley and me alone in the foyer. As the Överste, Ridley could've worn his uniform the way Kasper had, but instead he'd chosen a well-tailored suit.

As we waited, he readjusted the cuff links in the sleeve of his black dress shirt. I stood with my hands clasped neatly in front of me, watching as Kasper stiffly greeted everyone in the room.

"Are you heading out tomorrow?" Ridley asked, still fixing the diamond cuff link.

"I believe that's the plan. We're leaving first thing in the morning to head back to Storvatten."

"It's a really good opportunity for you." He'd finished his readjustment and folded his hands behind his back, standing tall and proper. "Working with the Högdragen like this. And you've earned it. Nobody has worked harder for recognition than you have."

"Thank you."

"But I have to be honest," he said in a low voice. "It's not gonna be the same here without you."

He looked at me then, his deep-set eyes under a veil of thick lashes. The heat I'd been longing to see in them had returned, and for a moment, there was nothing else. It was only me and him, and the warmth growing in my belly, and the way he made me feel so light-headed and wonderful all at once.

And then, "Ridley Dresden, the Överste of the Kanin," Reid announced so loudly it almost felt as if he were shouting inside my head.

Ridley walked away from me, leaving me behind to catch my breath. Which was just as well, because I'd never have made it through the introductions without a moment to gather myself.

I was seated next to Lisbet, and after I'd gotten settled in I realized that must've been a deliberate choice. All the Skojare—me, Lisbet, Linnea, and Mikko—were on one side of the table, a row of pale blonds across from the darker complexioned Kanin: Ridley, Evert, Mina, and Kasper.

For a second, before I got myself under control, I felt a wave of anger wash over me. I hated being singled out or deemed as "other" simply because of the color of my hair and skin. Even though this hadn't been done out of malice, it still stung every time I was deemed "un-Kanin."

But then I reminded myself that it was an honor to even be here, that I was still seated next to royalty. And maybe the decision had to do with ranking, and since I was the lowest one here, I was seated with our guests instead of next to our King.

Maybe. But I didn't really believe that.

Mikko started off dinner with a toast, standing and raising his glass of sparkling wine. The last time I'd seen him in Storvatten, he'd been a wreck—an overacting wreck, I'd suspected. But now he showed no signs of wear. His handsome face was unreadable, even when he looked down at his wife.

"I want to thank you all for returning my wife to me and for showing her so much hospitality," Mikko said, his deep voice betraying no emotion. "Your kindness and bravery will not soon be forgotten, and the Skojare are indebted to you." He raised his glass higher. "*Skål!*"

"*Skål!*" We all cheered in unison, then took a drink of our wine.

"I would also like to extend a special thanks to both Kasper Abbott and Bryn Aven," Mikko went on, still standing and taking turns looking between Kasper and me. "You are taking on the responsibilities of another tribe, which goes far beyond your duties. While I don't know if the Skojare *need* you, it will provide my wife great comfort, and it is as she wishes."

"It is." Linnea smiled up at her husband, and then she got to her feet.

It was a faux pas for her to speak while another person was toasting, and it was especially unheard of for her to stand up and join him. But when she looked out with sparkling eyes at the table, beaming with such wild delight, it was obvious that her excitement would not be held back by propriety.

"We both want to offer you our immense gratitude," Linnea said. She lifted her glass high in the air, spilling a few drops in her haste, but she didn't seem to notice or mind. "So to Kasper Abbott and Bryn Aven, I'd like to drink to you!"

She quickly took a drink from her glass, but everyone else was slower to follow suit. Kasper reddened and smiled thinly at her before taking a very quick sip. A King and Queen were never supposed to drink to their staff, but since Queen Linnea had suggested it, everyone had to do it or they would seem rude.

I finished my glass in one long swig because I had a feeling that it was going to be the kind of night where I'd want the wine to take the edge off, and as the dinner progressed, I was repeatedly proven right.

Linnea was almost giddy, and while Lisbet was much more composed and reserved than her granddaughter, she was also brimming with happiness. The two of them talked and giggled, steering most of the conversation. Queen Mina was determined not to be left behind, so she laughed louder and spoke quicker than she normally did.

King Evert, for his part, tried to look amused and interested, but he'd never been a good actor. I always thought that being a leader meant having a good poker face, but Evert proved me wrong in that regard.

Despite the antics of Linnea, it was her husband that kept drawing my attention. He didn't seem annoyed or embarrassed by her behavior, nor did he seem to enjoy it. He rarely spoke, instead sitting quietly and eating his food without reacting much to what was happening.

He seemed so cold and distant. I couldn't imagine that

Linnea actually loved him or missed him the way she claimed to have.

And even as the happy haze brought on by several glasses of wine settled over me, I found myself once again wondering what exactly Mikko was hiding behind his blank stare.

FIFTEEN

intemperance

My boots came up to my knees, and my jacket went down to the ground, but the cold air still managed to get through, sending a chill down my spine. Not that I minded. As the evening dragged on, the dining hall had grown increasingly warm and stifling.

Just beyond the palace door, I breathed in deeply, relishing the icy taste of the air as it cooled my flushed cheeks. The combination of being free from the dinner, the minor promotion in job duties, and the buzz from the alcohol all seemed to hit me with the exhilarating headiness of the wind. The night suddenly felt so very alive.

"I'll meet you at the garage at seven in the morning," Kasper reminded me. He and Ridley had been standing just behind me, making small talk about the dinner, and now Kasper had begun to say his good-byes.

"I'll be there," I said with an easy grin.

Ridley waved at him as Kasper left, watching as he walked away—nearly jogging in his hurry to get to Tilda's apartment. It was less than eight hours until he would have to be up, getting ready to depart for Storvatten, so I'm sure he wanted to make the most of their last evening together for a while.

"I'm surprised you're in such a good mood," Ridley said, turning his attention to me. He moved a few steps closer, filling in the gap that Kasper's absence had left. "After that *interesting* evening we had."

I laughed. "Yeah, but it's over now."

"It makes me glad we're not royalty. I'd hate to sit through those all the time."

"It's getting late." I exhaled deeply, letting my breath fog up the air. "I should be heading home and to bed, since I have a long day tomorrow."

"Yeah, I suppose." Ridley glanced up at the night sky, then back at me. "You be careful this time, all right?"

"I will," I promised him.

Then, since there really wasn't anything more to say, I gave him a small wave before turning to walk away. I'd only made it four steps before he stopped me.

"Bryn," he said, and I looked back over my shoulder at him. "Let me walk you home."

They were five simple words that sounded almost inconsequential, especially since Ridley had walked me home on several occasions. But somehow tonight they felt like so much more. There was a weight to them that had never been there before.

It was in Ridley's tone, which held a hint of urgency, his voice low but strong enough to carry. In his eyes that burned so intensely, I could almost see the hunger hidden in the darkness.

Finally, I answered him, and I didn't even know what I would say until the word came out of my mouth. "Okay."

He looked relieved, and then he walked over to meet me. His steps matched mine easily. I wrapped my arms around myself to keep from shaking—if it was from nerves or the cold, I wasn't sure—and he kept his hands in his pockets. The night was quiet, the streets were empty, and neither of us was saying anything.

It was a two-minute walk from the palace to the stables, and it had never felt so strange. My heart was racing, quickly pumping blood that felt too hot in my veins, and it caused a delirious heat to wash over me.

It was really the strangest feeling. Like teetering on the edge of a precipice. I *knew* something was going to happen. And the anticipation was killing me.

My apartment was a loft above the stables, and when we reached the staircase that ran alongside the building, I started to go up. But Ridley had stayed behind. I turned back to face him, standing at the bottom of the stairs and staring up at me with the same look he'd had outside of the palace.

"Aren't you coming up?" I asked, and for one terrifying moment, I was certain he wouldn't. And then he began to climb the stairs.

At the landing, I unlocked the door, acutely aware of Ridley's body behind me. My hair had been pinned up in a loose updo, and I could feel his breath warming the back of my neck.

We went inside, pretending this was normal, that this was like every other time he'd been in my loft, but the air felt electrified. He commented on the dirty laundry overflowing my hamper, and I apologized for the cold while starting a fire in the woodburning stove.

I kicked off my boots and jacket then lit a few candles while he set aside his own jacket and shoes. Now we stood in the center of the room, a few feet of empty space between us, gawking at each other. The floorboards felt cold underneath my feet, and I kept staring at the few buttons of his shirt that had been left undone, showing off the smooth skin of his chest.

I opened my mouth, planning to ask him if he wanted to sit down or have a drink, but the words suddenly felt like a waste. I didn't want to sit down or have a drink. I only wanted *him*.

I went over to him, and without hesitation, without thinking, without worry, I kissed him, knowing he would kiss me back just as hungrily. And he did not disappoint. He wrapped his arms around me, pulling me to him, but I didn't feel close enough. I pushed him back until he hit the wall.

Ridley stopped kissing me long enough to smile crookedly as I started to undo the buttons of his shirt, but even that quick separation felt too long. Then his fingers were in my hair, and his lips were on my mouth, and I didn't know if I'd ever wanted anything as badly as I wanted him. My body literally ached for him, starting in my chest and working its way down to a desperate longing between my legs.

His shirt was gone, and I'm not sure if he pulled it off or I did, but either way I was grateful. I ran my hands over the firm ridges of his chest and stomach, surprised by how warm his skin felt against mine. Then I felt his hand on my thigh, curious and strong.

Just as his fingers looped around the thin waistband of my panties, Ridley pulled his mouth from mine and looked me in the eyes. "Are you sure—"

But I silenced his question by kissing him again, and I put my hand over his and pushed down, helping him slip off my panties. I stepped out of them and back from him. As he watched me, I pulled my dress up over my head and tossed it to the floor.

His eyes widened in appreciation, and he whispered, "We should've done this a long time ago."

Ridley started to unbutton his pants as he stepped closer to me. He reached out for me, but I pushed him on the bed so he was lying on his back. Grabbing his pants with my hand, I yanked them off in one swift move, and then I climbed over him, letting my body hover just above his.

I leaned down, kissing him again, savoring the moment. Our bodies were so close, I could feel the heat from his. He put one hand on my hip, his fingers gripping me desperately, begging for more.

And then finally, I lowered myself on him, and my breath

caught in my throat. He gasped, almost in relief, and closed his eyes at first until we found our rhythm together.

I sat up, taking more of him and moving faster. He was breathing heavier, and just as the delicious heat exploded deep within me, Ridley sat up, still inside of me. He wrapped his arm around me, holding me against him at the moment he finished.

We both leaned against each other, panting, and my body felt like jelly. As if all my bones and muscles had melted into this wonderful, contented goo, and all I wanted to do was stay melded to Ridley like this forever.

But I couldn't. I leaned back a bit, trying to catch my breath. My hair had come free, and Ridley brushed away a lock that had fallen in my face. He let his hand linger, warming my cheek, and by the look in his eyes, I knew he wanted to say something he wouldn't be able to take back.

"Don't," I whispered.

He shook his head. "Don't what?"

"Don't say anything that would spoil this. Let's just leave this as it is."

He let out a deep breath. "Okay."

I smiled at him, pleased that he wouldn't push anything, and I climbed off him. I blew out the candle on my table and the one next to my bed, so the loft was in near darkness with only the fire in the stove casting light.

I climbed back in bed, lying on my side with my back to Ridley. He waited, sitting on the bed where I'd left him, but now

I felt the bed moving as he settled in behind me. I scooted back on the bed, moving closer to him, and he put his arm around my waist, strong and warm against my bare skin.

His body felt wonderful against mine, spooning me to him. I closed my eyes, wishing I could fall asleep like this every night, but knowing I never would again.

SIXTEEN

annul

The fire had gone out in the stove, so it was cold and dark as I scrambled around my loft. I'd pulled on a sweater and moved onto digging through my top drawer for a clean pair of panties and a bra, but I kept coming up with mismatched socks instead, making me curse myself for not doing laundry more often.

The bed creaked behind me, and I hurried to yank on my underwear. I could make out the dim outline of Ridley as he sat up, and my whole body tensed up as my stomach dropped. I'd been hoping to sneak out of here before he woke up, so I could avoid an awkward morning-after conversation.

"Sorry if I woke you," I said, since standing in tense silence wasn't making the situation any better.

"No, it's no problem." He leaned forward and clicked on my bedside lamp, bathing the room in dim light.

Ridley sat at the edge of my bed, the covers draped across

his lap and covering the more intimidating parts of his naked body. He was hunched forward slightly, staring down at the worn floorboards, and he ran his hand through his tangles of sleep-messy curls.

I waited, hoping he would say something, *afraid* he would say something. But when he didn't, I burst into motion. As uncomfortable and even painful as this morning was, I still had a job today. I had twenty minutes to pack and meet Kasper at the garage before heading out to Storvatten.

"Sorry, I have to get going," I tried to explain so he wouldn't think I was rushing out on him, even though I would've wanted to rush out on him whether I had somewhere to be or not.

"No, I get it."

Throwing my duffel bag on my old couch, I quickly made trips from my dresser and armoire, loading it up with everything I thought I might need. It was a little tough packing, because I wasn't entirely sure how long I'd be gone. It could be a few weeks—maybe even longer.

Plus, I need clothing for every occasion. Jeans for working, suits for meetings, uniforms for formal affairs, and even a couple of dresses. Thankfully, in tracker school, we'd actually had classes on learning to pack quickly and efficiently.

"Listen," Ridley said.

I paused long enough to look at him, and I realized that I'd been so focused on packing that I hadn't noticed him getting out of bed and dressing. His shirt still wasn't buttoned, and he was fixing the collar as he spoke. Still only wearing a sweater and no pants, I suddenly felt exposed.

"We don't need to talk about last night." I tried to brush him off and run back to packing, but he put his hand on my arm as I darted by, stopping me.

"I want to, though," he insisted.

Swallowing hard, I looked up at him. "Okay."

"Last night . . ." Ridley's eyes were slightly downcast, so he wasn't looking directly at me. He took a deep breath. "Last night was kind of amazing."

"Yeah," I said, since I couldn't think of anything more to say.

Last night actually had been amazing. I could still taste his lips on mine and feel his hands on my skin. In the moment afterward as I lay in his arms, my head against his shoulder, both of us gasping for breath, our bodies entangled—I'd never felt closer to anyone. I'd had this sense of utter completion that I'd never felt before.

Now, I felt a strange, cold emptiness inside me, an absence where he'd been.

"I don't know why it happened. I mean, I'm not complaining." He gave a weak smile that quickly faded away. "But it doesn't matter why, I guess. It just . . . We both know that it can't happen again."

"It can't," I agreed, somehow managing to force out the two most painful words I'd ever spoken. My throat wanted to close up around them, swallowing them completely, but I had to say them.

I knew that Ridley was saying this so I wouldn't have to. He was doing this to spare me the discomfort of actually having to form the words. But that didn't make this conversation any less painful.

"It's too much of a risk for you." Then Ridley shook his head, correcting himself. "For both of us, really. I could lose my position as the Överste, and before I honestly wouldn't have cared that much. But with us going after Viktor Dålig, I want to be there on the front lines."

"As you should be," I said. "Working with Kasper, this is my big chance to make a good impression for the Högdragen. I can't blow that by giving anyone any reason to think I might have gotten where I am by sleeping with my boss.

"And you'll be busy with your work," I continued. "And I'll be gone for a long time. There's not even any point to us, even if we wanted there to be."

Ridley looked me in the eyes for the first time since we'd woken up. There was so much unsaid, so much hanging between us, the air felt thicker. All I wanted to do was kiss him one last time, but I knew that would only make things harder.

"And there's Juni," Ridley said, breaking the moment, and I lowered my eyes. "She's not my girlfriend, but she deserves better than this."

"She does," I said, and I meant it. Juni had to be one of the nicest people I'd ever met, and I sincerely doubted she would approve of Ridley spending the night with me.

"Whatever has been going on with us lately . . ." He trailed off, waiting several moments before finishing. "It has to be over now. Last night was it. That was the last time."

I nodded, because I was afraid I wouldn't be able to speak if

I tried. He was right, and I agreed with him entirely. If he hadn't said it, I would've.

But it still broke my heart. The intensity and the severity of the ache in my chest was something that I hadn't been expecting. It hurt so badly it almost took my breath away.

So I bit the inside of my cheek, focusing on the pain, and stared down at the floor, waiting for this moment to be over. Ridley finished gathering up his things, and I didn't look at him or say a word. I didn't even move until I heard the door shut behind him.

Then I ran a hand through my hair, took a deep breath, and finished packing. It was the only thing I could do to keep from screaming.

SEVENTEEN

recrudescence

Under the twilight sky, the palace in Storvatten left me just as awestruck as when I'd first laid eyes on it. Its walls were made of luminous pale cerulean, curved and molded to look like waves swirling around the palace. Several spires soared high into the air, and in the fading light, set against the amethyst sky, the glass always seemed to glow.

Kasper and I walked along the long dock that connected the palace with the shore, since it sat like an island fortress several miles out into Lake Superior. It was a long walk, but it gave us plenty of time to admire the beauty of the fantastical structure that rose from the water, leaving a mirrored reflection beside it.

It was much warmer in Storvatten than it had been in Doldastam, with all of the snow melted. There was no ice on the lake near the palace, but I suspected that had more to do with Skojare magic than it did with the temperature. A lake frozen through is no place to swim.

When we reached the doors of the palace, Kasper paused to smooth out his uniform, even though it didn't need smoothing. For our long journey south, we'd worn comfortable attire, but to greet royalty we couldn't look like we'd been traveling all day.

At the end of the dock, before we left our SUV with a valet, Kasper had put on his uniform, and I'd changed into a simple but elegant white dress. On the drive, I'd already touched up my makeup and put my hair into a cascading side braid. Fortunately, the bruise on my temple had faded enough that I was finally able to mask it entirely with concealer.

Kasper used the large, heavy knocker, which commanded a low booming sound that seemed to resonate through everything. While we waited for the footman to answer, I took a moment to admire the massive iron doors. The last time I was here, I hadn't noticed the intricate designs carved into them. They showed Ægir—the Norse god of the sea—with waves crashing around him.

As soon as the footman opened the door, I heard a voice booming behind him. Despite its cheery tone, it had a thunderous quality, much like King Mikko's, so I knew it had to be Mikko's younger brother, Prince Kennet Biâelse.

"Let them in, let them in," Kennet commanded. He shooed the footman away and opened the door wider, smiling broadly at me. "You've had a long journey. Come inside."

I returned his smile and stepped inside past him, noting that he smelled faintly but rather deliciously of the sea. But the scent was mixed with something else, something refreshing and cool, like rain on a spring day or an arctic breeze. I wasn't sure exactly what it was, but I couldn't help but breathe in more deeply anyway.

"The King, the Queen, and Lisbet arrived about fifteen minutes before you did," Kennet explained. "They extend their apologies, but they're exhausted from their trip and have retired for the evening. So I'll be showing you to your rooms and getting you anything you'd like."

"Showing us to our rooms will be enough," Kasper said as he admired the main hall.

The rounded walls were sandblasted glass—opaque with a hint of light turquoise showing through. Like the outside of the palace, they were shaped to look like waves. They curved around us, making it feel as though we were standing in the center of a whirlpool.

Beneath our feet, the floors were glass, allowing us a glimpse of the pool below. It was empty now, but when I'd been here before, I'd seen royalty swimming in it. Above us, chandeliers of diamonds and sapphires sparkled, splashing shards of light all around the room.

"To your rooms it is," Kennet said with a bright smile, and he turned to lead us out of the main hall down to the quarters where we'd be staying.

Even though it was late, Kennet still wore a suit, and I'd never actually seen him in anything else. This time it was a frosty gray that shimmered silver when the light hit it right, and it was perfectly tailored for his well-toned frame.

Both Kennet and his older brother, Mikko, were very handsome: golden hair, dazzling aqua eyes, strong jaws, perfect complexions, and deep, powerful voices. Kennet was slightly shorter and more slender than his brother, but he didn't appear any less muscular.

"I didn't expect you back so soon," Kennet said, lowering his voice as though he were confiding in me. He walked beside me down the corridor, while Kasper followed a step behind. "But I have to admit, I'm happy you are."

"I'm just happy it's under much better circumstances," I replied carefully.

"Ah, yes. With the Queen back, it is a time of much celebration." His voice rose with excitement when he spoke, but then he looked down at me, smiling with a glint in his eye. "Hopefully that means our time together will be much more fun this time around."

It occurred to me that Ridley had been right when we were here before (as painful as it was to think of Ridley in any capacity right now). He'd thought that Kennet had been flirting with me, and I'd brushed it off as nonsense. But now I was beginning to see the merit in the idea.

Ordinarily, I would consider it a bad idea to flirt with a Prince. It could be rather dangerous, in fact. But considering that something very strange was going on in this palace, having another member of the royal family on my side wouldn't be a bad thing.

"I'm certain it will be," I said, attempting to match Kennet's playful grin with my own, and he laughed warmly.

Kennet led us down the spiral staircase toward the private

quarters. The main floor was entirely above the surface of the lake, while the private quarters and the ballroom were located underneath the water. As soon as we went downstairs, the musty scent grew stronger.

While an underwater palace sounded like a magical and grand thing, the impracticality of it seemed to have taken its toll. Wallpaper lined the hallway—blue with an icy sheen—but it had begun to peel at some of the corners. Even the navy-and-white checked tiles on the floor had begun to warp in a few places. All damage from the constant moisture of being in a lake.

As I suspected, Kennet led me to the room I had stayed in before, after first dropping Kasper off several doors away. The valet had already carried my bags down, and I was pleased to find them sitting on the lush bedding.

The wall to the outside bowed out, like a fishbowl, and the darkness of the water seemed to engulf the room. Despite all its luxurious trappings, the room filled me with a sense of unease. Like I was a dolphin on display at a zoo.

"In case you don't remember from last time, the bathroom is across the hall," Kennet explained; he'd followed me inside the room, standing directly behind me as I stared out at the lake. "My room is in the other wing, should you need me for anything at all."

I turned back to face him, and despite the gnawing ache in my heart over Ridley, there was something in Kennet's smile that made it . . . not exactly easy to smile back, but at least not so hard and not quite so painful.

"I trust that the room is in order for you," Kennet asked, and I realized he hadn't taken his eyes off me since we'd entered the room.

Smiling, I gestured around me. "It's perfect, thank you."

"If there's anything you desire, I'll be happy to get it for you." And there it was again. A glint in his eye that somehow seemed both dangerous and a bit charming.

"Thank you, but right now the only thing I desire is a good night's sleep," I told him politely.

He arched an eyebrow. "You will let me know if that changes?"

"Of course."

When he left, shutting the door behind him, I let out a deep breath and collapsed on the bed behind me. The day had left me exhausted in ways I didn't even know were possible. It still felt as if a hole had been torn inside me, as if my very insides had been ripped out, leaving a cold shell.

But there was no time to cry or mourn what might have been between Ridley and me. It was over, the way it should've been a long time ago, and the only thing I could do was push past it and hope that eventually the pain would get more bearable.

EIGHTEEN

exchequer

First thing in the morning, Kennet took Kasper and me down to the guard station. The last time I'd been here, when Ridley and I had been investigating Linnea's disappearance, we'd been denied access to the guards.

This time, Kasper and I were here specifically to see if there was any truth to Linnea's concerns and to implement new standards for the guards so they'd be better protection for the royalty. That meant we had to be directly involved with the guards.

The guard station was a small round room at the center of the lower level of the palace. It was sparsely decorated, with three large paintings of the royal family the only adornments on its white walls. Four large desks were placed at odd angles, along with several filing cabinets.

Much like the rest of the palace, everything in this room looked as though it had seen better days, save for the steel vault on the other side of the room. It appeared to be sterling and new, as though it would fit better in a bank vault than an old office.

Hunched over one of the desks, a guard scribbled something down on a notepad. His golden hair was slicked back until it curled at the nape of his neck, with just a hint of silver at his temples revealing his age. Under the tailored sleeves of his dress shirt, his shoulders were broad and his biceps were rather thick.

Another man—younger than the first, closer to my age—with a slender build and a slightly upturned nose, sat perched on the edge of the desk. He'd been leaning over, watching what the older man was writing, but he instantly hopped to his feet when we walked into the room.

"Your Highness," he said, bowing before Kennet.

The other man, who had been working on something, rose more slowly.

"No need for the formalities." Kennet brushed them off and glanced back at Kasper and me. "Bayle can be old school at times. He's a relic from Father's reign." The older guard grimaced, not that I blamed him, but Kennet turned back to him with a smile. "I'm just here to make the introductions. These are our friends from the Kanin, Bryn Aven and Kasper Abbott."

"Nice to meet you," the younger man said, but he didn't really looked pleased to meet us, nor did he introduce himself.

"I'm Bayle Lundeen." The older man came around the desk to shake our hands. "I'm the head guard. Anything you need, I should be able to help you."

"They're actually here to help *you*," Kennet reminded him.

"We need to revamp things so the Queen feels safe in her own home."

"Yes, of course." Bayle smiled wanly at us. "I'll do my best to implement any changes that the King and Queen see fit to impose."

"I just hope a uniform isn't one of them." The younger guard snickered, and Bayle shot him a glare.

Kasper had worn his Högdragen uniform, the way he did any time he was working. Since I wasn't officially on the Högdragen, I wasn't allowed to wear one, so I'd gone with a modified version of a tracker solider uniform: tailored black linen with epaulets, but not nearly as flashy as the silver and black velvet one Kasper wore.

"I'm sorry. I didn't catch your name," Kasper said, his tone even and polite.

"Cyrano Moen." The younger man straightened up, raising his chin. "I'm the Queen's personal guard."

"Well, Cyrano, it's funny that you mention uniforms, because I was actually going to suggest them," Kasper said, causing Cyrano to scowl.

"We've always had a dress code here." Bayle gestured to his and Cyrano's outfits, which were very businesslike—dark trousers, dress shirts, ties. Cyrano even had a suit jacket.

"A dress code isn't the same as a uniform," Kasper explained. "The Kanin have found that not only do those wearing a uniform tend to exhibit more pride and integrity on the job, but they also have more of a presence since they give the guard greater visibility. Ultimately, we've found that a uniform provides a sense of security and helps curb assaults."

Cyrano looked at Kennet, almost pleading with him to stop Kasper, but Kennet shrugged and smiled.

"We actually do have uniforms," Bayle said. "We only wear them for special occasions, like weddings or coronations, but it wouldn't be unthinkable for us to start wearing them on a daily basis."

"You're all working together!" Kennet beamed and clapped Bayle on the back. Still grinning, he looked at me. "Is there anything more you need from me before I leave Bayle to show you around the place?"

"No, I'm certain Bayle will be more than helpful," Kasper replied.

I didn't say anything, but my gaze had wandered back to the strange vault door at the other side of the room. It stood in stark contrast to the worn look of everything else. I wondered if the armory was behind it, but I doubted the Skojare had much in the way of weapons.

"You wanna see what's behind that door?" Kennet asked with a wag of his eyebrows.

Bayle cleared his throat. "My Prince, I'm not sure if that would be wise."

"Nonsense!" Kennet strode across the room. "There are several guards here. Nothing will go wrong."

I shook my head. "I don't need to see anything if it will cause trouble."

"It's no trouble at all." Kennet punched a few numbers on a state-of-the-art keypad next to the door, then scanned his thumb—both of which were light years ahead of the lock-and-key system the Skojare had for the dungeon.

Kasper pursed his lips and glanced over at me, as if I had intentionally brought this on. While Bayle seemed to have misgivings about Kennet opening the door, Cyrano had walked up behind Kennet, almost standing on his tiptoes so he could peer inside the second it opened.

There were several loud clicks, followed by a strange wooshing sound, and then the door slowly opened a bit. Kennet glanced around and, seeing that I wasn't beside him, he waved me over.

"Come have a look," he insisted with a smile. As soon as I'd reached him, he threw open the door, and I was nearly blinded by the sparkling inside.

I wish I could say that it didn't hit me the way it did—that my jaw didn't drop and my heart didn't skip a beat for a moment. But despite my education, and even my career in service, I still had troll blood coursing through my veins, and if there was one thing trolls desired in life it was gems.

The round room behind the vault door wasn't very large—maybe the size of standard swimming pool. White lights from the ceiling were aimed perfectly so there could be no shadows. Nothing could hide in here.

But the space was packed with sapphires. It actually seemed like a rather childish way to store them, with jewels simply piled up around the room. There were a few shelves where larger, more precious stones were displayed, but mostly they were just strewn about. Millions of dollars in gemstones were lying around the way a messy child might leave toy cars.

While most of the sapphires were a darker blue, they came in all shades ranging from pale turquoise to nearly black, not to mention some that were pink or red. Some were translucent, like diamonds, while others were opaque, like opals. But all of them sparkled like the night sky.

I didn't know enough of Skojare history to say for certain where they'd gotten all of these, but I knew they had once traded with humans for jewels. If I went far enough back in their history, I'd heard tales of them stealing, some of their ancestors even taking to the sea and pirating.

But really, it didn't matter how the Skojare had gotten the sapphires; they were here now, and I realized they were the only things in the palace that were safely guarded.

The gems also didn't completely mesh with what I'd seen of the palace and what I knew about the Skojare tribe. My understanding was that their funds were drying up. I'd heard they still had some jewels, but they were hoarding them so they wouldn't go completely broke.

The hoarding definitely did appear to be true, but apparently the term *some jewels* was very subjective.

"Beautiful, aren't they?" Kennet asked, breaking my trance, and I turned back to him, forcing myself not to admire the gems anymore.

"Yes, they're quite lovely," I admitted.

"I suppose that's enough for today then," Kennet said, and

he closed the door almost reluctantly, locking the treasure back up.

After that he left, allowing Bayle and Cyrano to give Kasper and me a tour of the palace and explain its inner workings.

The palace was filled with the wealthiest members of the Skojare, living in small apartmentlike spaces, and the guards, who lived in smaller dormitories on the second floor. The guards in their suits were nearly indistinguishable from the rich, and in part, I think that was because the lower-class didn't want it to be obvious who worked for whom.

Eliminating class distinctions was commendable, but somebody had to protect the royalty. Even public leaders in the human world had a secret service. Everybody couldn't run around and play together. Somebody had to do the work, but here in Storvatten, it seemed that nobody wanted to.

It could even be seen in how rundown everything was. But as I saw the cracks in the walls, the warped floor tiles, and even the broken locks, I couldn't help but think back to the vault filled with sapphires.

Why did the Skojare let the palace fall to disrepair when they had so much money? Was their greed so strong that they would rather sit on the gems and let everything fall apart around them than spend the money on necessary repairs? It was like one of Aesop's fables, where the outcome couldn't be good for them.

NINETEEN

de rigueur

"It's insane to me that they've lived like this for so long," I said for the hundredth time.

After Kasper and I had spent a long day going over the palace with Bayle and taking notes, we'd retired to my room to start making a plan for how we would improve things. The problem was that there were *so* many areas that needed improvement, it was hard to know where to begin.

Bayle had provided us with all kinds of paperwork on training processes, job descriptions, schedules, dress codes, pretty much everything we might want to look at, and it was spread out all over my bed.

I had a notebook on my lap so I could jot down ideas, and Kasper was pacing the room, looking over a training sheet and shaking his head. He'd taken off his uniform jacket, so he wore only the T-shirt underneath.

"They have zero combat training." Kasper hit the paper in

his hand. "How can you be a guard if you have no ability to protect anyone?"

"I don't know." I shrugged. "I can't believe that something bad hasn't happened already."

"Everyone here is almost completely unprotected!" Kasper was nearly shouting in his frustration. "The only things they've got properly secured are those ridiculous sapphires, and I can't believe they even thought of that."

I was about to join in Kasper's rant about the severe inadequacies of the Skojare guard when a small knock at the door interrupted us. Pushing the papers aside, I got up and answered it to find Marksinna Lisbet, dressed in a flowing gown.

"Dinner starts in twenty minutes, and we'd be so pleased if you both could join us," Lisbet said, smiling in her aristocratic way that I'd begun to find charming.

I glanced back at Kasper, even though I knew exactly how he'd respond. Even more so than me, he had a strong sense of propriety. When he was on duty, he took his work very seriously, and I admired that about him.

"We would be honored to, Marksinna," I told Lisbet. "But since we're working for your kingdom now, it wouldn't be appropriate for us to share a table with you or the King and Queen."

Lisbet laughed, an effervescent sound that nearly matched her granddaughter's. "It's never appropriate to turn down the King and Queen's request, and they've invited you to join us for dinner. So I suggest you get dressed and meet us in the dining hall in twenty minutes. We're excited to hear your thoughts on the kingdom."

Since she'd really left us with no choice, I scrambled to get dressed and fix my makeup. Kasper should've had an easier time, because he only had to put his jacket back on, but he ended up spending roughly fifteen minutes reapplying gel to his dark curls to keep them perfectly in place.

"When they ask us how we think their palace is, what should we say?" Kasper asked in a hushed voice as we made our way down a long corridor toward the dining hall.

"We'll just have to be as vague as possible," I suggested. "The truth is too brutal to say all at once over dinner."

"I just hope we can make it through the meal without someone saying, 'Off with their heads,'" he muttered.

"Even if they did say that, who do they have to enforce it?" I asked dryly.

Kasper laughed. "Good point."

We reached the hall to find Mikko, Linnea, Kennet, and Lisbet already seated around the table. Four guards were standing at attention in the corners of the room, including Linnea's personal guard, Cyrano, and they were all wearing matching uniforms—a frosty blue satin number that rivaled the Högdragen uniform in style and flair. They weren't exactly practical, although the guards did have swords sheathed on their hips in flashy metallic sashes, but the uniforms did identify their station.

As I made my way over to the table, I couldn't help but notice the icy glare from Cyrano. I wasn't sure if it was because of the uniform, although I was certain he wasn't happy about that, or because he had to stand guard while Kasper and I got to eat at the table.

Kennet stood up. "Bryn, why don't you take the seat next to me?" He pulled out the chair beside his. I'd been planning to sit next to Kasper at the end of the table, but I didn't want to seem rude by denying the Prince's request.

"Thank you." I smiled at him and allowed him to push my chair in for me, even though that was definitely not proper etiquette.

"So, how are you enjoying the palace?" Linnea leaned forward to speak to me, not minding if her elbows were on the table, and pushing elegant dinnerware to the side to get a better look at me.

"I can honestly say there's nothing else quite like it," I said.

"It is truly magnificent," Kasper said, echoing my sentiments.

A butler came around to begin serving the first course. Before I had the chance, Kennet slipped my silk napkin off the table and dropped it artfully on my lap. His hand brushed my thigh when he pulled it back, but neither of us acknowledged it.

"This is your first time here, isn't it?" Linnea asked, turning her attention to Kasper.

He nodded. "Yes, it is."

"My husband and I are *dying* to know what you think of our security here." Linnea leaned back in her chair so the butler could place her napkin on her lap, then he set a bowl of tomato bisque before her. "We already love the suggestion about the uniforms."

Behind her in the corner, Cyrano snorted a bit. He was doing a horrible job of keeping his expression blank, the way any good guard would do when they were working. Tomorrow, I knew that Kasper would have a long talk with him about the appropriate way for guards to behave.

"I've been saying they should be back in uniform for years," Lisbet commented between spoonfuls of her soup.

"They used to be?" I asked in surprise.

Lisbet dabbed at her mouth with her napkin before answering. "Yes, when I was a young girl, things were different. Much stricter."

"Things change, Nana." Linnea chose her words deliberately, looking over to Lisbet. "Mikko is leading us into a more equitable era."

Since she was home, the Queen had begun to wear lipstick again. Fortunately, she'd gone with a dark pink instead of the usual bright red, which suited her pale complexion much better. Her shoulder-length ringlet curls sprang free around her head, and her wrists were draped in several jeweled bracelets.

Everyone at dinner was dressed formally, including Kennet, whose steel-gray suit appeared to be sharkskin, since it had a subtle sheen to it. I'd like to say I didn't notice how striking he looked in it, but it would be impossible not to.

"Equity should never come at the cost of safety," Lisbet said, and her tone challenged anyone to disagree with her.

"Safety should never come at the expense of fun." Kennet

defied her with a broad grin, which caused Mikko scowl at him from across the table.

"Forgive my brother. He has never been known to take things seriously," King Mikko said, speaking for the first time since dinner had started. It always startled me a bit when he spoke—in part because he rarely did, and in part because of the sheer gravity of his voice.

"Forgive *my* brother," Kennet countered. "He has never been known to take a joke."

"Both of you, behave," Linnea said in a firm but hushed tone. In that moment, she had a weariness beyond her years, and I suspected this hadn't been the first time she'd had to remind the brothers to act appropriately. "We have guests."

"You spoke of making changes," I said, trying to change the subject. "Have there been changes to the guard in recent years?"

"Not dramatic ones." Mikko pushed the soup bowl away from him, having only eaten a few bites, and a butler hurried to take it away. "Most of the alterations were under my father's reign. He streamlined the guard and appointed Bayle Lundeen to implement the changes."

Kennet took a drink from his wine and smirked. "The kingdom says it was out of his strong sense of justice and commitment to an egalitarian society, but the truth was that our father was a tremendous cheapskate. He'd much rather have kept the vault full than paid the guard their rightful due, which meant we needed a smaller guard."

From behind Linnea, I saw Cyrano nod his head in agreement.

"Kennet!" Linnea gasped. Her level of shock was almost comical, especially considering that Mikko and Lisbet seemed unfazed. "It's not right to speak ill of the dead, especially your King."

"Perhaps it's best if we don't discuss business over dinner," Mikko said. I wasn't sure if he was coming to the aid of his wife, or if he also disapproved of Kennet's statement. It was impossible to tell since Mikko's face was an unreadable mask.

"I've always found that to be the best policy," Kennet agreed amiably.

Looking at Kennet and Mikko staring at each other across the table was a bit like a funhouse mirror. They looked so much alike, even though Kennet was younger and slimmer. But Kennet was very expressive, often grinning and raising his eyebrows, while Mikko rarely seemed to emote at all. Not to mention that Kennet was talkative and flirtatious, and Mikko barely said a word.

The waitstaff began to clear the first course before bringing in a massive salad of arugula, pressed melon, and goat cheese. While they exchanged our dishes, nobody spoke, and the only sound was the clearing of silverware and the setting down of plates.

"There are so many other things we have to talk about," Linnea said, since no one else seemed eager to pick up the conversation. "I am disappointed that I wasn't able to see either of you more today."

"Tomorrow you should make time for a little fun, Bryn," Kennet said. "You must take a break and have lunch with me."

I paused, trying to find a polite way out of it, until I came up with the perfect solution. "If you insist, then Kasper and I would be happy to join you."

But Kennet would not be appeased. "Unless of course Kasper has more pressing business to attend to?" He raised an eyebrow at Kasper.

"Kennet, you've met beautiful girls before," Lisbet said in exasperation. "Certainly you know how to contain yourself around them."

For once, Kennet didn't have a snappy comeback, and I just kept my head bowed, focusing on the salad before me. Even though I wasn't the one putting on the display, I still felt the maddening urge to blush, but I suppressed it as best I could.

"What is on your agenda for tomorrow?" Linnea asked, doing her best to keep the conversation flowing.

"I believe Bayle has a few more things he'd like to show us," Kasper said. "We haven't seen the towers yet."

"How exciting! The towers are my *favorite* part of the palace," Linnea enthused.

"When do you think you'll be ready to brief me on the changes you'd like to make?" Mikko asked, surprising me by showing an actual interest in what we were talking about.

"A few more days, I think," I said.

He nodded. "Let me know when you're ready, and we'll get something on the books."

"We're all excited to hear what recommendations you have," Linnea said.

"We'll certainly be honored to share them with you," Kasper said.

"Queen Linnea, how are you finding being back in the palace?" I asked her.

Since we'd gotten back, I'd had hardly a moment to check in with her, and I was curious to find out if she still felt out of sorts. I'd have preferred to ask her when we were alone in hopes of getting a more honest answer, but since I wasn't sure when that would be I thought now was better than never.

"I couldn't be happier to be home. I'm a bit embarrassed for all the trouble I caused for disappearing like I did. That strange man spooked me, I suppose, but I'm glad that you brought me back where I belong." She reached over and squeezed Mikko's hand on the table, looking up at him in adoration, but he barely glanced at her.

"We have already tried to make a few changes to keep her safe," Mikko said, lifting his eyes briefly to look at me. "Her personal guard was sent away and replaced with a new one."

"I graciously offered her the use of Cyrano until they find a more permanent solution," Kennet said. "I am a very generous man. In every aspect of my life," he added, winking at me.

"I do already feel safer," Linnea said, turning the conversation back and smiled brightly at me. "But it does help knowing that you and Kasper are here."

I wanted to reassure her that she was indeed safer with us, but honestly, I wasn't sure who exactly she needed protection from, so I remained quiet.

TWENTY

belfry

With the icy wind blowing through my hair, I leaned farther out the window than I knew I should have, but I couldn't help myself. We were in the highest room in the tallest tower of the castle, and the lake had to be at least a hundred meters below us.

"I think that's far enough, Bryn," Kasper said, doing his best not to sound nervous.

"He's right," Bayle Lundeen agreed, and that's when I reluctantly pulled myself back inside.

I wasn't sure what it was about being here, but the power of the Skojare in my blood seemed to be stronger. The water seemed to call to me more than it normally did, and when I'd been in the sapphire room yesterday, I'd felt an uncharacteristic moment of greed.

Maybe it was being around Skojare people that amplified

something inside me. Or it could simply have been the room we were in, since it was full of magic.

The tower rooms themselves weren't overly spectacular. They were somewhat small, cylindrical spaces at the top of about a thousand stairs. (There were actually several landings along the way with couches, water fountains, and restrooms, since you'd inevitably have to take a break getting up there.)

The walls were iridescent, reminding me of the inside of clam shells, and there were two windows: one facing the shore in front, and one facing the lake to the back. Both windows opened outward, with no screen. Kasper pointed out that it seemed dangerous, but Bayle assured us there'd never been any accidents and only three suicides over the past century.

A bed curved along the wall, covered in soft blankets and plush pillows. To one side of the room was what appeared to be a large white armoire, but when Bayle showed us the inside, it contained a small toilet and pedestal sink.

Across from it was a desk made of marble, also built to curve right against the wall. Ornate designs were carved into the legs and edges, and rising from the desk was a tall bookcase, lined with all kinds of books ranging from tomes dating back hundreds of years to the latest novel by George R. R. Martin. It was a small yet varied library.

This room was a self-contained little unit meant to house the tower guards.

"So this is how you keep the palace hidden?" I asked, admiring the room around me.

Bayle nodded. "We used to have a guard in each of the five towers, but with the cloaking abilities dwindling, we don't want to run the risk of burning out the guards we have, so we only have three on duty at all times. Since this is the tallest tower, it's the least used."

That made sense. If I had the choice of walking up several hundred stairs instead of a thousand to go to work, I would gladly choose the smaller tower. But Bayle had wanted to show us the full breadth of the kingdom, and we weren't disturbing anyone by checking out this one.

The tower guards were more like trackers than they were like the Högdragen. The Skojare might not have had changelings, but like trackers, the tower guards had special abilities that were specifically nurtured in their bloodlines.

Most of the Skojare lacked psychokinesis. Like all the tribes, our abilities had begun to wane over time. The royalty tended to blame this on diluting bloodlines. I suspected there was truth to that, but I also wondered if declining use and losing touch with our heritage impacted it.

Regardless, there were still some Skojare who possessed the ability of cloaking. They couldn't make themselves invisible, only objects and places. The power didn't seem to work as well on trolls as it did on humans, meaning a troll could see their tricks while a human would be fooled into seeing nothing.

But that was really who they needed it for. It was how they kept humans from spotting their massive palace on the lake, and it was how they kept Lake Isolera hidden.

Unlike the palace, though, which required upkeep from

tower guards, Lake Isolera had been placed under a spell long ago by one of the first Skojare queens. Her power had to have been incredibly strong, since her enchantment was the only thing that kept it cloaked. Eventually, the spell would fade, and Isolera would become an ordinary lake in the Canadian wilderness.

From what I understood, the tower guards would sit in the room and project the idea of a force field—thinking of an invisible wall that would hide everything behind it, and pushing out with their mind the way I would push against a boulder with my hands. It was a very taxing job, one that could burn people out quickly, so the guards worked in shifts and took frequent breaks lying down or reading a book.

It was necessary work, if the Skojare didn't want to be discovered by humans, and I couldn't imagine that discovery would go for well them.

"Since this tower isn't used for anything else, you could have two guards up here, watching the perimeter for enemies," Kasper said, motioning to the windows on either sides of the room. "I know the tower guards are too busy to be able to do that, but regular guards would work."

"We could, but that seems unnecessary," Bayle said. "The tower guards are protecting us from outsiders."

"What about Konstantin Black?" I asked, and he stiffened.

Bayle cleared his throat. "He was an exception, and I doubt he'll be coming back."

"You can say that, and you may be right," I allowed. "But do you know why he was here? How he got in? What he was hoping to achieve? Or why he warned the Queen to get out?"

"Of course not," Bayle replied icily. "We don't know that any better than you do."

"Then how can you possibly know that he or someone else like him won't strike again?" I asked.

Bayle inhaled sharply through his nose. "I suppose I don't." Then he lowered his dark blue eyes to gaze at me. "But from what I gather, Konstantin Black is Kanin, and he was *your* problem first. Whatever he was doing here, it was your people that brought him upon us, and it was you who lost him."

"I wouldn't have lost him if you'd been doing your job!" I snapped. "If you had even a halfway decent guard set up, he never would've gotten inside the palace in the first place."

"I work with the guard that I am given!" Bayle shouted. "You think I wouldn't want a guard as well trained and dedicated as the Högdragen? Of course I would! But that's not what King Rune designed."

King Rune was Mikko and Kennet's father, who had apparently decided to tie the purse strings much tighter than they needed to be.

"King Mikko refuses to undo his father's changes, which means we have no money, no training, nothing for any of that," Bayle continued in frustration.

"And that's why we're here!" Kasper spoke loudly in order to be heard, but there was no anger in his voice. He stepped between Bayle and me, holding his hands palm out toward each of us. "We're here to help, and to make sure that somebody like Konstantin Black can never get in here again. We're on the same page here."

Bayle huffed, but he seemed to relax a bit. He smoothed the satin of his uniform. He looked much more like a leader in it, and he even carried himself better. Kasper had definitely been right about the effect clothing had on the psyche.

"Kasper is right," I said. "I'm sorry."

Bayle nodded, and I suspected that was as close to an apology as I would get.

"It has been a great shame that the Queen went missing on my watch," he said finally. "I've tried to pinpoint how exactly Konstantin got in here, but the truth is that there are too many holes in our fence for me to know for sure."

"The Queen had begun to fear for her safety before Konstantin even arrived," I said. "There's a chance someone on the inside was working with him."

Bayle lowered his eyes. "I have considered this."

"And do you have any idea who it could have been?" Kasper pressed when Bayle didn't go on.

"No." He shook his head. "I simply don't know how any of the guards could benefit from the disappearance of Queen Linnea. She's kind and fair to everyone. The kingdom has a policy that doesn't allow us to pay ransom, and I doubt King Mikko would go against the rules of his ancestors, so no one could profit from her kidnapping."

"What if she had been killed?" I asked. "Would anything have changed?"

"I can't see how," Bayle said. "The crown follows the Biâelse bloodline. There would be no transfer of power, since Queen Linnea only has the title by marriage."

My thoughts circled back to where they'd started—the only person who could benefit from Linnea being gone was the one who didn't appear happy to be married to her.

"As the head guard, who are your official bosses?" I asked.

"The King has final say in all matters of the kingdom, but to a lesser extent, I am sworn to obey the entire royal family, including the Queen, the Prince, and Marksinna Lisbet as the Queen Grandmother," Bayle answered.

"What would you do if any of them asked you to commit murder?" I asked, and both Bayle and Kasper stiffened. It was a taboo topic among guards.

"In times of war, I am to defend the kingdom and fight our enemies," Bayle said, practically reciting the answer from a textbook. "In times of peace, I am to protect the King at all costs. It is my duty to kill if necessary, but never to murder. Taking a life must only be done in preservation of the kingdom."

"I know what you're supposed to do, but I'm asking you what you would personally do," I said.

"I would follow the tenets of my position, and I would not murder anyone," he said, but his eyes darted just slightly when he spoke.

"Would you tell the person you'd been instructed to kill?" I pressed. "Because if you turned down the King, I'm sure he could keep asking until eventually he found a guard who would do as he asked."

"I . . ." Bayle stopped for a moment, thinking, and when he spoke again, his shoulders had sagged. "I would like to believe that I would do the right thing."

Later, when we were walking down the spiral stairs to the main floor, Bayle had gotten quite the lead on Kasper and me, and he was well out of earshot. Just the same, Kasper slowed his steps and lowered his voice.

"There is no right answer to that question, you know," Kasper said, and I looked sharply at him.

"Of course there is. Murder is always wrong."

"When you're a civilian, that's true," he conceded. "But the King has the power to declare war and name anyone a traitor, worthy of death. He decides what is and what isn't murder. When you swear to serve him, you give up your own individuality; you forsake your own beliefs and morals in the name of the higher calling of serving the kingdom, for honor and duty."

I shook my head. "You can serve the King without betraying your own morality. They don't have to be mutually exclusive."

"I would like to think so, and I like to live my life that way," Kasper said. "But if the King commanded me to do something, and I denied him, he could have me locked up or banished. Even executed. So it's not just morality that would influence my decision. It's also self-preservation."

I stopped, and Kasper walked down a few more steps before pausing to look back up at me. Until this moment, I'd viewed him as one of the most upstanding people I knew, worthy of admiration. He was honorable, noble, and seemed to embody every quality that a member of the Högdragen was supposed to possess.

"But you wouldn't do it," I persisted, almost begging him

to agree with me, to pretend that this was all a misunderstanding. That the most virtuous members of the Högdragen couldn't be as fallible as everyone else.

Kasper sighed heavily. "I believe I would do my best to sway the King to the correct course of action and to protect the innocent. But in the end, I am nothing more than a sword at the end of the King's arm. I do as he directs."

TWENTY-ONE

entanglement

From out in the hall, I could hear Kasper talking, followed by the fainter sound of Tilda's laughter. His bedroom door was open, so I peered around to see him holding his cell phone out toward the dome glass wall that held the murky water at bay. He was video chatting with Tilda and giving her a tour of our accommodations.

"The water is so dark," Tilda was saying, her voice coming out weak and metallic from the phone. "I'd expected it be clear and bright."

"Everything here is darker and dingier than you might guess," Kasper admitted.

"Well, good. I was afraid you'd get too enchanted with Storvatten and not want to come back to me, so I'm glad it's not all that magical," Tilda said, laughing a little.

Kasper turned the phone back around to face him, so she

could see him again. "There's nothing in this world that can keep me from coming back home to you."

Since I'd accidentally eavesdropped on a private moment, I cleared my throat and knocked on the open door.

Kasper turned back to me with a start, so Tilda asked in concern, "Is someone there?"

"It's Bryn." Kasper pointed the phone toward me so I could see Tilda's smiling face on the small screen.

"Hey, Tilda." I waved toward the tiny camera on the phone, causing her to laugh.

"How are you enjoying the palace?" Tilda asked.

"I'm enjoying it as much as I can, I guess." I shrugged.

"Good." She paused, seeming to hesitate. "Ridley asked me how you're doing, and he'll be happy to hear that you're looking well."

"Thanks." I swallowed back a lump in my throat and looked away from her. "I didn't mean to interrupt your moment here, but I was just checking to see if Kasper wanted to join me for lunch."

After we'd toured the towers, Bayle had shown us around the palace for the rest of the morning, but he'd given us an hour on our own for lunch. Kennet had said that he'd meet me at my room at noon, but I was getting hungry and decided it would be better if I got something on my own.

"I thought you were having lunch with the Prince?" Kasper asked.

"Lunch with the Prince?" Tilda raised an eyebrow that

others might have misinterpreted as intrigue, but I knew it meant nothing but disapproval.

Tilda had already witnessed my out-of-class dating once, and heard me vow that I'd never do it again. Back when I was sixteen and freshly graduated from tracker school and I thought I knew everything, I'd pursued a crush with a slightly older Markis.

Even though I was determined to be a Högdragen, and inter-dating between a tracker and a Markis was forbidden, I was at a stage in my life where I thought I could do what I wanted—that I was smart enough to play around the rules.

I hadn't been in love with him, but initially I had been enamored by his charm and good looks. He seemed to enjoy me too, and there was something about the danger of getting caught that made it all the more exciting.

After we'd been sneaking around for a few weeks, I began to detect an arrogant, mean streak to him. Once when we were fooling around in his room, I noticed a polar bear rug on his floor. Hunting wasn't prohibited by the Kanin, but doing so purely for sport was frowned upon.

I asked him about it, and he proudly boasted of killing it himself. Not long after that I began to realize that thanks to my exotic blond hair and blue eyes, I was just like the polar bear—a trophy from a conquest.

When it was all over, Tilda did her best not to say "I told you so," even though she had repeatedly warned me this was a bad idea and expressed her disapproval. But she was more than relieved when I told her that it would never happen again, and I swore off romance with royals forever.

Of course, I did have this awful habit of breaking promises I'd made to myself.

"I've been waiting in my room for fifteen minutes, and the Prince hasn't shown up," I told Tilda, doing my best to display a lack of interest in him. "I thought I'd head up to the kitchen and grab something."

"I already called up to the kitchen and had them bring me something." Kasper pointed to a half-eaten sandwich on a silver tray next to his bed. "Otherwise I would."

"No problem." I waved it off. "Enjoy your lunch with Tilda."

"Take care of yourself, Bryn," Tilda called after me as I turned to leave.

With nothing else to say, I preferred to hurry out with my head down, trying to pretend it didn't hurt to hear that Ridley had been concerned about me. It hurt because he cared, and it hurt because he shouldn't, and it hurt because things with us would never be the way they were with Tilda and Kasper.

I had my eyes on the floor, my mind desperately trying to push away any thought of Ridley. My heart throbbed painfully in my chest. That was how I didn't notice Prince Kennet until I'd run right into him—literally hitting my head against his chest.

"Sorry, Your Highness, I'm sorry, I didn't see you there." Apologies tumbled out of my mouth.

"No need to be sorry," Kennet said, his deep voicing lilting as he smiled. "In fact, I should be the one saying I'm sorry."

"Don't be ridiculous." I brushed my hair out of my face and looked up at him. "I'm the one who ran smack into you."

"You did do that," he agreed. "But running into you is never all bad. Especially when I've left you waiting so long for our lunch date."

"Oh, right, that." I hurried to think of a way to contradict him on the term *date*.

"You must be ravenous by now," Kennet went on before I could correct his statement. "The good news is that lunch is waiting for you." Then he frowned. "The bad news is that it won't be with me. Queen Linnea has requested that you join her instead, and since the Queen outranks me, I am obligated to step aside. This time."

"She and I do need to talk about the things going on in the kingdom, so it's just as well," I said.

"A working lunch?" Kennet wrinkled his nose. "That sounds terrible."

"I enjoy the company of the Queen, and this may come as a shock to you, but I enjoy my job a great deal."

Kennet put his hand over his heart in mock surprise. "I can hardly even fathom the idea."

"I thought as much," I replied with a laugh.

"There is some good news though," Kennet said. "I get to escort you to the Queen's tea room."

"She has her own tea room?" I asked, following Kennet as he started to walk away.

"She's the Queen. She has her own *everything*."

"Do you think that's why she was targeted?" I asked.

He shrugged. "I don't know why anyone went after her. I know I just said she has everything, but in truth it all actually belongs to my brother. She just has access to it."

That was essentially what Bayle had already told me. There wasn't really any reason for anyone to go after Linnea, unless it was personal. But I'd been hoping that Kennet might be able to shed a different light on things.

"Do you share any of the Queen's concerns?" I asked.

"You mean do I feel that someone is lurking around the corner waiting to nab me?" Kennet seemed to consider it, but when he looked down at me he was grinning. "How could I feel unsafe when I know I've got you here to protect me?"

"I'm here to protect the Queen."

"Technically you're here to help the royal family, which does include me."

"You didn't really answer my question though," I said. "Do you think something is going on here?"

"I think that our guards have been horribly trained and commanded for years now," Kennet said, and he seemed to be choosing his words with an unusual level of care. Normally, he'd say any little thing that flitted into his mind, but for once he appeared cautious.

"As a result of the guards' ineptitude," he went on, "it's entirely plausible that something troublesome is afoot. But it would be near impossible to discern what is due to incompetence and what's due to actual nefarious intentions."

"Bayle told me your brother has been reluctant to make

changes," I said. "If the guard is awful, do you know why that is?"

"The exact machinations of my brother's mind have always been a mystery to me," Kennet said with a sigh. "I do know that during his coronation speech, he promised to continue our father's reign, upholding everything that he'd put in place. But why the King refuses to change in the face of all the evidence telling him it's necessary . . ." He trailed off.

He stopped and turned to me, his blue eyes softening. "You have to understand. Our father was a very difficult man, and Mikko got the brunt of Father's . . . *difficulty*. Mikko never learned how to stand up for himself, and he's uneasy about change or responsibility."

"That doesn't sound like a good combination in a King," I pointed out.

"No, it doesn't." Kennet smiled bitterly for a moment, but it quickly fell away. "Anyway, it's not my place to speak ill of the King—either my brother or my father."

"Thank you for being so candid with me, my liege," I said, since Kennet had been more honest with me about his family than many other royals I had encountered would be.

He stopped, turning to face me, so I did the same. "You know, you really don't have to do all that. You can just call me Kennet. I feel like we are on a first-name basis."

"That seems like a very dangerous territory to venture into," I said. "You are the Prince. I am a tracker from a neighboring tribe. It would be very unwise for the two of us to mingle, which is why it is for the best that we don't reschedule our lunch . . . meeting."

"That hardly seems fair." Kennet scoffed. "I see absolutely no reason the two of us can't be friends."

"There is that whole business where I could be jailed and you could be stripped of your title," I reminded him. "That seems like a good reason."

"It's only if we procreate and dilute the bloodline that the offense is punishable by incarceration." Kennet brushed it off, as though it weren't a big thing. "There's no law against us fraternizing."

"Perhaps I don't want to fraternize," I countered.

"Are you asking me to procreate then?" Kennet asked with a wag of the eyebrow.

"I think it's best if we stop this conversation, and I get to my lunch with Queen Linnea," I said. "It's never good to keep the Queen waiting."

"Right you are." Kennet smirked, but he started walking again.

"Thank you, Prince," I said as I followed him.

"Anytime, tracker," he replied.

TWENTY-TWO

doubts

Sunlight flooded the tea room. The outside wall was domed glass, starting in the middle of the ceiling and curving down until it met the floor at the surface of the lake. The windowed wall was divided into three pie-shaped panes of glass, separated by ornate golden sash bars.

Since it was on the main floor, it was one of the few rooms in the palace that let in the warm spring sun. It shimmered on the lake outside, casting shards of light through the tea room like a disco ball.

The walls had wainscoting halfway up, where it met wallpaper covered in pale blue roses and light green vines. A chaise sat against the wall with an antique coffee table surrounded by several tufted chairs.

In the center of the room was a round table, directly underneath an elegant gold chandelier that hung where the glass met the ceiling. Piles of fresh fruit, trays of pastries, and an array of tea bags were spread out on a lace tablecloth. Delicate saucers and cups were hand painted with roses of pink and blue.

Linnea sat at the table with a raspberry tart in her hand, smiling at me as I came in. In her knee-length azure sundress, she reminded me of a little girl playing tea party and pretending to be a princess. But of course, she wasn't playing pretend—all of this was real life for her.

Kennet had dropped me off at the door, promising to see me later, and then left me alone with the Queen. Her personal guard—who should've been in the room with her, or at the very least standing at the door—was nowhere to be seen, and I would have to remember to make a note of that when I returned to Kasper. The King and Queen should never be left unguarded.

"I'm so glad you could make it!" Linnea said effusively and gestured to the empty seat across from her. "Sit, sit. Eat and drink, and we have so much to talk about!"

"Thank you, Your Highness." I sat down and added fruit and a cucumber sandwich to my plate, while Linnea began to rattle off all the reasons it was so great to have me there.

"Everyone here is *so* stuffy and dull," she said with a dramatic eye roll and took the last bite of her tart. Today she'd gone for minimal jewelry, wearing only her large diamond wedding band along with white lace fingerless gloves. "Even the ones my age."

Since I'd known Linnea, she seemed far more excited about the idea of having a new friend to talk to than having a guard to watch her back, and I wasn't exactly sure how I felt about that.

While I liked Linnea just fine, I didn't want to be chosen for a job because she thought we'd make great pals. I was here to show my merits as a guard and to get to the bottom of what Konstantin had been doing here in the first place. But perhaps I could use the Queen's need for a friend to get her to confide in me about what was really going on around here.

When Ridley and I had been looking for her before, we had suspected that she might be too demanding or childish for Mikko. Maybe she annoyed him, or he simply didn't want to spend the rest of his life trapped in a loveless arranged marriage to her.

How Konstantin tied into a possible plan to do away with her, I had no idea. But maybe she knew something that could help.

"The King must be happy to have you back." I poured myself a cup of tea and watched for her response out of the corner of my eye.

"Yes, he's thrilled!" Linnea laughed. "The first night we were back together, I didn't think he'd ever let me go. He held on to me for hours and made me promise that I'd never leave him again."

"*Really*?" I asked, then hurried to correct myself so I didn't sound quite so shocked. "I mean, he seems so . . . in control of his emotions."

"I know, I know." She laughed again. "It's the craziest thing, because he's such a big strong man, and he's the King of an entire kingdom. A small one, but a kingdom nonetheless. You'd think he'd be so brave and tough, and oh he tries to be. But do you want to know a secret?"

I nodded. "Yes. I would."

Linnea leaned forward over the table, so I did the same, and even though we were alone, she whispered. "Mikko is terribly shy. Almost pathologically."

"Really?" I asked.

"Yes, it's really so sad." She leaned back in her chair and returned to her normal volume. "That's why whenever he's at dinner with people, he's so quiet, and he seems so cold and stoic, but that's not who he is at all."

"I never would've guessed that." I settled back in my chair, trying to run through all my encounters with the King.

"Before we were wed, I did *not* want to marry him," Linnea confessed. "It had all been arranged since I was twelve, but with the age gap, we'd hardly spent a moment together before the wedding, and when we did he said nary a word to me."

"That sounds dreadful," I said.

"It really was." She nodded, her transparent gills flaring slightly under her jawline. "I mean, it was just after my sixteenth birthday, and I wanted to fall in love, and I thought there was absolutely no way I could do that with this cold brute of a man.

"But the truth is that Mikko is one of the kindest, most loving, most caring men I've ever met." Linnea smiled, the soft, wistful kind that barely graced her lips—and her aqua eyes sparkled. "And as I got to know him—the *real* him—I began to fall madly in love with him."

"That's . . . amazing," I said, unsure of how else to respond.

She leaned forward again and lowered her voice. "It wasn't until we'd been married for four months that we even, you know . . . *shared* a bed together. Mikko wanted to wait until I was completely comfortable with it."

"He sounds like a very honorable man," I said.

If what Linnea said was true, then he definitely was. But I was having a hard time reconciling this information with the cold, aloof King I'd considered him to be.

Although, when the Queen had been missing, a different side of Mikko had emerged. He'd been visibly distraught and inconsolable. At the time, I'd thought it was all a melodramatic act, but if Linnea was telling the truth, he might have been so afraid of losing her that he'd let his guard down and shown his real feelings.

Of course, that made everything even more confusing. If Mikko hadn't grown tired of or irritated with his wife, then why had anybody wanted to get rid of her?

Not to mention the fact that Mikko had thwarted our investigation when Linnea was missing. We'd wanted to interview guards and look at reports, but we were denied access.

"Have you talked to Mikko about what happened before you went missing?" I asked.

"I talk to Mikko about everything," Linnea said, and with her love of chatting, I had a feeling that was very true.

That probably made them very compatible. She enjoyed talking, and Mikko was more of a listener, so they balanced each other out.

"Did he say anything about Konstantin Black?" I asked. "Does he know anything about him?"

"Everything he knows, he's heard from you." Linnea shook

her head. "He is grateful that Konstantin warned me to run away, though, and Mikko is relieved he wasn't executed. Konstantin may have saved my life."

I rested my arms on the table. "From whom, though? Does Mikko have any idea who might have wanted to hurt you?"

"No. He's tried talking to the guard, but the unfortunate truth is that he's been very hands-off about most things," Linnea admitted, frowning. "His social anxiety makes it so hard for him to interact sometimes, so he's really left Bayle Lundeen to handle everything."

"Do you trust Bayle?" I asked.

"I don't know." Her eyes widened, as if it had just occurred to her that she shouldn't. "Do you?"

"Honestly, I'm not sure I trust any of the guards around here. It's hard to tell who knows what," I said.

"I know." She nodded. "What I said the other night about overreacting and running away, that was for the benefit of the guards. I have no idea who we can trust anymore. But to tell you the truth, I'd never considered that Bayle might be involved."

"He's the head guard, and this is all happening on his watch. Either he's involved, or he's too incompetent to stop it."

Linnea exhaled deeply and rested her chin on her hand. "Rune trusted Bayle and appointed him, and both Mikko and Kennet are loyal to him and seem to trust him. Their father was a terrifying man, and even after his death neither of the boys wants to defy him. But . . ." She chewed the inside of her cheek, pondering the situation. "You're right, and I know you're right."

"I know it's tough for the King to go against what he believes his father's wishes were, but the guard needs an overhaul to keep you all safe," I said. "Whether your husband is comfortable with it or not, he needs to start taking control of his guards. If he wants to keep you safe, the King needs to be in charge."

Linnea nodded. "He needs to hear it from you though."

"What?" I asked.

I'd gone into this luncheon thinking that Mikko might be the one behind everything, or at the very least a participant in Konstantin's plot. But Linnea had just turned that theory on its head, and now she wanted me to go to Mikko and tell the King he needed to get rid of his top guard.

"You're an expert on these matters, and you're right." Linnea pushed back her chair and stood up. "We should go now. He's down in his office. It's the perfect time for you to go tell him what you think."

"We should set up a meeting with Kasper, maybe even your grandmother and the Prince," I suggested, since I felt unprepared to present my case to the King—especially considering I didn't completely know what my case was.

"We'll have a proper meeting later." Linnea waved it off. "Let's go."

The Queen had given me an order, so I had to obey. As we walked downstairs toward the King's office, Linnea chattered the whole way, although I'm ashamed to admit that I'm not entirely sure what about. My mind was focused on trying to figure out what exactly I would say to the King, and how I should phrase everything.

Linnea pushed open the door to her husband's office without knocking. I was still lost in thought, but Linnea's scream pulled me into the moment instantly.

Mikko's desk faced the water, so his back was to the door. He was hunched over his desk, hard at work on something, so he didn't see the man standing behind him with a sword raised above his head, about to strike and cut off the King's head.

TWENTY-THREE

impact

Training kicked in, and I didn't have to think—my body just sprang into motion. I ran at the man, knocking him to the ground and grabbing his wrist. I slammed it into the floor, forcing him to drop the sword.

He tried to crawl toward it, and the satin of his uniform made it easier for him to slip out from underneath me. But I knelt on his back, pressing my knees into his kidneys as I pinned him in place.

With one swift move, he tilted to the side and thrust his elbow up, hitting me squarely in the chin. It was just enough to throw me off balance, and he scrambled out from under me. He grabbed the sword, but I was already on my feet when he jumped up and pointed it at me.

There was a split second of shock when I realized who it was—Cyrano Moen, Linnea's personal guard.

Cyrano tried to run at me. I dodged to the side, avoiding the blade of the sword, then I grabbed his arm. I turned him around, bending his arm at a painful angle, and he let out a yelp. If I applied more pressure, I would break his arm, and that caused him to release his sword again.

I took it from him this time, letting him go so he fell on the ground. Cyrano lay before me, panting, and I hoped this meant the fight was over. In the background, I heard Linnea crying and demanding to know why he would do this.

But he didn't answer. Instead, he reached for the spare dagger in his boot.

"Drop it," I commanded, and his hard blue eyes were locked on mine. He had to know I meant it, but there was a determined mania in his gaze that I didn't understand.

He slowly got up, still holding the dagger, so I repeated, "Drop it."

"Cyrano!" Mikko's voice boomed from somewhere behind me. "Do as she says!"

"I'd like her to make me," Cyrano snarled, and then he lunged at me.

In my days of training as a tracker, I had run a sword through hundreds of dummies. They were built to have the same feel as a troll, so we'd know how much resistance a body would give and how much force we'd need to get the sword through.

Still, I can't explain how different it felt, or even what the difference was, when I pushed the blade straight through Cyrano. It was easier than I expected—the flesh gave way, and when the bell of the sword handle pressed against his stomach, I felt the warmth of his blood as it spilled over.

The only light came from a desk lamp, casting too much of the room in shadows. Everything seemed to have an eerie, yellow hue to it, thanks to the way the light played off the reflective glass and the water outside.

We had turned, so the window was behind me, and the light bounced onto Cyrano's face. It cast a shadow across his mouth and body, but his eyes were wide and I could see the yellow dancing in them, like fiery waves.

His eyes stayed locked on me still, filled with that strange mania. Not until the final seconds, when I was lowering him back to the ground and pulling the sword out of him, did the frenzied look finally give way. A glassy peace seemed to come over him, and he was dead.

Linnea ran over to Cyrano's body, pounding on his chest and screaming, demanding why he'd want to hurt her husband. She'd never been anything but kind to him. How could he betray her like this?

Her words eventually seemed to fade away, becoming a distant foggy sound, like something from a dream. Mikko came over and pulled her off.

I don't remember letting go of the sword, but I remember the sound it made, clattering against the floor. I didn't move or speak until Bayle Lundeen came in, asking me questions.

I answered them as directly and simply as I could, but the words felt detached from me, as if they were coming from someone else. It was my voice, it was the truth about what I'd done, but it wasn't me.

Nobody told me that I was acting strangely or that I didn't seem present, so I must've been performing normally. I have no idea how long I talked to Bayle and King Mikko. It might have been minutes. It might have been an hour.

Eventually, Kasper came and took me back to my room. He suggested I shower, since I had Cyrano's blood all over me, and then he headed back upstairs, promising to help with the investigation.

The shower lasted a very long time. I know this because it started out hot, but when I'd finished, the water was icy cold. I walked across the hall from the bathroom, wearing only a white robe. I'd thrown my clothes away in the trash can. I didn't need them anymore.

When I went into my room, I still felt vaguely as though I was in a dream. I just couldn't seem to feel my body. It was as if I were floating above everything, not a part of this world, and I wondered if this was what it felt like to be a ghost.

"Bryn?" Kennet asked, and I looked over to see him sitting on my bed. His usual smile was gone, and his eyes were dark.

"How long have you been there?" I asked.

"Long enough," he said, like I would know what that meant, and he stood up so he could walk closer to me. "Are you okay?"

"I don't know," I admitted, and I wasn't sure I had the ability to lie right then. It seemed out of the realm of my abilities to make things up. "I just killed a man."

"I know."

I waited a beat before adding, "I've never killed anyone before."

It was so much simpler than I expected. Taking a life seemed like it should be a much greater challenge, but my sword had gone through him just like it would through anything else. And then he was dead.

There was a weight to that that I hadn't expected. No amount of training or even belief that I had done the right thing could change the way it felt. A man had been alive. Now he wasn't. And it was because of me.

"You were doing your job, what you needed to do," Kennet said. "That's why I came here. To thank you for saving my brother's life."

"Is the King okay?"

I tried to collect myself, realizing that I had a job to do. I was a tracker. I'd been training for years to do what I'd just done. I just needed to get through the shock of it all.

"Yes, he's fine, thanks to you." Kennet smiled. "Mikko wanted me to extend his gratitude to you, and I'm certain he'll do it personally later on. He thought you might need time to collect yourself."

"No, I'm fine." I brushed my fingers through my tangles of wet hair and turned, walking away from Kennet and toward the window. It was still daylight out, and a few rays of light managed to break through the murky water. "I'll do whatever they need me to do."

"No one needs you to do anything right now." Kennet followed me, his steps measured to match my slow place, before stopping behind me. "The King has given you the night off to do as you wish."

"But isn't there an investigation to be done?" I turned back to face him.

"The King, Kasper, and Bayle are handling it right now," Kennet reassured me. "You can join them tomorrow. But for now, I think it's best if you get some rest."

I shook my head. "I'm fine. I don't need rest. I need to figure out what's going on."

"Bryn, take a break when you've earned it." Kennet sounded weary, probably growing exhausted from trying to convince me that there was more to life than work. "And by Ægir's might, you've earned it."

I closed my eyes and took a deep breath. Kennet was close enough that I could breathe him in again—the heady scent of the sea and fresh rain and ice. He smelled of water in all its forms, so wonderful and soothing.

Without thinking, I leaned into him, resting my head against his chest, and he responded by wrapping his arms around me and holding me to him.

"I'm sorry if I come on too strong." His words were muffled in my hair as he spoke. "It's just that this palace can be awfully lonely day after day. But I don't want anything from you that you don't want to give."

I buried my head deeper in his chest.

"You smell like home," I whispered, realizing too late that my inability to lie had also become an inability to filter. Words were tumbling out without hesitation. "But not like the house I grew up in."

"It's water that you smell," he explained, his words muffled in my hair. "And water is your home."

Home. It was the last word that echoed through my mind when sleep finally overtook me that night.

TWENTY-FOUR

afflicted

I remembered nothing from my dreams, but I couldn't shake the fear. I was sitting in my bed, in the strange darkened room of the Skojare palace, covered in a cold sweat and gasping for breath, and I didn't know why I was so terrified.

Kennet had slipped out after I'd fallen asleep, which was only proper. But I missed the comfort of his presence, and I realized that in spite of all my best intentions, I now considered Kennet a friend.

"Bryn?" Kasper cautiously pushed open my bedroom door and looked in. "Are you awake?"

"Yeah." I sat up straighter and used the blanket to wipe the sweat from my brow. "Yeah, you can come in."

"Are you okay?" Kasper asked. Even in the darkness, my distress must've been apparent.

"Yeah, I'm fine." I brushed it off. "What do you need?"

"I know I told you to rest, and I understand if you want to—"

"Just tell me what's going on," I said, rushing him along.

"We're going to check out Cyrano Moen's house, and I thought you'd want to join us."

The clock on my nightstand said it was nearly midnight. "Now? Why haven't you already gone?"

He let out an irritated sigh. "I don't know. Bayle insisted that we do all this other pointless stuff first." He shook his head. "Honestly, I want you to join me so I can have another set of eyes that I can trust."

"I'll go with you."

I hopped out of bed, and Kasper turned away since I'd been sleeping in just a tank top and underwear. I hurried to throw on a pair of jeans and a shirt, and then we left my room.

Cyrano Moen's house was three miles from the palace, counting the long walk on the dock that connected the palace with the mainland. Storvatten itself was a strange, quiet village with no street lights and no real roads to speak of, just dirt paths meandering through the darkness.

Most of the houses were burrows—squat little houses half-buried in the ground with thatched roofs and moss growing up over them. Cyrano's was no different, but unlike the other houses surrounding it, his actually had the lights on.

The front door was open, and five steps led into a living room. Bayle was already inside when Kasper and I arrived, looking around the small space. The house was round, and everything inside it was visible from the front door—the living room, the kitchen, even the bedroom in the back corner where a crib sat next to a full-size bed.

"Cyrano had a family," I realized, and guilt hit me like a sledgehammer.

"Neighbors said they left earlier today," Bayle said, then motioned to discarded clothes on the bed and a pacifier on the dirt floor. "By the look of things, I'd say they went in a hurry."

A picture hung on the living room wall of Cyrano with a lovely young wife and a small, pudgy baby with a blue ribbon in her hair. She was an adorable baby, but there seemed to be something off about her eyes, something I couldn't place.

That wasn't what struck me, though. It was that this man had a family, one I'd taken him away from.

"Bryn." Kasper touched my arm, sensing my anguish. "You were protecting the King."

"What was that?" Bayle asked, looking over at us.

"How old is the little girl?" I asked, not wanting to let Bayle in on my private feelings, and pointed to the picture.

"A little over a year, I think," Bayle said. "Cyrano talked about her from time to time. Her name was Morgan, and I think she was diagnosed with some sort of disorder a few months ago."

"Disorder?" I looked at him. "What do you mean?"

"I can't remember what it was." Bayle shook his head. "Something with her brain. She started having seizures, and she couldn't crawl because she didn't have any strength. And there was something with her eyes. They kept darting all around."

"Salla disease," Kasper said, filling in the name Bayle had forgotten.

Bayle nodded. "Yeah, that's it."

I'd heard of Salla disease before. It was some kind of genetic disorder that affected a small percentage of the troll population, but it wasn't common enough that I knew much about it.

"My little sister Naima has it," Kasper said, and his whole face softened when he mentioned her.

"What is it exactly?" I asked.

"It affects the nervous system, and it made it hard for Naima to talk or move, not to mention the seizures," he said. "Fortunately, my parents caught it early with Naima, and they got the medics involved right away. With a combination of medication and their healing powers, along with a couple other things, they really helped her."

Our medics had the ability to heal with psychokinetic powers, but they weren't all powerful. They couldn't undo death, and they couldn't eliminate most diseases. They could take away some symptoms, but they couldn't eradicate disease entirely.

"I mean, she's not cured, and she never will be," Kasper elaborated. "But Naima's ten now, and she can talk, and she *loves* to dance." He smiled. "She's really happy, and that's what counts."

"I'm glad she's okay now," I said.

"Me too," he agreed. "But the treatments my parents got for her cost a fortune. My dad had to get a second job to help cover them."

"That's terrible, but if the two of you are done talking about your families, do you wanna start looking around to see if we can find any clues about Cyrano?" Bayle asked, sounding awfully patronizing for someone who had hired Cyrano in the first place.

"Yes. Of course." I saluted him, which made him scowl, and I started to look around the room.

In reality, there wasn't much to investigate. The house was small and ordinary, and it didn't appear that Cyrano had left behind a manifesto. But since Bayle had been condescending, I wasn't going to leave a single stone unturned.

I lifted up the blankets on the bed, riffled through the baby's toys in the toy box, and leafed through the few books on the shelf. None of them were too exciting—there were a few books on parenting and Salla disease, a dog-eared copy of *Atlas Shrugged,* and a book by Jordan Belfort.

While I dug around their living room, Bayle walked around not doing much of anything, and Kasper scoped out the kitchen. I was flipping through one of the books when I glanced over at the kitchen to see that Kasper had dropped to his knees and was reaching underneath the stout wood-burning stove.

"What are you doing?" I asked, setting aside the book to check it out.

"I thought I saw the light catch on something." He squeezed himself against the stove, reaching all the way to the back, then he scooted back out.

"What is it?" I asked, and Bayle came to look over my shoulder.

Kasper sat back on his knees and opened his hand, revealing two blue stones each about the size of a marble but not quite as round. Their dark blue color sparkled as Kasper tilted his hand.

"Those are big sapphires," I said.

Kasper looked up at me. "This has to mean something."

TWENTY-FIVE

incentives

"What is going on in my kingdom?" Marksinna Lisbet asked, and for the first time since I'd met her, she truly appeared her age.

Her golden hair fell in loose curls down to the middle of her back. Her satin dressing gown flowed around her, creating a half-circle of shimmering fabric on the marble floor of her chambers. She sat at her vanity, her makeup and jewels spread out on the table beside her.

The only jewelry she wore was the large sapphire wedding ring from her long-deceased husband, and even though it wasn't yet six in the morning she'd already applied a coat of mauve lipstick.

"Nana, it's not so bad," Linnea said, attempting to comfort her. She sat on a plush chaise behind her grandmother, and based on her lack of makeup and loosely tied robe that revealed a lace-trimmed camisole underneath, I suspected she hadn't been awake long either.

Lisbet had summoned Kasper and me very early this morning to have a private meeting in her chambers, with only her and her granddaughter. When we arrived, she apologized for the early hour, but said she thought it was the only way a meeting among us would go unnoticed.

"It's not so bad?" Lisbet shot a look over her shoulder at Linnea and scoffed. "Just two weeks ago someone attempted to kidnap you, and last night *your* guard tried to murder your husband! How can you say it's not so bad?"

"Well . . ." Linnea faltered for a moment, frowning. "Both Mikko and I are alive and well. So it can't be *that* bad."

"My child, you know you are the world to me, but things are very bad indeed when the only positive thing you can say is that you're simply alive," Lisbet said. "You're a vibrant, healthy, young Queen. You are *supposed* to be alive!"

"Kasper and Bryn are here," Linnea tried, gesturing toward where we stood at attention near the door. "They'll help us sort out this mess."

The Marksinna looked toward us, an unsettling weariness and fear in her eyes, and she nodded once. "You are here, and I am very grateful for it, because without you I have no idea what would have become of my grandson-in-law. But what do we do about all this?" Her gaze fell heavily on Kasper and me. "Who is behind these attempts on my family's lives? And how do we stop them?"

"Bayle Lundeen has launched a full-scale investigation—" Kasper began, but Lisbet immediately held up her hand to stop him.

"I don't trust that man." Lisbet grimaced. "I haven't trusted him for so long, but Mikko refused to hear anything about it. Lundeen was his father's lackey, which really tells you something about him. Rune Biâelse was an awful, cold tyrant, and anybody he trusted can't be good news."

"Nana!" Linnea exclaimed.

"I'm just stating a fact, my dear," Lisbet said, brushing her off. "And worse still, Rune left his son too terrified to act even long after his death."

"I don't trust Bayle Lundeen either," Kasper agreed. "But now I'm a part of the investigation, and I'm hoping to steer it in the right direction."

"A noble intention, but I'm not certain it will bear any fruit," Lisbet said. "That is why I called you both here. You have no connection to this guard, and you've already proven yourselves to be far more intelligent and capable than anyone we have here. I want you to look into it, separate from whatever farce it is that Bayle Lundeen is spearheading."

I exchanged a look with Kasper, who nodded his encouragement.

"That was already our intention, Marksinna," I said. "We did not trust the guard when we arrived, but after the incident with Cyrano, we trust them even less. Now we must determine how widespread the betrayal is, and who is behind it."

"Excellent." Lisbet smiled at us. "What have you uncovered so far?"

"Cyrano was supposed to be guarding Queen Linnea over the lunch hour, but he informed her that he had a meeting with Bayle he needed to attend," Kasper began.

"I already know that," Linnea said. "I'm the one who told you that."

"Right." Kasper gave her a look but kept his voice even. "We have confirmed that the meeting did exist and that Bayle was there with ten other guards who all vouch for him, along with the kitchen staff and footmen. Cyrano wasn't supposed to attend because he wasn't allowed to leave the Queen unguarded, which he did."

"He told me I would be fine because I would be with Bryn," Linnea said. "And as it turns out, I was much safer with Bryn than I would have been with him."

"So Cyrano lied to get a moment alone with the King so he could kill him?" Lisbet shrugged. "That doesn't tell us *why* he wanted to."

"No, but it does suggest that Bayle wasn't directly involved," Kasper said.

"It's also worth mentioning that Cyrano had a wife and a young child," I said, and by the surprised looks Lisbet and Linnea gave each other, I guessed this was news to them. "His daughter has a rare disease that requires costly treatment, which makes money an excellent motivator. Both the wife and the child appear to have left in a hurry."

"Clothes were scattered over the beds, but there were no signs of a struggle," Kasper said. "They seem to have left very suddenly but of their own accord."

"That's not that surprising if they heard Cyrano was a traitor who'd been killed," I continued, not letting the darkness of his death cloud my words. "We would expect them to run away lest they be punished for his crimes."

"If they are innocent, they have nothing to fear," Linnea piped up, and that was her naiveté showing.

Another time, I would have to explain to her how Viktor Dålig's young children had been punished for his transgressions. The world was not a fair place, and a Queen needed to know that if she wanted to help rule a kingdom.

"We did find something odd, however," Kasper went on. "Under the stove were two sapphires, a little smaller than a marble. We suspect that in the commotion of leaving, they fell out and rolled under the stove, and Cyrano's wife either didn't notice or was in too much of a hurry to be bothered with them."

"Sapphires nearly as large as a marble?" Lisbet shook her head. "Are you certain they were real?"

Kasper nodded. "Based on the color and size, Bayle estimated they were worth at least twenty thousand dollars apiece."

Linnea gasped. "How could a guard have sapphires worth that much? And how could his family be so careless as to leave them behind?"

"That is an excellent question," I said. It was one that Kasper and I had been quick to answer last night. "The only way Cyrano's wife wouldn't have noticed or wouldn't have cared about leaving behind nearly fifty thousand dollars was if she had a lot more."

Queen Linnea shook her head with her forehead scrunched up, clearly still baffled by what I was saying. "We pay them a decent wage, but it's nowhere near enough to have that kind of money. Was Cyrano stealing them?"

"That is one consideration," Kasper allowed. "The other is that Cyrano was paid off."

Lisbet rested her chin on her hand, staring off at nothing, but her eyes darted back and forth as she thought. The Mark-sinna had most likely come to that conclusion long before her granddaughter had and was trying to make sense of it.

"With his daughter's illness and the rising cost of medical bills, Cyrano was very vulnerable to bribery," I said. "He probably believed that it was worth risking his life to take care of his family."

That would explain the intent mania I saw in Cyrano's eyes. He'd had no reason not to drop his sword yesterday, but after talking with Kasper, we'd both begun to suspect that Cyrano planned on going after me until I killed him. In fact, the payment to his family might have been contingent on his death. It would be the only way that whoever had paid him off could be certain that Cyrano would never talk.

I wasn't sure if that made me feel any better about what had happened. Killing a desperate man intent on dying to save his family didn't exactly sound like justice.

"Who here has that kind of money?" Kasper asked.

"Well . . . nobody." Linnea shrugged her shoulders. "I

mean, the women have jewels." She motioned to her grandmother's table, covered in gaudy necklaces and rings. "One of my necklaces might cost ten thousand dollars, but it would have to be filled with sapphires and diamonds. We don't have massive gems like that floating around."

"They came from the vault," Lisbet said, looking at Linnea in the mirror. "That's the only place where we have stones of that caliber."

"Those belong to the kingdom," Linnea said, trying to dissuade her grandmother. "They belong to everybody. Why would Cyrano steal from himself?"

"He didn't steal it—he was paid off," Lisbet corrected her, and Linnea sank down in the chaise. "And it may 'belong' to the kingdom, but only the royal family has access to it. Only the King is allowed to spend it."

"But Mikko's saving it," Linnea argued weakly. "He's trying to do what's best for the people."

Lisbet closed her eyes and sighed. "You can't have a room full of precious stones and expect no one to get greedy."

"Who has access to the vault?" I asked. "Who could have gotten in there to take the sapphires?"

Lisbet turned back toward Kasper and me and looked up. "The system requires thumbprint recognition that you need to get the door open, and that's calibrated for only four people—the royal family. That would be myself, Linnea, Mikko, and Kennet."

"There must be some mistake," Linnea said, disputing Lisbet's assertion. "None of us would do this. I know I didn't, and of course you wouldn't do it. Mikko didn't try to kill himself, and Kennet would never do anything to hurt his brother." She shook her head. "This is a mistake. Someone else is behind this."

Lisbet regarded Kasper and me gravely, ignoring the Queen's insistence that it couldn't be any of the people she loved.

"Talk to the people and do what you need to do," Lisbet told us. "This must end."

TWENTY-SIX

stoic

The marble bench felt hard and cold underneath me, and I leaned forward, resting my arms on my legs. My mouth felt dry, so I licked my lips. I let out a shaky breath.

"You okay?" Kasper asked, his voice soft so it wouldn't echo in the cavernous round hall outside of the King's chambers.

"Hmm?" I'd been staring at the pattern of tiles on the floor, trying not to think of anything at all, and I turned to look at him.

"You seem kind of out of it." Even though Kasper worked to keep his expression neutral at all times, his face had softened and his dark eyebrows were pinched with concern.

"I'm fine," I lied, sitting up straighter.

We were waiting outside the King's chambers with the intention of questioning him about the sapphires in Cyrano's possession. After our meeting with Lisbet and Linnea, we'd gone straight down here, hoping to talk to him before Bayle or anybody else had a chance.

When we'd arrived, he'd still been sleeping, but his valet had gone in to see if Mikko would be willing to see us. A few minutes later, the valet had informed us that Mikko would, but he needed some time to wake up and ready himself, and Kasper and I had been patiently waiting for the past fifteen minutes.

"I know I've been really fortunate to have been a member of the Högdragen in a time of peace." Kasper still spoke low so his voice wouldn't carry. Not that he needed to worry, since we were alone. "I've only been on it for a little over a year, but even when I was a tracker, things were mostly quiet and peaceful."

"Konstantin Black did try to kill the Chancellor," I reminded him, not unkindly.

"I said *mostly,*" he said. "I was out on a mission away from Doldastam when that happened, so I missed all the commotion surrounding it."

"You didn't miss much," I muttered. "Konstantin is insanely good at disappearing in the blink of an eye."

"My point was that I've never even had to draw my sword on someone and mean it, let alone take another person's life," Kasper said, and I involuntarily tensed up. "I can't imagine what that must be like."

"It's part of the job." I wanted to brush it off, change the subject, do anything other than actually talk about it.

"I know, and I know you did what you needed to do." He waited a moment, letting that sink in. "But it couldn't have been easy for you."

"It was surprisingly easy, actually," I said thickly. "From start to finish, it was all over in a matter of minutes."

Kasper put his hand on my back. The gesture felt awkward and a little stiff, but there was something oddly comforting about it.

"You were trained well, and you did what you were supposed to do. That won't change what happened, but maybe it can make it little easier on you."

I offered him a wan smile. "Thank you."

The valet came out and told us that the King would see us now. I stood up and straightened my clothes, and then I followed Kasper inside.

We found Mikko in the sitting area of his chambers. He was dressed but unshaven, with a blond scruff on his chin. The high-backed, tufted chair he sat on looked cushy, but he sat rigidly with his shoulders back, appearing rather uncomfortable.

His blue eyes landed on us briefly, then went back to staring at the rug on the floor. His lips were pressed together in a thin line, and as he breathed in deeply through his nose, his gills seemed to flutter in agitation.

There was a couch and several other chairs that Kasper and I could have sat in, but since Mikko made no motion to them, we remained standing. We never sat in the presence of royalty unless we were invited to.

"I'm assuming this is about the investigation," Mikko said.

"We just had a few things we wanted to talk to you about. This won't take long." I tried to keep my tone soft to calm any anxiety he might have.

Linnea had said he was painfully shy—although to be honest, he seemed more angry than he did nervous. But it was probably better for a King to seem cross all the time than afraid.

Mikko nodded once. "Go ahead."

"Do you know how Cyrano Moen could have come into possession of sapphires?" Kasper asked.

"No." Mikko's hands were resting on his lap, and he began to rub one palm against his leg anxiously. "Sapphires are the most plentiful stones in our kingdom, though. Perhaps he bartered with someone for them."

"We had considered this, but the ones he had were very valuable," Kasper explained. "Bayle estimated their worth at upwards of twenty thousand apiece."

Mikko's expression remained hard, unchanged by the news Kasper had given him, and his eyes were now locked on the floor. He sat stoically, not responding, for nearly a minute before he said, "He shouldn't have had those."

"What do you mean by that?" I asked.

"I don't know how a guard would come by those." Mikko looked up at us and shook his head. "I have no idea how he would've gotten them."

"We suspect he might have been paid," Kasper said, "for his attempt on your life."

The King lowered his eyes and didn't say anything. He'd stopped moving his hand on his leg, and aside from the subtle movement of his gills when he breathed, he was as still as a statue.

"Do you know who would have access to those kinds of

sapphires and would want to hurt you?" I asked him, speaking slowly and carefully.

Of course, Kasper and I already knew who had access to the sapphires, and that list was only four people long. The only person I'd really crossed off was Marksinna Lisbet. I believed she cared too much about her granddaughter to risk anything that might get Linnea hurt.

But even Queen Linnea—who seemed friendly and naive—could be putting on an act, and she could be behind everything. Most of what I knew about things here in Storvatten had come from her, and I really had no way of knowing if she was lying or not.

Despite my newfound friendship with Prince Kennet, I still didn't trust him farther than I could throw him. As the younger brother of the King, I could think of a very obvious motive for him to want his brother out of the way, but I had no idea why he'd have planned an attack on Linnea.

That was assuming of course that Cyrano's attack on Mikko and Konstantin's on Linnea were related, which was the theory that Kasper and I were going on at the moment.

And as for Mikko, with his hardened expression and clipped answers, I honestly had no idea what to make of him. I had been hoping that talking to him would clear things up, but he seemed even more cagey than usual.

"No." Mikko shook his head. "I can think of no one."

"According to Marksinna Lisbet, only four people can get to the vault," Kasper said, pushing Mikko a bit since he wasn't being forthcoming.

"Sapphires can come from anywhere, not just the vault," Mikko replied curtly.

I glanced over at Kasper. We had considered this too, but given how many sapphires were in the vault and how poor the rest of the community was, it seemed very unlikely that they came from anywhere else.

"The four people who can get into the vault are your grandmother-in-law, your brother, your wife, and yourself," Kasper went on as if Mikko hadn't said anything.

"Thank you for informing me of things of which I'm already aware, but I don't think I can be of help to you." Mikko stood up abruptly. "I'm sorry I don't know more, but I should begin preparing for the day. Bayle Lundeen is running a meeting later today, and I am certain that I'll see you both there."

Both Kasper and I were taken aback, and it was a few seconds before we could gather our wits. We thanked the King for his time and then left his chambers, since there was nothing else we could really do.

We saw ourselves out, and once we were in safely in the hall with the door closed behind us, I turned to Kasper. "He knows something."

"But who is he protecting?" Kasper asked. "Himself, or someone he cares about?"

TWENTY-SEVEN

augur

Kasper told me to go rest, but I had other plans in mind.

After spending the morning going over our notes and talking to anyone we could, we still had an hour left until the meeting with Bayle Lundeen was set to start. Kasper and I had tried to speak with him, but he kept insisting that he was busy and he'd talk to us during the meeting.

Apparently, I still wasn't looking so hot, so Kasper had all but commanded me to go lay down, promising he would get me in time for the meeting. I considered it, but I knew sleep wouldn't make me feel better. So I changed into a tank top and leggings and headed outside.

On the back of the palace was a stone patio, curved along the edge to mimic the waves on the outer walls. A hundred rounded stairs led down from the patio to the bottom of the lake, and I descended them slowly, pushing through the shock of the cold as I waded into the water.

Even in May, Lake Superior barely got above freezing. The Skojare kept the ice at bay through a combination of practical tools and magic, but that didn't mean the water was warm by any means.

A human would succumb to hypothermia in as little as fifteen minutes, but I was no human. The Skojare thrived in the cold water. Spending their entire existence in Scandinavia, northern Europe, and Canada, they had adapted to handle the harsh temperatures of swimming in freezing lakes.

Even the Kanin had adjusted to the cold, but I doubted Kasper or Tilda would fare as well stepping into the icy lake as I would. It wasn't exactly a pleasant feeling—like an electrical current running over my skin. But I couldn't deny that there was something strangely enjoyable about it.

The chill took my breath away, and it felt as though it was waking up parts of my body I hadn't even known were sleeping. I lay on my back, floating on the surface. The sun warmed me from above, while the cold water rocked me from below.

I just needed to be able to clear my head. The last twenty-four hours had been a blur of insanity, and I couldn't seem to process any of it.

I knew that I'd killed Cyrano, and I knew that it had been the correct thing to do given my job and his actions. But I couldn't make sense of how I felt about it. Numb perhaps, the numbness was mixed with sadness and regret and pride.

Sadness because a man had died, and regret because I was convinced I could've done something differently so he'd still be alive. And pride because I had done exactly what I had been trained to do. When it came down to it, I had acted and saved the King.

It seemed nearly impossible to reconcile those three emotions.

I tried to let the water wash over me, desperate for a reprieve from constant worries about work and Konstantin and Ridley. No matter how hard I tried, Ridley kept floating back into my thoughts, leaving an ache that ripped through me.

Thinking of him hurt too much, and I pushed away my memories of his eyes and the way his arms felt around me.

I closed my eyes, trying to clear my mind of everything, and I just focused on the sound of the lake lapping against the palace, the iciness of the water holding me up underneath the contrasting warmth of the sun.

That was all that mattered for the moment. Soon, I'd have to go back inside and try to untangle the mess of who was trying to kill whom and why here in Storvatten. But right now, I just needed *this*—to have a few minutes when nothing mattered and I didn't need to think.

With my eyes closed, I could see the sun through my lids. Then the yellowish-red of my eyelids began to change, shifting into pure white bright light that filled my vision. It was disorienting and confusing, and when I tried to open my eyes, I realized they already were.

I was standing in the snow, but there was no horizon around me. Just whiteness, as if the world disappeared into nothing a few meters beyond where I stood. My heart began to race in a panic, and I turned in a circle, trying to understand where I was and what was happening.

Suddenly Konstantin Black was there, standing in front of me dressed all in black, smiling at me. "Don't be scared, white rabbit."

"What's happening?" I asked.

This didn't feel anything like a dream, but it had to be. There was no other explanation for how I could have been in the lake one second, and here in an impossible place with Konstantin the next. I didn't remember falling asleep, but it was a possibility, given how exhausted I had been lately.

"I can't stay long," Konstantin said.

Already, his smile had fallen away. This was the first time I'd seen him without his hair pushed back, and his dark curls fell around his face. His eyes were the color of forged steel, the kind used to make our swords, and he stepped closer to me, looking at me intently.

"Why are we here?" I asked.

"Here is nowhere." He shook his head. "You are in Storvatten, and you must leave."

I narrowed my eyes at him. "How do you know where I am?"

"I know a great many things, and it doesn't matter how I know. You are not safe in Storvatten, and you need to leave."

"It seems safe to me, now that you and Viktor Dålig are gone," I said.

Konstantin pursed his lips, and for a moment he looked pained. "I am glad to see you're okay after what he did to you."

"Why?" I shook my head. "Why do you even care?"

"I don't know," he admitted with a crooked smile. "I just don't want to see any more innocent people hurt."

"Then you need to stop working with Viktor Dålig."

The sky—if you could call the whiteness that surrounded us the sky—began to darken, turning gray, and the snow underneath my feet started to tremble.

"This won't hold for much longer," Konstantin said. Thunder seemed to come from nowhere and everywhere at all once, and he had to shout be heard over it. "You must leave Storvatten! They plan to kill you because you're getting too close!"

"Too close to what?" I asked, and by now the sky was nearly black. "How do you know?"

"Viktor Dålig gave the order. He wants anyone in his way dead."

Konstantin receded from me, but he didn't step or move himself. It was as though he were slowly being pulled into the darkness around us.

"Run, white rabbit," he said, his voice nearly lost in the rumbles, and then he was gone.

I opened my eyes to the bright sun shining above the Skojare palace, and even though I was still floating above the water, I was gasping for breath.

Everything seemed peaceful and still. There was no thunder, no darkness, no Konstantin Black. I tried to tell myself that it was just a strange dream brought on by stress and exhaustion, but I couldn't shake the feeling that I had really been talking to Konstantin. That somehow he'd managed to visit me in a lysa to warn me that there was a bounty on my head.

TWENTY-EIGHT

denunciation

It was in the fishbowl of the meeting room that everything went completely insane, and this was coming from someone who'd just been visited in a dream by Konstantin Black.

The meeting room stuck out from the rest of the palace in a bubble, with one interior wall and one exterior wall of glass domed out around us. It left me feeling as if the lake were engulfing us, as if it were a sea monster trying to swallow us all.

At the end of the long table in the center of the room sat King Mikko, with his Queen sitting to his right and his brother to his left. Lisbet sat next to her granddaughter. Other than Kasper and me, they were the only people in the room.

"This is Bayle's meeting, isn't it?" Kennet asked, looking over his shoulder at the large bronze clock hanging on the wall. "Doesn't he know it's rude to arrive late to your own party?"

"When you arrived late to your own birthday party, you told me that was arriving in style," Linnea reminded him.

Kennet smirked. "That's because everything I do, I do in style."

Kennet might have joked, but nobody else here seemed to be in good spirits. Bayle's making us wait—twenty minutes so far—wasn't making things any better. Kasper and I were close to the end of the table, a polite distance away from the royalty, and Mikko kept shooting icy glares in our direction.

I had a feeling if we didn't solve things quickly, we never would, because it seemed like we had begun to wear out our welcome.

"Oh for Ægir's sake." Lisbet let out an exasperated sigh. "My King, perhaps you should send someone to fetch Bayle. This is getting tedious."

"He will be here," Mikko said, apparently immune to the same tension the rest of us were suffocating under.

Fortunately for the rest of us, Bayle finally arrived, with guards in tow. They were senior guards I'd met earlier in the week, decked out in their uniforms. Bayle had added a vest made of platinum, with carvings of fish scales. It was real metal that he wore over his jacket, armor to protect against attacks.

Looking back, that was the first sign that something was going on. Who wears armor to a meeting?

"I'm glad you could grace us with your presence," Kennet said dryly.

"I am very sorry, my liege, but I had important business to attend to, which will become very clear to you all in a moment," Bayle said. To his credit, he actually sounded winded, like he'd been hurrying.

He seemed nervous, though—staring about the room, swallowing and licking his lips a lot, and stammering a bit when he spoke. The guard behind him held a thick manila envelope, and he would only stare at the ground.

"That's fine," Mikko said. "Just get on with it."

Bayle began to rehash what we all already knew—Cyrano's attempt to kill Mikko, my thwarting of it, Cyrano's wife and daughter running off, the sapphires, and the fact that the only people who had access to the vault were in this room.

"We spoke to all of you this morning, asking when and why you last accessed the vault," Bayle said, and he put his hand on the bell of his sword. "Marksinna Lisbet had been there three months ago with the record keeper, for accounting purposes. Prince Kennet was there two days ago, showing Kasper and Bryn."

Bayle cleared his throat. "Queen Linnea and King Mikko claimed it had been so long ago that they couldn't recollect when they'd last opened it."

"So?" Kennet arched an eyebrow. "That doesn't really tell us anything does it?"

"No, not by itself." Bayle turned to the guard behind him and took the envelope. "We checked the database to see if anybody else had gotten in the vault, and according to the, uh, the computer, the last person in the vault was, uh, King Mikko, two hours before the attack on his life."

Mikko didn't say anything immediately. He just shook his head. "That's simply untrue. I wasn't in there. I had no reason to go in."

"Sire, the fingerprint scanning says you were," Bayle said.

"The King is not a liar," Linnea hissed.

Lisbet held up her hand to hush her granddaughter, her eyes fixed on the guards. "What does all this mean?"

"Well, it, uh . . ." Bayle cleared his throat again. "We believe that King Mikko paid Cyrano Moen to attack him, making it appear that Cyrano would kill him but knowing that a guard would intervene and protect him."

"That's preposterous!" Linnea shouted. "Why would Mikko fake an attempt on his life? That makes no sense."

"We believe that King Mikko is the one behind your attempted kidnapping, and that to shift blame from himself, he planned the assassination attempt," Bayle explained. "He wanted us to think someone else was behind everything going on here."

Kennet sat back in his chair, almost slouching, and only glanced over at his brother once. Mikko, for his part, seemed unmoved by what Bayle was saying. He just kept shaking his head.

"Mikko would never hurt me," Linnea insisted. She leaned forward on the table, as if that would make Bayle believe her.

"It's with all that in mind that we have come here to arrest King Mikko Biâelse for the attempted kidnapping of the Queen, Linnea Biâelse, as well as hiring Cyrano Moen for a feigned assassination attempt," Bayle said, and for the first time since he'd come in the room, his voice sounded strong.

"That's treason!" Linnea was practically screaming now. "You cannot arrest the King!"

"Linnea, hush." Lisbet put her hand on Linnea's arm. "Let them sort this all out."

Technically, a monarch could be arrested for breaking any of the laws of the kingdom. And while I wasn't as familiar with Skojare history I was with Kanin, in the Kanin lore, I only knew of two monarchs ever being arrested—a Queen for poisoning her husband, and a King for stabbing the Chancellor in the middle of a party.

Kings had been overthrown. A few had been forced to step down, and a couple had even been executed. But they were almost never arrested. In theory, laws might apply to royalty, but in practice, they never really did.

"I haven't done anything," Mikko said, his voice a low rumble. "I'd never hurt my wife, and I never hired a guard to pretend to hurt me."

But he didn't threaten to have them banished or thrown in the dungeon. He simply denied the charges, and that emboldened the guards to come over and put Mikko in shackles.

Linnea began screaming at them, telling them that they couldn't do this and that they had to let him go, and Lisbet had to physically hold her back. Throughout the whole display, Kennet never said a word.

As the guards escorted Mikko out of the room, he walked with his head bowed and his broad shoulders slumped. He seemed almost resigned to the position, and since he was a King with all the power in the kingdom to fight the charges, I didn't understand why he was just taking it like this.

It did fit in line with what both Kennet and Linnea had said about him—that he would rather take what was given to him than fight back. But that made it feel all the more tragic to see the tall hulk of a man with his head hanging down as the guard he refused to depose escorted him out of the room.

Before Bayle left, I got up and ran after him, stopping him at the door. "We'd like to take a look at the records."

"In due time." Bayle was talking to me, but his eyes were directed out the door, following Mikko's figure down the hall. "There's a case we're working on, and you'll have your turn when we're done."

"No, we should be part of the case—" I tried to argue, but he cut me off.

"Excuse me," Bayle said brusquely. "I've just arrested the ruler of our kingdom. I have more pressing matters to deal with."

While Lisbet struggled to get Linnea to calm down, I walked back over and collapsed in the chair next to Kasper. He looked just as shocked as I felt, and considering Kasper prided himself on keeping his emotions hidden, that was really saying something.

"What the fuck just happened?" he asked.

I shook my head. "I have no idea."

TWENTY-NINE

quandary

"Miss! You can't go in there!" the footman called after me, but if I wasn't going to heed Konstantin's warning of imminent death, I wasn't about to listen to a servant worrying about propriety.

I pushed open the door to Kennet's chambers without knocking and without waiting for anyone to let me in. He stood next to his bed loosening his tie, his suit jacket already discarded on a nearby chair.

"Miss!" The footman had hurried in after me. "You must leave."

"It's all right," Kennet told him, but he kept his eyes on me. "She can stay."

"If you are sure, my Prince," the footman said, eyeing me with disdain.

"Give us a moment alone. And make sure you don't let anybody get by this time."

The footman bowed then turned and left, closing the door behind him. Kennet's room didn't appear all that different from my own, except the finishings were nicer. The wallpaper wasn't peeling, and sheer silver curtains ran along the window that faced the water, giving the room a greater sense of privacy.

Kennet took off his tie and tossed it on the bed. "By the look on your face, I'm assuming this isn't a friendly visit."

"You know why I'm here," I snapped.

"No, I really don't." He sat on the bed, sounding tired, and most of his usual swagger had disappeared. He seemed world weary in a way that I hadn't thought Kennet capable of.

"Why didn't you defend your brother?" I asked.

"Why didn't you?" he shot back.

"Because he's not my brother, and I'm not the Prince. They never would've listened to me."

Kennet stared down at his satin bedspread. "They were arresting the King, Bryn. They weren't going to listen to me either." Then he shook his head. "I'm not sure he's innocent."

"You think he did it?" I asked.

He looked up at me. "You don't?"

"I don't know," I admitted.

Kennet motioned to me. "Well, there you go."

"You still should've defended him."

"Just because he's my brother? Or because he's my King? You think he should get a free pass?"

"No. Of course not."

Kennet cocked his head and narrowed his eyes. "You think I had something to do with it."

"I haven't ruled out any possibilities yet." I chose my words carefully.

"You don't trust me?" Kennet smirked a little and stood up, walking toward me.

"I think it would be unwise to trust anybody in Storvatten right now."

"That is probably very true." He stopped mere inches away, looking down at me. "Why did you come to my room, Bryn?"

"I want to find out the truth about what is going on here."

"But you don't trust me."

"Maybe I can tell when you're lying," I countered.

"Oh yeah?" Kennet raised an eyebrow. "Am I lying when I say I want to kiss you right now?"

I took half a step back, surprised by his frank declaration, and it took me a moment to figure out how to counter him. "Prince, I value your friendship, but that is all."

He stepped closer, smiling down at me. "You would deny your Prince a simple kiss?"

I looked up at him sharply. "You would order me to?"

"No, of course not," Kennet corrected himself quickly. "You know I didn't mean it like that."

"How do I know that?" I asked as I studied his face. "I don't know you, and I don't trust you."

For once, he didn't have a smart comeback. The weariness I'd seen in him earlier was creeping back in, and I felt a small pang of sympathy.

"Today has been a very long day, and the days ahead are only going to be longer," Kennet said, his voice a low, resigned rumble. "And as much as I'd usually love to play these games with you, I don't have it in me today."

"I don't want to play any games," I told him. "I just need you to be honest with me."

He let out a deep breath. "I will answer any questions you ask me as honestly as I can."

"Did you try to kidnap or hurt the Queen?"

He pulled his head back in surprise. "No. Of course not."

"Do you know who did?"

"It's my understanding that it was that Konstantin Black fellow."

"Do you know him?"

"Konstantin?" Kennet shook his head. "No. I never met him."

I narrowed my eyes, appraising him. "You're not lying?"

"No, I swear," he insisted, and for once I actually believed him. "I never met him. I never even heard of him until you told us about him."

"Did your brother have anything to do with the Queen's kidnapping?" I asked.

Kennet opened his mouth but seemed to think better of it. His gills flared with a deep breath, and finally he said, "I think my brother is involved in a great number of things that I know nothing about. He is a good man, and he tries to be a fair King, but he's been in over his head since the day he was crowned. No matter what he has done, I'm certain that he never meant to hurt anybody."

"What about you?" I asked.

"What about me?" A smile began to play on his lips.

"Are you a good man?"

"No, I would say I'm not a very good man," Kennet admitted. "But I would never do anything to hurt my brother. Despite our occasional differences, I love Mikko, and I won't let anything bad happen to him."

"You let him go to jail," I reminded him, and he flinched.

"Mikko is in jail," he contended. "But I'm not the one who arrested him, and there will be a trial. He will have the chance to clear his name, and I'll stand by him.

"Besides, there are worse things than jail," Kennet added.

"Did you hire Cyrano to kill you brother?" I asked.

Kennet rolled his eyes. "I already told you I'd never do anything to hurt Mikko. Haven't I answered enough of these questions?" He stepped backward and sat on the bed.

"I have one more question," I answered. "Do you know why anyone would want me dead?"

"What?" Kennet shook his head, appearing appalled by the idea. "No. Of course not. Who wants you dead?"

"No one. Never mind." I tried to brush it off, since that was easier than explaining that Konstantin Black had visited me in a dream to tell me that Viktor Dålig had put a hit out on me.

Kennet smirked. "I can't imagine a single reason anyone wouldn't want you around. Other than your incessant questions, of course."

THIRTY

desperation

The darkness of the water outside my window made it impossible to see if the sun had come up yet. I lay in bed not sleeping, the way I had spent most of the night not sleeping, waiting for my alarm to go off and tell me it was morning and I could get up and actually accomplish something.

Not that I was sure anything could be accomplished. Kasper and I had spent a large portion of yesterday trying to get Bayle to hand over papers to us, but he insisted that they needed to be locked up for safety before King Mikko's trial.

Bayle refused to tell us much of anything, citing confidentiality. We tried to push it, but since we didn't have much standing here, we didn't get anywhere. When we tried to talk to Mikko, his barrister shut us down.

There wasn't much more we could do for him, so Kasper suggested we go back to working on the mission we came here for in the first place—creating recommendations to help the palace guard function better. And that's what we did, staying up late into the night to write a report about the changes we thought the guards could make so the royal family would be safer.

It did seem a little like a moot point, with the Skojare King locked up and their kingdom in a panic. Not to mention that Bayle Lundeen still had more power than he should—but for the moment, things were in too much chaos to add reorganizing the guard.

Whoever stepped up in the interim for King Mikko—most likely Linnea, Kennet, or Lisbet—could replace Bayle, and that was our number-one recommendation. The guard needed a complete overhaul, starting at the top. Once Bayle was gone and the trial was over, it would be good for the Skojare if they could get a fresh start with a properly functioning security system in place.

A timid knock at my door interrupted my not-sleeping, and I rolled over to check the alarm clock. It wasn't even six in the morning yet, so I suspected that whoever was here wasn't bearing good news.

I opened the door to find Linnea. The hood of her dressing robe was up, hiding her mass of curls, and her eyes were red rimmed. Her porcelain skin somehow seemed even paler than normal, and she sniffled as she stared up at me in desperation.

"Please, you have to help us," Linnea said, almost sobbing already.

"Help who?" I asked.

"Mikko and me." Linnea came in past me, wringing her

embroidered handkerchief. "I saw him last night, and it was awful, but they would only let me stay for twenty minutes, and he can't live like that, Bryn! He can't!"

I closed the door and held out my hand. "Calm down. I know you're upset, but everything will be okay."

"How can you say that?" Linnea cried. "My husband is in the dungeon!"

"Getting hysterical won't get him out any sooner."

"I know. I'm sorry." She wiped at her eyes with the handkerchief, then she sat down on the bed. "I don't even know how this can happen. How can the King be arrested?"

"The laws apply to the King and commoners alike," I said, reciting what we were taught in school—but even then, everyone had known it wasn't true.

"They say they're doing it to protect me," Linnea went on, ignoring my comment. "But why would I need protection from Mikko? He *loves* me!"

"They're still investigating." I tried to placate her.

Her lips trembled as she stared up at me from underneath the hood. "I don't even know what's happening in the kingdom. How can I trust Mikko will even get a fair trial? What if they find him guilty? What will become of him? And what will become of me?"

I shook my head sadly, wishing I had something better to give her. "I don't know."

"I just can't believe this is all happening. I'm the Queen! I should have some say!" Linnea cried out in frustration.

"It's isn't fair," I agreed.

For the most part, both Kanin and Skojare societies were patriarchies—women could only rule in extreme cases and for a short period of time, usually after their husband the King had died and before their son the Prince came of age. Other tribes were more socially progressive than ours, allowing women to rule in the absence of a male bloodline, but the Kanin especially were much more rooted in tradition than most.

Linnea's power as Queen only came from her husband, or her son if she eventually had one while Mikko was King. If Mikko were to lose his crown, she would lose hers as well. With the King thrown in the dungeon, her power was locked up along with him.

"What's going on?" Kasper threw open the door my room, his sword in hand.

His hair was disheveled from sleep, and he wore only a pair of pajama pants, revealing a tattoo of a rabbit above his heart. I knew that many of the Högdragen had that same tattoo, but I'd never seen Kasper's before.

"Nothing." I held up my hands to calm him. "Everything is fine."

"I heard a noise," he said, probably referring to Linnea's yelling, and he looked around the room in bewilderment. "Why is the Queen here?"

"Am I even the Queen?" Linnea asked, growing more despondent by the second.

"She just needed someone to talk to," I explained to Kasper, and he relaxed and lowered his sword.

"What I *need* is answers," Linnea said.

"Your grandmother carries a great deal of weight in the kingdom," I said. "You should be talking with her. I'm sure she knows more about what's going to happen than I do."

"She does," Linnea agreed, but she didn't sound too happy about it. "She's on the committee to decide who should rule in the King's absence, but she won't listen to me. Whenever I say anything about Mikko, she just tells me to be patient and that the truth will come out."

"That is very sound advice," Kasper said.

Something must've occurred to Linnea, because she suddenly perked up, her eyes bright and excited. "But she'll listen to you. She trusts the pair of you. If you talk to her about Mikko, she'll *have* to listen to you."

"My Queen, I think you're being a bit a rash," I explained carefully. "Marksinna Lisbet is far more likely to listen to you than she is to two guards from another kingdom. As the Queen and her blood, you possess far more clout than we ever could."

"Nonsense." Linnea jumped to her feet, undeterred. "Nana still thinks of me as a child. She respects your opinions. You must come with me to talk to her at once."

"At once?" Kasper asked.

"Well, I'll give you a moment to get dressed." Linnea glanced over at his shirtless torso. "But as soon as you're finished."

I sincerely doubted that we could change the Marksinna's mind, not to mention that I wasn't convinced Mikko was innocent. Of course, I wasn't convinced that he was guilty either.

THIRTY-ONE

sequester

Linnea held my hand as we ran down the hall, practically dragging me along behind her, and as we entered Lisbet's chambers, she continued to do so. I wanted to let go or pull free, but she squeezed so tightly I thought she needed it.

"What are you all doing here?" Lisbet asked, sounding more harried than surprised.

Despite the early hour, Lisbet was already up and getting ready for the day. Instead of her usual gowns and dresses, she wore suit pants with flowing wide legs and an elegant top, while her matching jacket lay carefully on her bed. She flitted about the room, putting in large dangling earrings, barely stopping to look at us.

"We want to talk to you about Mikko," Linnea said, summoning all her strength.

"I have a great many meetings today, all centered on him," Lisbet replied tiredly. She began rummaging through the drawer on her vanity. "I can't imagine there's anything more I have to say about him."

Linnea stepped away from me, letting go of my hand. "But Nana, he's innocent! Bryn and Kasper think so too!"

Kasper appeared startled by this declaration, since he'd never said anything indicating he felt that way.

Lisbet apparently found what she was looking for—a heavily jeweled bracelet—and she straightened up and looked over at us as she put it on. "Is that true?"

"I haven't seen any evidence that's shown King Mikko's guilt definitively," I replied, choosing my words very carefully so as not to alienate Linnea, but I need to be truthful. "But I haven't been allowed to see very much evidence at all."

Lisbet nodded. "That is an unfortunate necessity."

Every time Kasper and I had tried to get more information yesterday, we'd hit a wall. While I wouldn't go as far as to suggest that Lisbet declare Mikko wrongfully accused the way Linnea had, I did realize that now was the perfect opportunity to see if Lisbet could remove some of those walls.

"If we had more access, I'm certain we could be of help—" I began, but Lisbet held up her hand, silencing me.

"You've already been more than enough help," she said. "But I'm afraid your time here has run its course. Members of another tribe—no matter how well-meaning and how educated—cannot be involved in deciding the fate of our King."

I lowered my eyes. "Of course."

"Things are changing a great deal here, and I truly believe my granddaughter is much safer, and that is because of you,"

Lisbet went on. "Both of you have been integral in improving our way of life here in Storvatten."

"We have been compiling a report of our recommendations," Kasper said, since it seemed clear that Lisbet was about to give us leave. "What would you like us to do with it?"

"I would like you to complete it. We will definitely be taking all your recommendations under advisement," Lisbet said.

"But Nana, Mikko . . ." Linnea whined, impatient with all the talk not about her husband—which was understandable given her desperation.

"Linnea, my love, we have already gone over this many times." Lisbet spoke sweetly, but strain was visible in her face—the tight smile, the irritation in her eyes. "The inquest will decide what happens. I know you love him, but you must wait—as I must, as the entire kingdom must—to find out the truth, and then you must learn to be satisfied with whatever that may be."

"But this isn't fair! It's not right!" Linnea shouted with tears in her eyes, then turned to me. "Bryn! Tell her!"

At first, I said nothing, caught off guard at being put in such a position, but I finally came up with, "My Queen, you know my thoughts on this won't affect the outcome."

"She is right, Linnea," Lisbet said. "You must learn to be patient."

Linnea pushed back her platinum ringlets and tried to stay collected, but she'd only had the most tenuous grasp on composure all morning. It all became too much for her, and she burst out sobbing. Her grandmother reached out to comfort her, but Linnea pushed Lisbet off. Mumbling apologies, she ran into the adjoining bathroom and slammed the door shut behind her.

"I'm sorry for her outburst," Lisbet said. "She's still very young, and the past few weeks have been very hard on her."

"No need for apologies," I assured her. "But it sounds as if you're saying our time here is done."

Lisbet walked over to the bed and put on her suit jacket, a large sapphire brooch already pinned to the front. "I do think you've helped as much as you can."

"What of the Queen's safety? And your own?" I asked.

In the back of my mind was Konstantin's warning that my life was in danger in Storvatten—assuming he had actually visited me in a lysa, and it wasn't simply a stress dream. Either way, it didn't matter. If I felt that Linnea wasn't safe or that I had a job to do here, I would argue to stay.

"I am looking into it, off the radar of the guard, and I will get to the bottom of things. And I can assure you that I value Linnea's life more than my own," Lisbet told me emphatically. "Her safety will be my utmost priority."

"Marksinna, I know how much you love your granddaughter, but with all due respect, the kingdom has already been falling down around you," I said. "And I fear the both of you will continue to be in danger. At least as long as Bayle Lundeen is in charge."

"Today, I will attend a meeting where the acting monarch is declared in Mikko's absence," Lisbet said. "I am going to do all I can to ensure that I get the position, and my very first act will be removing Bayle." She stared down at me severely. "This kingdom will not fall apart as long as I'm around."

I wanted to argue with her, but the truth was that Lisbet had far more power than I did. She was much better equipped to handle the heft of the Skojare problems than I was. By removing Cyrano Moen, and by convincing Lisbet to remove Bayle, I had done all I could to keep Linnea safe.

"I'm sorry I don't have more time to talk to you, but as you can imagine, it's a crazy time here in our kingdom," Lisbet said. "Once you complete the report, deliver it to me. Then you are free to head back to Doldastam."

THIRTY-TWO

valediction

In the week since Kasper and I had left, Doldastam had warmed up some, but it was still buried under snow, which was typical even for May. I'd gotten so used to looking out the windows of the Skojare palace and seeing the dark water surrounding us, it was a strange relief to see the overcast sky and snow-covered landscape.

After Marksinna Lisbet had told us our time was done, Kasper and I had spent the better part of the day perfecting our extensive list of recommendations. I wanted to be certain I wasn't leaving Linnea defenseless, and when I handed the list to Lisbet, I reiterated that they could call upon us should they need anything again.

My goodbyes with Linnea had been short and bittersweet. She didn't say much, instead preferring to sit with her head down and mumble her gratitude. I thought that would be it, but when I turned to go she lunged at me and hugged me fiercely as she cried against my shoulder.

"You mustn't forget about me, Bryn," she said between sobs.

I wasn't sure what to do, so I awkwardly patted her back and said, "Of course I won't."

"And you will come back, right?" She let go of me and wiped her eyes, trying to collect herself again. "If I need you?"

"Of course. I will always be here if you need me. I won't let anything bad befall either you or the King," I promised her, although I had no idea how I'd be able to keep that promise from Doldastam.

Linnea smiled at me with tears streaming down her cheeks. I didn't want to leave her like that, but Kasper insisted it was time to go. We'd been ordered to move on, so there was nothing more we could do there, and I left Linnea in the hands of her grandmother.

The Storvatten palace was in chaos, with people running this way and that down the halls. The meeting with Marksinna Lisbet, Prince Kennet, and an advisory board had been deadlocked most of the morning, and they had adjourned without reaching a decision on who would be King, in part because none of them agreed how long the King would be absent.

Usually, a footman would have carried our bags to and from our rooms when we arrived and departed, but today either the footmen were busy caring for arriving Skojare officials from other towns, or someone was too busy to instruct them. Either way, Kasper and I were left to tend to our luggage ourselves.

I didn't mind, except that the halls were inordinately crowded, making it harder to get by.

"We shouldn't be leaving," I muttered to Kasper as we made our way through the labyrinth the halls had become.

"This all comes with the Högdragen territory—you do what you're told as long as you're told to do it, and then you move on," he replied simply.

We managed to make it to the door in once piece with all our possessions. I paused, looking back at the icy palace around us.

"Do you think Linnea and Mikko will be all right?" I asked.

"I think that with Lisbet in charge, things will be safer here than they have been in a very long time," Kasper said.

He was right. We had begun to make changes to the guard, but Lisbet would be the one to finish them. Besides, Linnea could always reach me in a lysa, and I would come the second she called for me, if she did.

I had opened the front door to the palace when Kennet came running out to stop us, pushing through everyone bustling around the main hall.

"You were really gonna leave without saying anything?" Kennet asked, out of breath because he'd literally jogged over to us.

"You have a lot on your plate today," I said. "I wasn't even sure where you were, and I didn't think you'd have the time."

"I always have time for you, Bryn," Kennet assured me with a smile.

Kasper stood awkwardly next to us and cleared his throat loudly. I wasn't sure if it was to remind me that he was there, or to emphasize that openly flirting with the Prince was frowned upon. But it didn't matter. I planned on keeping things brief.

"Thank you for making time for me while I was here, Prince."

"It has truly been my pleasure." Kennet stared down at me, his eyes that brilliant blue that I'd thought only existed in movies, and a wry smile played on his lips. "Until we meet again."

And that's how I'd left Storvatten—feeling an odd mixture of pride and uncertainty. I had done the job I had been tasked with, and I had done it to the best of my ability. But leaving the palace while it was still so unstable didn't exactly make me happy.

It was midday on Tuesday when we drove through the walls that surrounded Doldastam. The gate was locked, and the two Högdragen manning it were incredibly thorough in checking our IDs and credentials. I was honestly a little surprised they didn't search the SUV at the rate they were going.

After my time in Storvatten and the long drive back, all I really wanted to do was put on something comfortable, go brush Bloom, and then maybe curl up in bed with a good book and lose myself for a while.

Of course, there wasn't time for that. At least not right away. Kasper and I had just completed a mission, which meant that we had to debrief King Evert.

Because of the added security, Elliot Väan—a Högdragen guard—met us at the door instead of a footman. He and

Kasper worked together a lot, and they were good friends. As Elliot led us down to the meeting room, he and Kasper made small talk, and I tried to adjust to being back home.

The Kanin palace definitely seemed darker after the glass walls and frosty wallpaper in Storvatten. Here the stone surrounded us, lit by kerosene lamps. Though there were elegant touches, with jewels and antiques in every corner, there was definitely something much more medieval about the Kanin palace.

As we got closer to the meeting room, Kasper asked Elliot, "How have things been while we've been gone?"

Elliot shook his head. "Things are not going well."

"How so?" Kasper asked, and I turned toward them, my interest piqued.

"It's too much to tell you right now." Elliot gestured toward the doors to the meeting room. "The King may fill you in anyway, and he should be here shortly."

I wished he would've said more, but meeting with the King took priority over small talk with a guard. As I went over to the table to take a seat, Kasper cleared his throat.

I looked back at him, standing tall with his hands folded behind his back. "What?"

"A member of the Högdragen stands."

"But we're having a meeting with the King. I always sit."

Kasper stared straight ahead. "A member of the Högdragen stands."

"Are you saying I should stand?"

"I'm not in a position to give you orders."

I rolled my eyes. "We've just spent a week working together. If you think I'm doing something wrong, tell me."

His mouth twitched, then he turned to me and said, "I think you get too familiar with people in authority."

My jaw dropped. I'd expected maybe a small admonishment about my posture or something. The only thing he'd really corrected me for in Storvatten was that I didn't stand tall enough.

"Don't look so shocked." Kasper sighed, and his shoulders relaxed. "I'm not trying to be mean, and it's good that they like you. It speaks well of how you carry yourself and interact with others, especially those in power who are generally slow to grow fond of those who serve them."

"You wouldn't have brought it up if you didn't think it was a bad thing," I said.

"I think it's a dangerous thing," he clarified. "Queen Linnea treated you more as a friend than a servant—which is what a guard is, when it comes down to it."

I lowered my eyes. "Things were strange in Storvatten. The Queen needed someone to rely on."

"It's not just there though," Kasper said. "You're too friendly with Ridley, and he's your boss. You talk back to our King and Queen."

"My job is to serve this kingdom to the best of my ability, and that means I won't stand idly by if I think the wrong thing is being done, even if the one doing it is wearing a crown." My voice grew louder as I spoke. Kasper had been speaking to me as gently as he could, but it was hard for me not to feel defensive.

"Bryn." He glanced toward the door, as if expecting the

King to come walking in, and he pushed his hand palm down in a gesture indicating that I should lower my voice. "I'm not attacking you. I know you have the best intentions, and you're good at what you do."

I folded my arms over my chest. "That's not what it sounded like."

"When I'm working, I set aside my opinions and feelings," he explained. "I simply do as I am told. My job is to follow the King's orders, and when I'm done, I'm done. My day is over, and I go home to Tilda, and soon I'll come home to a baby. There I have opinions and thoughts, because that's my life. That's where those things fit."

"You care about your job just as much as I do," I countered.

"No, I take my job as seriously as you do," Kasper corrected me. "The things that matter the most to me aren't my job or the King or the Queen. They're Tilda, and my family, and my friends. Those are things I'm passionate about. But at work, I keep my mouth shut and do my job."

I shook my head. "Well, I guess my service is more than just a job to me. I'm willing to sacrifice anything to help our people"—I couldn't help but think of Ridley, and I swallowed back the ache he always brought to my chest—"so if I overstep my role, it's only because this job matters so much to me."

"I'm not trying to upset you, Bryn," Kasper said. "I admire your devotion—everyone does. It's how you've gotten so far. All I'm saying is that it's not good when you make your job your whole life, and it's even more dangerous when you mistake the people who reign over you for your friends."

I opened my mouth to argue but stopped myself when I realized I was being defensive. Because what he'd said was true. Every night when he went home to Tilda and their future child, I went home to an empty loft.

It was the life I'd chosen for myself. But was it really the life I wanted?

THIRTY-THREE

operations

Even a ride on Bloom couldn't help me shake my unease. The horse tried his best, galloping along the wall that surrounded Doldastam as fast as he could, but when I took him back to the stable I still wasn't feeling any better. He nuzzled me more than usual, his mane as soft as silk as it rubbed against me, and I fed him an extra apple before leaving.

The debriefing with the King had gone about as I'd thought it would—he'd already heard about Mikko's arrest and mainly been interested in who would be ruling the Skojare in his absence. But Evert had seemed more distracted than normal, and he left the meeting within a few minutes with brusque congratulations on a job well done.

I wanted to work off the anxiety that Storvatten and Konstantin and even Kasper's lecture had caused, but that required dealing with everything that went along with going to work. So that left me walking around town, trying to clear my head.

My path took me by the tracker school, but I deliberately gave it a wide berth in case I spotted Ridley. I definitely wasn't prepared to see to him yet.

As I walked by, I glanced over at the training yard behind the school. A split-rail wooden fence surrounded the yard, in an attempt to keep out the children who mistook it for a playground. Most of it was flat, level dirt with the snow shoveled away, but there was a climbing wall and a few other obstacles.

With the temperature just below freezing and the air still, it was a perfect day for the trackers to be out running a course. Instead, I only saw two people, and because of the distance between us it took me a few seconds longer than it should've to realize that it was Ember training with someone else.

Her dark hair was pulled back into a ponytail, and she wore a black thermal shirt and boots that went halfway up her calf. Her sparring partner was a guy, dressed similarly to her but with the addition of a thick winter cap. Even though he was taller and broader shouldered than her, Ember had no problem pushing him around.

Since no one else was outside, I decided to walk over and say hi. I'd just reached the fence when I finally recognized her combatant, and I realized with dismay that Ember had just thrown Markis Linus Berling to the ground.

"What are you doing?" I asked, but instead of a friendly greeting it sounded much more like a demand.

I'd never seen a Markis or Marksinna training before, in large part because a tracker was never, ever supposed to lay their hands on one, especially not the way Ember just had.

"Bryn!" Ember grinned at me, apparently not noticing the accusation in my tone. "I heard you were coming back today."

"Hey, Bryn." Linus smiled at me, and Ember extended her hand and helped pull him to his feet.

"What are you two doing?" I managed to sound less angry this time as I leaned on the fence.

"Since you've been gone, I've been working as Linus's tracker, helping him acclimate and all that." Ember started walking over to me, and Linus followed, brushing snow off his pants as he did.

"That's great," I said, and I meant it. Ember was a good tracker, and I was sure she'd be a great help to him. "But since when did acclimation include combat training?"

"I asked her to teach me." Linus pushed the brim of his hat up so I could see his eyes better. Freckles dotted his cheeks, and there was something boyish in his face that made him seem younger than his seventeen years.

It'd been nearly a month since I first met Linus in Chicago, when I was tracking him and first ran into Konstantin Black, which set off this whole thing. Since that time, Linus seemed to be doing well at understanding his role in Kanin society as a high-ranking Markis, adjusting quicker than most, but he still hadn't lost his friendly innocence.

"A lot of the younger Markis and Marksinna are requesting defensive training," Ember explained as she leaned against the fence next to me. "Things have been crazy since you've been gone."

I instinctively tensed up. "Crazy how?"

"You know how Ridley was training those scouts to go out and look for Viktor Dålig?" Ember asked.

My stomach dropped, fearing that something might have happened to him while I was gone, and it took me a moment to force myself to nod.

"Well, last week, one of the scouts reported that he thought he'd found Viktor," Ember went on. "He managed to report back with Viktor's whereabouts, but then all communication went silent. Ridley went with a rescue team to go after him. When they found the scout, he was dead."

"But Ridley came back okay?" I asked, my stomach twisting painfully.

"Yeah, he's fine," Ember said, and relief washed over me. "But they found an abandoned campsite, where they're assuming that Viktor, Konstantin, and at least twenty or so other people were hiding out. They were long gone by the time Ridley and the rescue team arrived, of course, but the scary part was that the campsite was only three hours away."

My mind flashed back on Konstantin Black, telling me that I needed to get out of Storvatten because Viktor Dålig wanted me dead. But if Viktor was hiding out near Doldastam, it seemed like I would be an easier target for him here.

Admittedly, we had Högdragen gaurding at every door, and the Skojare had the worst security I'd ever seen. But it wasn't like I could trust Konstantin either. He could have just been leading me down the wrong path. If I wasn't dreaming the whole thing up in the first place.

"That's when I decided I needed to be able to defend myself," Linus said, and while I admired his effort, I'd seen firsthand how clumsy he could be. I hoped the training would work for him.

"Linus has even rallied some of the other Markis and Marksinna." Ember looked at him with pride. "He's been getting everybody to realize the importance of self-reliance."

Linus shrugged and lowered his eyes, kicking at the snow absently with his foot. "I was just talking, and I thought that we should all do what we can to prepare. If you're all going off to war, you can't be wasting your time and energy on us."

"Good job," I told him. "I knew you'd be good for Doldastam."

He smiled sheepishly. "Thanks. But it's no big deal, really."

"So along with Linus, I've been, uh, tutoring this other girl." Ember tucked a stray hair behind her ear and looked down at the ground, so she wouldn't have to look at me. "Marksinna Delilah Nylen. She's my age, and she's uh . . ." A weird smiled played on her lips, and her cheeks reddened slightly. "She's good. She can handle herself in a fight."

Ember smiled wider and laughed, almost nervously. I had seen this behavior before—Ember had a crush. I would've called her out on it if it weren't for Linus standing right there. She was open about her love interests, and it wasn't a big deal—except that Ember was a tracker and the object of her affection appeared to be royalty.

I gave her a look, trying to convey that we would talk about this more later. When she caught my eyes, Ember only blushed harder.

"So does anybody have any idea where Viktor and his band of merry men are headed?" I asked, changing the subject so Ember would stop grinning like a fool.

She shook her head. "Not at the moment. Scouts are looking into it, though."

"Well, the good news is it doesn't sound like Viktor has that many people behind him," I said. "Twenty guys does not an army make."

"That's true, but Ridley is fairly certain it's only a scouting mission, that Viktor and his men just want to scope out exactly what's going on here," Ember explained. "King Evert's freaking out because Viktor's coup fifteen years ago was only him working with a few other guys. And not only did he kill a member of the Högdragen, he got *really* close to killing the King.

"Imagine what he could do with twenty guys," she went on. "And who knows how many more guys he has stashed somewhere else? Those were just the ones he had with him. He could have hundreds."

I'd never been angrier with myself than I was in that moment. If I had just been able to stop Viktor in Storvatten, none of this would be happening. Everything would've been over before it started.

"It's not your fault," Ember said, reading my expression. "Viktor's obviously been planning this for a long time, and I'm sure that even if you'd gotten him, somebody would've stepped in to take his place."

"Maybe," I allowed. "I just wish it had never come to this."

"I know," she agreed. "When this all started, I thought King Evert was overreacting. But now it looks like this war is shaping up to be a big deal."

THIRTY-FOUR

polity

I had just stepped up to my parents' house when my dad opened the door, as if he'd somehow been expecting my unannounced visit. His glasses were pushed up back on his head, holding back his thick black hair that had silvered at the temples.

Dad smiled at me in the way he did when he hadn't seen me in a while—happiness with an edge of relief that I was still alive and well. Without saying anything, I came into the house and he closed the door behind me.

He pulled me into a rough hug, and it wasn't until he did that I realized how much I needed it. I hugged him back harder than I normally did, resting my head in the crook of his shoulder.

"Is everything okay?" Dad asked. I finally released him, but he kept his hands on my shoulders and bent down to look me in the eye.

"Iver? Is someone here?" Mom asked, and she rounded the corner from the living room. "Bryn! You're back!"

She hurried over to me, practically pushing my dad out of the way so she could hug me. She kissed the top of my head and touched my face. Whenever I came back, she seemed to almost pat me down, as if checking to make sure that I was real and in one piece.

"Oh, honey, what's wrong?" Mom asked when she'd finished her inspection. "You look like you have the weight of the world on your shoulders."

"I heard your mission in Storvatten went well," Dad said. As Chancellor for Doldastam, I assumed he'd already gotten the rundown on how things went. "Did something happen that you didn't tell the King?"

"No." I shook my head and let out a heavy sigh.

That wasn't entirely true—I hadn't told King Evert about Prince Kennet's flirtation with me, or how guilty I had felt leaving Queen Linnea, and I definitely hadn't been able to tell him about the lysa involving Konstantin Black.

But I didn't want to tell my parents about any of that either. Well, at least not the Kennet and Konstantin parts. The thing with Konstantin would only frighten them.

"I did my job in Storvatten," I said finally, looking up at my parents' expectant faces. "But I don't think I helped anybody."

And then suddenly, the words came tumbling out of me—all the concerns I'd been trying to repress. How I wasn't certain of Mikko's guilt, and how Kasper and I might have inadvertently been complicit in his unjust arrest. How Linnea seemed more like a child than a Queen, and it didn't feel right leaving her there like that, where she would be ostracized and unprotected if her husband was convicted, and how I knew if Marksinna Lisbet couldn't deliver on her promise to change things, I would have to go back to help Linnea and Mikko. How I didn't trust a single person in Storvatten when it came down to it—not even Marksinna Lisbet or Prince Kennet. How everyone seemed to have conflicted motives and acted cagey at times, like they were hiding something, and I could never be sure if it was because they didn't trust me for being Kanin, or if they were up to no good.

Eventually, my mom interrupted my long rambling tale to suggest we move to the dining room. I sat at the table, across from my dad, while Mom poured large cups of tea for each us.

"You did the right thing," Dad said when I'd finally finished, and Mom set a cup in front of me before taking a seat next to him.

"Then why doesn't it feel that way?" I asked. "It doesn't feel like I've done anything at all."

"Of course you did," he corrected me. "You helped get the Skojare's security in shape, and you brought comfort to Linnea. That's exactly what you set out to do."

"But there's so much left unfinished!" I insisted.

"That's the problem with working for the kingdom, the way you and I do." He motioned between us. "We can only do what we're commanded to do. Too many times, my hands have been bound by the law, and I know how frustrating it can be. But sometimes that's all you can do."

"There are so many limitations to your job," Mom said after taking a long sip of her tea. "That's why I've never quite understood the appeal of it for you. You've always been so strong willed and independent. But you want a job that demands complete submission."

"Runa," Dad said softly. "Now isn't the time for this kind of discussion."

"No, it's okay." I slumped lower in my seat. "She's right. All I've ever wanted to do was make this kingdom better. I wanted to do something good and honorable. And the only way I knew how was to be a tracker or on the Högdragen." I sighed. "But lately I just feel no good at all. I feel like I'm often choosing the lesser of two evils."

"Welcome to politics." Dad lifted his glass in a sardonic cheer and gulped it down.

Mom shifted in her chair and leaned on the table. "You know how I feel about your job, and I'm not advocating for it. But I think you're taking this mission too hard."

"What do you mean?" I asked.

"You were working with another tribe, and if we're being honest, the Skojare are *weird*," she told me knowingly. "I lived there for the first sixteen years of my life, and I was constantly surrounded by that 'cagey' feeling you described. King Rune Biâelse practically made it mandatory.

"Did I ever tell you why my mother named me after him?" Mom asked, and I shook my head. Her name, Runa, was the feminine version of Rune. "The King could be mercilessly cruel to everyone and everything, and my mom hoped—

futilely, I might add—that naming me after him would somehow endear me to him."

"I've heard stories about him being an awful King, but I never realized how bad it was until I was there," I said.

"That's not to say the that the Skojare aren't cold and secretive and just plain odd naturally," she clarified. "Because they are. But Rune just made everything worse for everybody.

"And so they sent you, a Kanin, to a place where outsiders are always distrusted," Mom went on. "The problem isn't with you or even with your job in general, but with the mission itself. You were sent someplace where you could never really be of help, so naturally you came back feeling defeated."

"Your mom is right," Dad agreed. "You were sent there more as a gesture of goodwill than anything else. You were meant to make the Skojare feel aligned with the Kanin, so that if something happens, our King might able to get his hands on the Skojare's jewels."

I leaned my head back so I could stare up at the ceiling. Even though I knew what my dad was saying was true, and I'd really always known it, it still didn't feel good to be a political pawn.

For as long as I could remember, my mom had railed against my working for the kingdom. And that entire time, I'd been completely convinced that she was wrong, that all her concerns and criticisms about our way of life were either unfounded or didn't take into account the bigger picture—that I was helping people. I was making it better.

But now I wasn't so sure about anything anymore.

"I remember feeling frustrated when I was growing up in Storvatten," Mom said after a long pause. "My kingdom demanded silence and obedience. It left me feeling cold and isolated, and I wanted something entirely different." She cast a warm glance at my dad. "I followed my heart, and I've never once regretted the choice I made all those years ago."

I looked over at my parents, feeling more lost and confused than I ever had before. "But what if my heart doesn't know what it wants anymore?"

THIRTY-FIVE

wedlock

The greenhouse seemed unable to contain all the plant life, and vines weaved around door frames to climb over the walls in the small adjoining room. It was usually used as a break room, but it was a perfect place to get ready for a wedding.

Flowers of pink and white and purple bloomed on the vines, and flourishing potted plants sat on every available surface. Even the two sofas in the room had floral designs stitched onto their cream fabric.

A pale pink rose blossomed at the top of the full-length mirror, and Tilda took a deep breath as she stared at her reflection. Her long hair hung in loose curls down her back. Her cheeks were flushed slightly, and carnation-pink lipstick brightened her full lips.

The light chiffon fabric of her off-white dress flowed over her growing baby bump, nearly hiding it, but still managing to highlight how curvaceous and tall she was. Soft sleeves draped off her shoulders just so, revealing her well-toned arms and olive skin.

Ember and I stood to either side of her, both of us looking short and rather plain compared to Tilda's radiance. Our hair had been styled the same way: small purple flowers were weaved into braids twisted into an updo.

We wore matching dresses: pale blue chiffon that landed just above the knees, in a similar empire design as Tilda's. Her mother, Ranetta, had made all three of our dresses, and she'd done an amazing job, especially given the short notice of the wedding.

Tilda's mother stood behind her, carefully adjusting the wreath of flowers on her head—the Kanin tradition instead of a veil. When she'd finished, she looked at her daughter's reflection and smiled with tears in her eyes.

"You look absolutely beautiful," Ranetta told her.

"It's true," Ember chimed in. "I don't think I've ever seen anyone look prettier."

Ilsa, Tilda's older sister, opened the door with a quick knock, then poked her head in. "I think they're all ready for you out there."

Ranetta once again assured Tilda that she looked beautiful and that everything was perfect, then departed with Ilsa to take their seats before the processional started. We could hear the soft music from the piano, and we were just waiting for our cue—"Winter" by Vivaldi to begin.

Tilda took a deep breath and stared straight ahead. "I don't know why I'm so nervous," she whispered.

"It's a big day. It makes sense," Ember said.

Her smoky gray eyes widened, and she nodded. "It's a *huge* day."

"There's nothing to be scared of." I tried to calm her nerves. "Do you love Kasper?"

"Of course." She looked down at me, her eyes misty. "I love him with everything I am."

"Just remember that, and everything will be okay."

Tilda smiled, then she reached out and took my hand. Ember was on the other side of her, and Tilda grabbed her hand too, squeezing it tightly. The three of us stood together like that until the first notes of "Winter" began.

Ember went out first, walking down the short aisle. Tilda was getting married in the flower garden of the greenhouse, and there were flowers everywhere. Potted plants had been moved to the side to make room for a white velvet carpet to run down the center, and the twenty chairs set up on either side of it were decorated with floral garlands.

At the altar, Kasper's two groomsmen were already waiting underneath the flowered arbor. His best man was Elliot Väan, the guard he worked with, and his fifteen-year-old brother, Devin, was the other groomsman.

Devin looked just like a smaller version of his brother, but his fidgety, hyper demeanor set them apart, especially in contrast with Elliot's severe Högdragen stance.

When it was my turn, I kept my head high and my eyes forward. I knew that Tilda had invited Ridley, and I didn't want to see him holding hands with Juni, who would undoubtedly be getting misty eyed at the beauty of it all.

The carpet felt soft on my bare feet, and I kept my eyes locked on the pale lilac and white roses that adorned the arbor. I listened to the music and counted my steps, and I tried desperately not to think about the night Ridley and I had spent together and how I'd wished it would last forever.

When I reached the altar, I took my place next to Ember and turned to watch Tilda. She came out a few seconds later and met Kasper. As soon as she saw him, her eyes filled with tears and she smiled. He took her hand, then he leaned over and whispered something in her ear, causing her to smile wider. Then hand in hand, the two of them walked down the aisle together.

It was only when they made it to the front, and the officiant had begun the ceremony, that I allowed myself to steal a glance around the room.

Kasper's family sat in the front row, and by the rigid way his father sat, it was obvious that he'd once been a member of the Högdragen. His mother seemed more relaxed, hanging on to her husband's arm, her eyes brimming with tears.

Naima, Kasper's little sister, was the spitting image of him. She couldn't have been more than ten, with black corkscrew curls and a wide toothy smile, watching Kasper and Tilda with intense fascination.

But soon my eyes wandered beyond them, and it only took

me a moment to spot Ridley, sitting in the third row. He was alone, no Juni by his side, and he was looking right at me. His dark eyes met mine, and for a moment I forgot to breathe.

Then Tilda turned to hand me her bouquet so she and Kasper could exchange rings, and I looked away from Ridley, forcing myself not to gaze in his direction again.

Tilda's hands were trembling as Kasper slid on the ring, and she laughed nervously. From where I was standing I could see Kasper, and how his love for Tilda warmed his dark eyes when he looked at her.

To seal their matrimony, they kissed. Tilda put her hands on his face, and Kasper put his arm around her, and the kiss was chaste but passionate. As they embraced, I wondered if I'd ever seen two people who loved each other more.

THIRTY-SIX

interlude

Ember never missed an opportunity to dance, and she was out on the floor, twirling around underneath strings of fairy lights. Devin had been chosen as her reluctant dance partner, and she pulled him along with her, forcing him to keep up with her moves whether he wanted to or not.

After the ceremony, we'd moved to the reception in the adjacent party room, which was really just a small ballroom built for occasions like these. A three-piece orchestra had been set up at one end of the room, with Tilda's sister Ilsa singing with them. Ilsa had an astonishing range and an amazing voice somehow suited perfectly for the covers of Etta James, Rosemary Clooney, and Roberta Flack that she was performing.

I sat at the side of the room, trying to hide in the shadows as I sipped my sparkling wine and watched the dance floor. Since Tilda and Kasper had invited so few people, it left the floor rather sparse, even when most couples were dancing together.

Unfortunately, that made it all too easy for me to see through them to Ridley at the other side of the room. He was standing near the buffet, absently picking at the vegetable skewers on his plate, and when he looked up at me I quickly looked away.

Tilda had been slow dancing with Kasper, their arms around each other as they talked and laughed, but she stepped aside so Kasper could dance with his little sister. As she walked across the dance floor toward me, Kasper spun Naima around, making her giggle uncontrollably.

"Is your plan to hide in the corner all night?" Tilda asked with a crooked smile, as she sat down in the chair next to me.

"I'm not hiding," I lied and took another sip of my wine.

"Mmm-hmm," she intoned knowingly.

"It was a beautiful ceremony," I said, changing the subject.

Her smile turned wistful as she watched her new husband. Naima had taken to standing on Kasper's feet, and he held her hands as they waltzed around the room, both of them smiling and laughing.

"It really was," she agreed.

"I've never seen Kasper happier."

Watching him now, so relaxed and beaming, reminded me of what he'd said the day before. Work was important to him, but it wasn't his life. It wasn't what defined him, and it wasn't who he really was. This—the guy dancing with his kid sister, smiling at his wife—was Kasper.

His words had stuck with me, and as I watched him I couldn't help but wonder—if the balance of working a job that mattered and having a life outside of it was possible for him, could it be possible for me too? Had I been wrong in assuming I had to choose one over the other?

"You'll have to talk to him eventually," Tilda said, pulling me from my thoughts, and I looked over to see her gazing at me seriously.

I thought about playing dumb and asking *who,* but I knew Tilda would see through that, the way she always saw through my acts.

So instead I simply said, "I know."

"I don't know *why* you're avoiding him, but I know you are," Tilda said, and she raised her hand to silence me before I could stutter out some kind of excuse. "It doesn't matter right now. I just think you should go talk to him before it gets even harder to."

Ridley was still standing on the other side of the room. Kasper's dad had been talking to him, but the conversation appeared to be finishing up, leaving Ridley alone again.

"The bride is always right on her wedding day," Tilda added. "So you know I'm right when I say that you need to do this."

I took a fortifying breath then finished my glass of wine in one large gulp. "Okay." I stood up, smoothing out my bridesmaid dress, and looked down at Tilda. "Will you be okay here by yourself, or do you want me to wait?"

"No, go!" She shooed me away with a smile. "I just wanna sit here another minute, and then I'm sure Kasper will have me out dancing again."

My heart was pounding so hard as I walked across the

dance floor, I could hardly hear the music over it. I kept reminding myself that it was only Ridley, that I'd talked to him a thousand times before and this wasn't a big deal.

Of course, I'd never talked to him after having a one-night stand with him.

He smiled thinly at me as I approached, and I wished I'd had another glass of wine before making my way over.

"Hey," I said when I reached him.

"Hey," he replied, and then I realized in terror that I couldn't think of anything more to say. I'd thought as far as saying *hey,* and now I was trapped in an awful moment where I could only stare at him.

"The wedding was great," I blurted out suddenly, because it was something to say.

"It was." He nodded, then motioned to me. "You looked beautiful."

I lowered my eyes. "You don't have to say that."

"I know." He paused. "I wanted to."

"Well, thanks." I offered him a small smile.

I wasn't sure if I should tell him he looked good too, because he definitely did. His dark hair was just slightly disheveled, as if he couldn't completely tame it. He was clean shaven, which he rarely was, and his tan skin looked so smooth. The vest he wore over his dress shirt was fitted perfectly across his broad shoulders, and the first few buttons of his shirt were undone, showing off just enough flesh to make me crazy.

"So, listen," Ridley said, filling the awkward silence that had fallen between us. "I've been looking for the right time to talk to you since you got back, and now seems as good as any."

"Yeah?" I asked, lifting my eyes to meet his.

"I ended things with Juni."

My heart skipped a beat, and I hoped I didn't look as excited as I felt.

"It wasn't fair to her," he elaborated. "The way I was treating her. Juni is fantastic, and I did like her. But the truth is, I didn't like her enough."

"Yeah, that makes sense," I said, just to say something.

He took a deep breath. "And there's no point in dancing around things anymore. I have feelings for you, Bryn, very strong feelings, and I think you feel the same way."

"I . . . you know . . . I . . ." I was too stunned to properly form a sentence, and I wasn't even sure what I wanted to say.

Of course I had feelings for Ridley, and while part of me was thrilled to hear he felt the same way, nothing had changed. He was still my boss, the Överste, actually, which meant that we would both be in serious trouble if we were to get involved.

So what could I say to him? That I loved him, but it didn't matter because we couldn't be together? What would even be the point of admitting how I felt?

Through my shock and confusion, I realized something in the room had changed. Everyone had stopped dancing, and as I looked around the room the musicians stopped playing. Ilsa had been singing "Why Don't You Do Right?" but just stopped mid-word.

Most of the light in the room came from fairy lights and

candles, but someone flipped on the overhead light, blinding everyone. I lifted up my arm to shield my face, and I finally saw the reason for the change.

Reid Kasten, King Evert's personal guard, stood at the entrance.

"Sorry to interrupt the festivities," Reid announced, speaking loudly and clearly. "The King sent me here to retrieve Bryn Aven."

I glanced over at Ridley, as if he would have some insight as to what this was about, but he shook his head.

"I'm right here." I stepped onto the dance floor so Reid could more easily see me.

"The King wants to see you immediately."

"What's this about?" Ridley asked, stepping up behind me, and Reid regarded him with derision. "I'm the Överste. If something's going on, I should go."

"The King didn't say what it was concerning," Reid said, showing Ridley a bit more respect. "He tasked me with returning with Bryn Aven."

Ridley looked as if he wanted to say more, so I held up my hand to stop him. "It's okay."

I cast Tilda an apologetic smile, since any summons had intruded on her celebration, and she pursed her lips in worry as Reid escorted me away from the dance floor and toward the palace.

THIRTY-SEVEN

lush

The walk to the palace had been cold. I'd put on boots out of necessity, but I hadn't changed out of my light bridesmaid dress, and I'd only grabbed a violet cloak to keep out the chill. Since I didn't know what was going on, I didn't want to waste any more time than I had to.

When we arrived at the palace, I slipped off my boots and cloak by the door. I expected Reid to lead me to the meeting room, but he took a different turn. Instead of going left toward the east wing of the palace where public affairs took place, he went right, taking me toward the private quarters.

"Where are we going?" I asked him.

"The King's parlor," Reid replied in a clipped tone, so I decided against pressing him further.

I'd only been in the private wing twice before, both for training purposes when I was still in tracker school, so it had been a while. Here the floors changed from cold, gray stone to pearlescent tile, purportedly brought in from Italy. Sheetrock covered the stone walls, painted ivory with faint silver flourishes to give it an added elegance. Instead of kerosene lamps, the halls were lit with bright dome lights.

Before we reached the room, I could hear Queen Mina. Her laughter carried through the closed door, and it sounded as if she'd affected the British accent again.

Reid knocked on the door and waited for us to be granted entrance, and I tried to figure out what exactly was happening. None of this made sense or was even remotely close to how things were usually done.

"Come in!" King Evert shouted, without checking to see who we were or what we wanted.

For his part, Reid continued to act as if it were business as usual. He opened the door for me then stood next to it inside the room and announced my arrival. But I barely registered it because I was too busy trying to make sense of the scene before me.

The King's parlor was smaller than I'd expected. It only had room for a love seat, a sofa, and two sitting chairs—all of them high-backed tufted seats in a cream color. Above them hung a small but bright chandelier.

The walls were covered in wallpaper with alternating vertical bands of white and silver. On the wall opposite the door was a carved marble fireplace with a painting of Evert and Mina on their wedding day hanging it above it. To the left and pressed against the wall was an elegant bar made of mirrors with white baroque details.

The King lounged in the chair closest to the fireplace, one leg draped over the arm. The sleeves of his gray shirt were rolled up, and several buttons were undone. His black bangs hung over his forehead, and he had a highball glass in his hand, half full of a dark liquid.

Next to the fireplace, the Queen stood, still laughing as I entered the room. Her hair hung down in loose curls, and she wore a simple gown of pristine white. Even though she looked more relaxed than I usually saw her, she still wore gaudy diamond earrings, and the heavy necklace that lay on her collarbone was encrusted with sapphires. I presumed the wineglass on the mantel directly beside her to be hers.

But the big surprise was the man standing next to the bar, pouring himself another drink. His back was to me, but his broad shoulders and blond hair were unmistakable. His sharkskin jacket was discarded on the sofa, and the sleeves of his white dress shirt had been pushed up.

Prince Kennet seemed to be having some kind of weird party with Mina and Evert.

"Oh, Bryn!" Mina exclaimed when she saw me. "You look so lovely!"

Kennet turned around to look at me and smiled appreciatively, but I didn't have time for that.

"Thank you, my Queen," I replied politely. "I was called away from a wedding to—"

"Doesn't she look lovely?" Mina asked Evert, interrupting me.

Evert narrowed his eyes, as if needing to get a better look at me, and I stood up straighter and repressed an irritated groan. "Yeah, yeah, she does," he slurred.

"The Skojare good looks help with that," Kennet said with a wink, making Mina erupt in laughter again.

"If you won't be needing me for anything more, shall I wait in the hall, sire?" Reid asked, and I didn't blame him.

The King and Queen were drunk, or at the very least buzzed, both of them bordering on obnoxious.

"Yes, of course." Evert waved Reid off, and the guard bowed before exiting the room and closing the door behind him.

"Your Highness, you summoned me?" I asked, trying to find out what exactly I was doing there in the first place.

"That was all my idea, I'm afraid," Kennet admitted. With drink in hand, he effortlessly climbed over the back of the love seat and sat down, extending his legs out on it.

"Oh yes, Prince Kennet came all the way here from Storvatten to thank us personally for our help in sorting out their troubles," Mina explained, and as she spoke, her hand went absently to her lavish necklace. "He wanted to extend his gratitude and strengthen the friendship between our tribes."

"As I understand it, the troubles are still being sorted out," I said carefully. "Storvatten is in great turmoil without a leader."

"That's all been sorted out." Evert waved his hand again, nearly spilling his drink as he did. "The Prince is the King."

I shot a look at Kennet, and the hair on the back of my neck stood up. When I'd left Storvatten, Lisbet had all but guaranteed that she would be appointed the ruler in Mikko's absence.

She had assured me that she would do everything in her power to get the position in order to ensure her and Linnea's safety.

So how exactly had Kennet gotten the title? There was a chance the Skojare in charge of making the decision had thought it would be best if they stuck with the Biâelse bloodline and overruled Marksinna Lisbet.

But as Kennet barely stifled his smirk, I couldn't help but suspect he'd fought Lisbet for the title.

"Acting monarch," Kennet corrected him, which meant he had all the power but not the official title of King. "And only until my brother is exonerated."

I stared at Kennet evenly. "What if your brother isn't exonerated?"

"That would only be if he is actually guilty of everything he's accused of, and if he is, he shouldn't be the King." Kennet sat up straighter. "It is still a terrible mess in Storvatten, you're right, but we're on the right path to figuring everything out and making it a safer place.

"And that," he said, lifting up his glass, "is all thanks to you and the Kanin. So here's to you."

Mina hurried to grab her glass off the mantel and raised it in a toast. "*Skål!*"

"*Skål!*" Evert shouted, then proceeded to drunkenly spill his drink all over himself.

Mina looked at her husband with pity as he tried to wipe the alcohol off his shirt. "Oh, Evert, my love. Let me help you." She rushed over, using the length of her dress to help dry him off.

"I don't even know how that happened." He shook his head in disbelief. "I don't . . . I think I'm drunk."

"I think you are, too, my King," Mina said with a bit of a laugh and smiled up at him. "Why don't we get you up to bed and into something dry?"

He reached out, stroking her face in a moment of tenderness that I hadn't even known the King was capable of. "You're so patient and beautiful. What did I ever do to deserve you?"

"All the right things," she assured him, and then she stood up. "I'm sorry, but I hope you can excuse us both."

"Yes, of course." I bowed slightly.

"I'm sure Bryn and I can entertain ourselves in your absence," Kennet said, wagging his eyebrows at me.

THIRTY-EIGHT

idyll

The very moment the King and Queen left us alone, Kennet leapt up from the sofa and bolted toward me. I had hardly a second to react before his arm was around me and his lips were on mine, but I put my hand on his chest and pushed him back.

"What are you doing?" I demanded, looking up into his startled blue eyes.

"Kissing you. Isn't it obvious?" he asked like a guy who was used to taking what he wanted without any protests.

I pulled myself from his arm and stepped back from him. "I already told you. We're only friends."

"You're saying you don't want to kiss me, then?" Kennet asked with raised eyebrows. I turned away, walking toward the love seat. "Why not? You should at least offer me a reason."

For one thing, I didn't trust him. Not that I ever really had, but now with his new appointment as ruler of the Skojare and ject to another. I'd dropped the formal titles, since I had no idea if Mikko was even King anymore.

"I don't know." Kennet had his back to me as he took a drink, and I watched his shoulders rise and fall with heavy resignation. "He won't let me see him."

"Why not?"

"You'd have to ask him that yourself." He swirled the alcohol in his glass around, watching it. "I do love him. I know a lot of people don't believe that now, maybe you included, but he is my older brother. I don't want to see him hurt."

"I'm sure it's hard for him," I said gently, trying to offer Kennet a bit of comfort. "With everything that happened, and now with you being the King. Mikko is going through a very difficult time."

"He never even wanted to be King," Kennet muttered, still staring down at his glass. "I offered to take the crown in his place, but Mikko refused to go against Father's decree." He shook his head and took a long drink.

"When I left, Marksinna Lisbet told me she thought she'd be placed as acting monarch," I told him.

"Did she?" Kennet laughed. "She is one crazy old bat."

The sharpness of his words startled me, but I quickly recovered and asked, "What do you mean?"

"I'm next in line for the throne." He looked at me like it should have been obvious. "If anything happens to Mikko, it goes to me. There's no way that a Marksinna with no ties to our bloodline would ever be in charge, even for a moment."

"Maybe it was just wishful thinking on her part," I said. "She was just worried about Linnea's safety."

Kennet scoffed. "I can keep the kingdom safe."

"Her biggest concern—and mine too, really—was continuing to allow Bayle Lundeen to remain in charge of the guard."

"Then you can both rest at ease," he smiled at me. "The first thing I did after being appointed was dismiss Bayle."

"You fired him?" I asked, almost breathless in my relief.

He nodded. "I did, but I think he feared an investigation, so he immediately took off. We have a few guards looking for him, but I'm not sure what a guard like ours will really turn up."

"So then are the charges against Mikko dropped?" I asked.

Kennet shook his head. "It's not quite that simple. There's still evidence against him, and we do have to wait for a trial. I'm sure this will all be sorted out soon." He walked over to me, probably because I'd softened since our conversation had started.

"Is Linnea holding up okay?" I asked, since I didn't know what to say to that.

"About as well as you'd imagine."

"But you'll keep her safe, won't you?" I asked, and I tried to play on his pride to ensure that he would do everything in his power to protect her. "As long as you're the acting King, you wouldn't let anything happen to her, would you?"

"No, of course not," he said, and a sparkle had returned to his eyes. "But if you're really concerned about her, why don't you come with me?"

"Prince—" I started to decline, but he silenced me.

"I know I was a little overzealous before, and I am truly sorry about that," Kennet said, his voice low and apologetic. "But I like having you around, and Linnea would love to have you back. You can help us, and honestly, we do need you."

"I appreciate the offer, I really do," I said. "But as much as I enjoy your company and Linnea's, I just don't think can. There's too much going on in Doldastam."

Kennet frowned. "So that's a no?"

"No." I shook my head. "My place is here."

"Oh, Bryn." He let out a sigh, and he reached out to fix a lavender flower that had come loose from my hair. When he finished, he looked down at me sadly. "I don't think you really know your place at all."

THIRTY-NINE

conciliation

It was time to get back to reality.

That's what I told myself after I'd finished getting changed in the locker room. I pulled my hair up in a ponytail and headed out to the gym, determined to head back to work.

With everything going on—Storvatten preparing for war, Viktor and Konstantin, not to mention things with Ridley, and Kennet's bizarre invitation last night, and Tilda's wedding, which was a good thing but still out of the ordinary—my life had been completely devoid of routine.

Since I'd joined tracker school when I was twelve, this place and this job had been my one constant. I was sent out on missions where I had to encounter changelings and deal with unique obstacles, but I always came back here.

And right now, when everything felt like it was crumbling down on me, I needed this more than ever. I needed to disappear into my work until I was completely gone.

So when I stepped into the gym, expecting my tiny little haven in the chaos of the world, I was caught off guard to see that things had been completely turned upside down.

All the trackers were training at once—some doing combat or sword fighting, others lifting weights, while still others were running laps—which filled the gym with far more people than I would've preferred. On top of all that there was also a group of around twenty-five Markis and Marksinna standing in formation as Ember commanded them.

I recognized a few of them, like Linus Berling, but the rest of them stood out thanks to their designer workout clothes. One girl was even training while wearing a diamond tennis bracelet and chandelier earrings.

"Down!" Ember shouted as I walked over to her, and her ragtag troops dropped to the floor.

Some of them moved more quickly than others, and I wasn't surprised to see that Marksinna Tennis Bracelet had trouble keeping up. Linus did relatively well, but he relied more on effort than skill. A girl in the front was doing astonishingly well, though, as if she had been training for years.

When she hit the ground, I noticed a subtle change in her skin color—the deep olive darkening to match the black of her workout clothes for a second. Her long dark hair was in a loose braid that bounced when she dropped. Her large eyes were almost almond shaped, and she kept them locked on Ember as she awaited her next order.

"Up!" Ember commanded almost as soon as they hit the floor, and they hurried to get back on their feet. When Ember saw me, she smiled. "Why don't we all take five? You've been working hard."

"How's it going?" I asked Ember as her troops took a breather or got something to drink. Linus offered me a quick wave before jogging over to the drinking fountain.

"Good." She nodded. "They're shaping up really well."

"That's only because we have such a good teacher." The girl in the front wiped sweat from her brow, and she had a water bottle in her hand.

"Thanks." Ember smiled, maybe a little too widely, and they looked at each other for what was beginning to feel like an uncomfortable amount of time. "Uh, sorry. Bryn, this is Delilah, I mean, Marksinna Delilah Nylen."

Delilah rushed to fill the gap between us so she could shake my hand, and I noticed she was a little taller than Ember. "I've heard so much about you. You're a real hero."

"I'm not even close to being a hero, but thank you," I said.

"Sorry, sure." When she released my hand, she stood up straight with her shoulders back, the way I knew Ember had taught her. Then she tapped her water bottle. "I need to refill this, so I should do that before we start up again."

"Go ahead," Ember told her, and the second Delilah was out of earshot, Ember turned to me and asked in an excited whisper, "What do you think?"

"Well, she has good posture," I said.

"That's it?" Ember stared up at me. "That's all you've got?"

I glanced over to where Delilah was refilling her bottle at the fountain at the edge of the gymnasium. "She's obviously a hard worker, and she seems to know her stuff." Ember kept staring at me, so I added, "And she's very pretty."

Ember practically beamed. "She's great, right?"

"She is," I admitted hesitantly.

But not only was Delilah a Marksinna, she was one who could change her skin color, meaning she had an important bloodline. No one in a position of authority would look kindly on Ember messing with that.

"Just be careful," I advised.

"I always am." Ember looked so pleased that I didn't want to completely spoil her mood.

By then it was time to start training again, and Ember began barking commands. Delilah seemed more than happy to follow them, which boded well for their burgeoning relationship. Even though Delilah was nobility, she seemed to respect Ember's experience and leadership.

I realized I had my own forbidden romance that I needed to deal with, and before I could really head back to reality, I needed to talk to Ridley.

Over at the other end of the gym, Ridley held a clipboard, reading the papers attached to it. Since Tilda had gotten married last night, she was off today, which left him working her job for the day.

His brow was furrowed in concentration when I reached him. I didn't want to disturb him, so I waited next to him until he noticed me, which thankfully didn't take long.

"Tilda is *really* good at her job, but her handwriting is atrocious," Ridley said, telling me something I already knew. "I will be so relieved when she gets back from her honeymoon in a couple days."

"They're taking a short honeymoon, so it won't be too bad."

He finally looked up at me, and I suddenly felt sick. I didn't know what to say to him. All I wanted was for him to pull me into his arms, but I knew he couldn't.

"Now probably isn't the best time for this conversation," I began, swallowing down my fear. "I just wanted to tell you that I, um, want to talk to you, I guess."

"About what I said last night?" he asked.

I nodded. "Yeah."

"Now's perfect," he replied instantly. "Come on."

A gym filled with people obviously wasn't the best place to have a private conversation, and Ridley walked away. I followed him out into the hallway, which was quiet and deserted. Trackers-in-training should've been in class, but they were all either in the gym doing drills or out in the yard doing obstacle courses.

"So?" Ridley folded his arms over his chest and stared down at me expectantly.

"Well . . ." I exhaled shakily. "You know how I feel about you."

"What if I told you I don't?"

I looked up at him, his eyes filled with that dark intensity that made my heart race. "Ridley."

"I said it. Would it be so bad if you said it too?" he pressed.

"I care about you," I admitted, saying it aloud for the first time, and there was something terrifying and exhilarating in that. "I care about you a lot."

One corner of his mouth pulled up in a crooked smile. "Good."

"But you know the deal," I said, and his smile fell away. "We would both lose our jobs, and as much as I do care about you, I'm not willing to do what my parents did. My dad sacrificed a lot, but my mom gave up *everything*. I know she loves my dad and she loves me, way more than she ever cared about Storvatten, but that doesn't mean she wants this life that's been thrust upon her either. And unlike my mom, I do really care about Doldastam and my job, even as imperfect and insane as it has been lately."

"You're not your mom, and I'm not your dad," Ridley countered. "I would never ask you to give up the life you've chosen. I know how much your job means to you, and I wouldn't let you sacrifice it for me, even if you wanted to."

"But that goes for you too," I argued. "You have to go after Viktor. I can't let you lose your position as the Överste, not when it's so important to you, and the kingdom needs you. But where does that leave us? Neither of us can give up the things that are standing in our way."

"I can," he said simply.

"No, Ridley, you can't."

"Not right now, that's true. But as soon as we have Viktor, and I mean the very second, I'll quit."

I shook my head. "I can't ask you to do that."

"You don't have to. I *want* to," he insisted. "I've done this job long enough, and I'm sure that Tilda would be twice as good as me, and she'll probably want a desk job soon. So I'll find something else."

"What else?" I asked.

"*Anything* else." Ridley grinned. "That's the point. I don't care. I can do whatever I want. But the thing I want most is to be with you."

Suddenly, I felt dizzy. It almost sounded too good be true.

"You really wanna do this?" I asked breathlessly.

"Yes. Once we catch Viktor, I want to give us a real shot." He took my hands in his. "What do you think?"

I nodded, too excited to speak at first. "Yes."

Ridley stepped away from me to look through the narrow windows in the gymnasium door, checking to see if anyone was watching. They must not have been, because he rushed back over and pushed me back against the wall, so we were more hidden if anyone decided to pry, and he kissed me full on the mouth.

It ended much too soon, with him pulling away from me as he tried to catch his breath. "I have to get back. And so do you. And right now I'm still your boss, so that's an order."

FORTY

honeymoon

Lunch usually meant hurriedly devouring salads and hard-boiled eggs in the cafeteria at the school, all the trackers crammed in together like sardines since we were working at full capacity.

So that was why I didn't mind skipping out on lunch to head over to Tilda's apartment. Yesterday, while we'd been getting ready for her wedding, she had asked me if I could come over to get the keys to her place so she could show me how to feed her goldfish while she was on her honeymoon. She and Kasper were leaving this afternoon, so this was the last chance to do it.

I left the school feeling lighter than I had in days. After the conversation with Ridley, the future felt like it actually held the promise of something good. The dark days that had been surrounding me might actually be making a turn for the better.

We were still at war, and things weren't over yet, but for the first time in a while, I felt optimistic. As I walked downtown, I caught myself humming.

A Land Rover was parked in front of the electronics shop below Tilda's apartment, presumably rented from the King's fleet, since other than a few of the very rich, nobody owned a vehicle in Doldastam. The tailgate was open, and Kasper was loading up two large duffle bags in the back.

"I thought you guys were only gonna be gone for a couple days," I said and motioned to the overstuffed bags in the back.

"Three days, two nights at a bed and breakfast in Churchill." Kasper shut the back of the SUV and turned to me with a look of resigned exasperation.

With everything that was going on, the King didn't want them to be gone for very long, and for their own safety, Kasper and Tilda had chosen a human town only an hour's drive from Doldastam.

"And Tilda actually has a bag upstairs still. But the pregnancy is making her worry more, and if what she needs to relax on this honeymoon is everything and the kitchen sink, then I'll be more than happy to load it up."

I smiled at him. "You're gonna make a great husband."

Kasper laughed. "Just remind Tilda of that when she gets mad at me, okay?"

We went down a narrow alley squished between the electronics shop and the taxidermist next door. Around the back of the shop was a doorway that opened to a set of stairs leading up to the small two-bedroom apartment. Tilda had lived there for two years by herself, and it had to be one of the most contemporary places in all of Doldastam.

I opened the door expecting her usual immaculateness. Tilda always kept it looking like something out of a magazine showcasing trendy New York apartments. Instead, I was greeted by an unexpected mess—clothes were strewn all over her sofa, several cardboard boxes were stacked up in the living room, and dirty dishes were piled up in the sink.

Tilda came out from her back bedroom and gave me a sheepish smile. "I know, I know. It's a total disaster, but I haven't had time to clean."

"No, don't worry about it," I said as I made my way through the labyrinths of boxes and stepped over a glass punchbowl, which I assumed had been a wedding gift.

On the peninsula that separated the kitchen from the living room, Tilda had a fishbowl with two of the fattest goldfish I had even seen. Not only were they several inches long, they were completely rotund.

"These are Odin and Odessa." Tilda pointed to the one with the longer fantail flowing out behind it as it swam. "That one's Odessa. Odin is the fatter one. Kasper got them for me on my birthday in February." She opened the cupboard below them and pulled out a cylinder of fish food. "They were smaller when I got them, but they've just kinda ballooned. Usually when I'm on missions, Kasper takes care of them, but I think he over-feeds them, which is why they've gotten so fat."

Kasper had followed us, and he rested his arms on the granite countertop, leaning forward. "Thanks, dear."

"Well, it's true." Tilda shrugged and went onto explain the exact right amount of food to give the fish and how to properly care for them in case of some kind of fish emergency.

"I think I can handle that," I said when she'd finished.

"Knowing that you're taking good care of them and that you're watching the apartment will give me one less thing to worry about," Tilda said.

"Yeah, thank you, Bryn," Kasper added. "And not to change the subject, but what ended up happening last night with you at the palace?"

After Kennet and I had had our conversation, I'd gone home, since the night already felt exhausting. I'd texted Tilda to let her know I was okay, so she wouldn't worry, but I hadn't said anything more because I didn't want to ruin her wedding night with work talk.

"That's right!" Tilda put her hand on her face in distress. "I totally forgot to ask you about that! What happened?"

"It was just . . . strange." I shook my head. "Prince Kennet came from Storvatten to personally thank the King and Queen for helping, and I guess he wanted to thank me too."

Kasper's brow creased in bewilderment. "That is rather strange."

"Yeah, I thought so too," I agreed. "Apparently, he's the acting ruler now."

"What?" Kasper appeared as surprised as I'd felt when I found out. "I thought Lisbet was gonna get that."

"I don't know exactly what happened, but Kennet is the King now." I shook my head. "He got rid of Bayle, which is good, but the trial with Mikko is still on, which seems bizarre to me. I mean, if Kennet is in control can't he just make it go away?"

"Yes, unless he doesn't want to make it go away," he replied.

I chewed the inside of my cheek, taking in Kasper's response. "He gave Mina a necklace of sapphires."

"Buying her loyalty?" Kasper asked, and I nodded. "The exact same way someone bought Cyrano Moen's."

The way Kasper said that made something click in my brain. Pieces that hadn't fit together started falling into place.

"When Ridley and I went down to find Linnea before, Mikko barely spoke to us," I remembered. "Kennet worked as his liaison, and he kept saying that all the attempts at blocking the investigation were coming from Mikko, but how would we know that? Kennet could've just as easily been doing it himself. And Boyle refused to let anyone look at the records, so he could've easily fabricated evidence to frame Mikko."

"He planned the kidnapping of Linnea, and then he was involved in the investigation, so he could shift the blame however he wanted." Kasper straightened up. "And he wanted to shift it onto his brother."

"He wanted Mikko in jail so he could get the crown," I said, thinking aloud. "First he hired Konstantin to kidnap Linnea and make it look like Mikko either kidnapped or killed her. I don't know how he got in touch with Konstantin, but if Konstantin and Viktor Dålig are working some kind of operation with hired hands and weapons, they needed financing."

"And we saw how well Cyrano Moen was paid," Kasper added.

"Kennet told me that after he fired Bayle, Bayle had run off," I said. "But if Bayle has been working with Kennet this whole time to make it all happen, it would make sense for Kennet to send him away before they could question him and find exactly how he was tied to this whole mess."

I'd been suspicious of Kennet since I met him, but I'd also been suspicious of Mikko and nearly everyone else I met in Storvatten, so it had been hard for me to decide how culpable he might have been.

I looked over at Kasper. "Kennet did it all, didn't he?"

"I don't know if we can prove it, but yes. I think he did."

"He's here right now, celebrating with Evert and Mina," I said. "And they should know. They probably can't do anything, but they need to know they're aligning themselves with someone who has connections to Konstantin and is helping to finance the attacks on our kingdom."

"Holy shit." Tilda expressed my sentiments perfectly. "Evert is gonna be *pissed* when he finds out. I honestly wouldn't be surprised if he declared war on the Skojare."

She was right, and while that would have very negative ramifications for the Skojoare, it didn't change anything. The King needed to know the truth.

"I have to tell him, and it'll be better to do it before Kennet leaves," I said. "Maybe he'll just lock up Kennet, and we can avoid an all-out war."

I started to make my way to the door, since I didn't have time to waste.

"Wait. I'll go with you," Kasper said, then he looked over at Tilda. "I mean, if it's okay."

"You don't have to." I shook my head. "I can do this alone."

He turned back to me. "I know you can. But we worked in Storvatten together. This is kind of our job, which means I should be there too. I want to help you make this case." Then he looked to his new wife. "As long as it's okay with Tilda."

"The bed and breakfast will still be there in a few hours," Tilda told him with a smile. "You should go and do this. It's important. And besides, I wouldn't mind a little more time to make sure I've packed everything."

"Thank you." Kasper went over to her and kissed her quickly. "I love you."

"I love you too." She watched us go with an anxious smile, and as we walked out the door, she added, "Good luck."

FORTY-ONE

recrimination

We stood inside the meeting room, under the cold gaze of King Evert's coronation painting. Kasper stood rigidly beside me like a true member of the Högdragen, even though he was wearing a T-shirt and jeans instead of his uniform.

I had taken to pacing and chewing absently at my thumbnail. In my head, I tried to organize my thoughts and the best possible way to tell Evert about what was happening. It was important that he believe me, but it was also important that he didn't react rashly and attack Storvatten.

When we'd reached the palace, Elliot Väan had been standing guard at the door. Fortunately for us, Elliot had been Kasper's best man and was a good friend. Kasper managed to convince him to let us in and request that the King come and meet us.

The door opened behind us, startling me because I'd been deep in thought, and I turned to see Elliot holding the door open. A few moments later, almost as if she'd been deliberately trying to make an entrance, Queen Mina walked into the room. Elliot closed the door behind her, standing guard inside the room.

I wasn't sure what Mina had been doing before Elliot summoned her, but she looked more regal than ever. The train of her white gown flowed out over a foot behind her. Her hair was done up in twisted braids nestled at the top of her neck, and she'd donned a silvery fur stole that complimented the sapphire necklace.

Her crown—a platinum tiara encrusted with diamonds, including a massive one in the center—sat atop her head. Whenever she wore it, she seemed to carry her head a bit higher, lifting her chin slightly. I wasn't sure if it was to counteract the weight of the jewels, or if she was just putting on airs.

"Elliot claimed that you need to see the King urgently on important business." Mina walked around the table, eyeing Kasper and me with her cool gaze. She stopped directly across from us, beneath the painting of Evert. Instead of sitting down, she remained standing and rested her hand on the tall back of the King's chair.

"Yes, we did," I said.

"The King is very busy. As you can imagine, with the impending war, he has much to do and can't possibly take the time to meet everyone who wants to see him," Mina explained in a tone far frostier than the one I was used to hearing from her, and I wondered if she was suffering from a hangover that was making her so cross. "He has asked me to see you and find out if what you have to say is as important as you believe it is."

I glanced over at Kasper, but he kept his gaze straight ahead. This already wasn't going the way I'd hoped, and now I wasn't sure what to do.

The Queen could be maddeningly night and day. Even without a possible hangover in play, she vacillated from warmth and kindness to ice queen on a regular basis.

Mina didn't seem that open to hearing what we had to say, but I didn't know how else we'd get to talk to the King.

"Thank you for taking the time to see us, my Queen," Kasper said. "I know how busy your schedule must be."

"I'm often busier than the King, so let's get on with this, shall we?" Mina drummed her fingers along the back of the chair in impatience, causing the many rings on her fingers to sparkle in the light.

"We have reason to believe that Prince Kennet Biâelse is behind the events in Storvatten, not his brother King Mikko." I plunged right in, deciding that we had a better chance of getting through to her if we played it straight.

Mina arched an eyebrow but her expression remained otherwise unmoved. "Is that so?"

"We have a great deal of evidence to back up our claims, and we'd be happy to go over all of it with you and the King," Kasper said.

"You're getting ahead of yourself," Mina told him. "I haven't heard anything yet that would make me want to summon the King."

"In order to stage the kidnapping of Queen Linnea Biâelse three weeks ago, Prince Kennet enlisted the help of Viktor Dålig and Konstantin Black," I explained. "As a result, we believe that Prince Kennet may be funding Viktor Dålig and Konstantin Black's terrorist activities."

"Terrorist?" Mina nearly scoffed at the idea, totally overlooking the part where I connected Kennet to Konstantin. "Is that what you're calling them these days?"

With war preparations fully underway, I was floored by the Queen's response, but I pressed on. "They have used violence and fear by attacking our changelings, presumably to gain some sort of control over the Kanin, so yes, I would say that that's an accurate descriptor," I replied, matching her icy tone.

"Well, then, what's your great evidence that Kennet is connected to Konstantin? How did they meet each other?" Mina snapped. "These are high claims you're making, so what do you have to back them up?"

"We don't know how they met each other yet," I admitted. "But we know that Konstantin Black warned Queen Linnea of a plot against her, presumably because he and Viktor Dålig were hired to hurt her in some way. Possibly even kidnap or kill her."

"That proves that Konstantin was involved, but we already knew that. What more do you have to place blame on Kennet?" Mina persisted.

"He had the means to enlist Viktor and Konstantin's help," Kasper said. "He had access to all the same things as King

Mikko, but unlike the King, the Prince had a motive—he wanted the crown. So he framed his brother to get it."

Mina pursed her lips and inhaled deeply through her nose. "You're sure of this?"

I nodded. "I know he did it. And if you were to interrogate him, I think he'd eventually reveal his connection to Konstantin Black and Viktor Dålig."

"All right then. If you're sure." Mina looked past me to where Elliot stood by the door and motioned to him. "Let the Prince in."

"What?" I exchanged a looked with Kasper.

Kasper swallowed, trying to hide his nerves. "This is highly unorthodox."

I'd expected the King to interrogate Kennet himself, most likely with the help of the Högdragen. With that kind of pressure, I thought Kennet had a good chance of caving and confessing what he knew.

But with just Kasper and me accusing him, I couldn't imagine why he'd be honest in front of Mina.

"The Prince and I happened to be having lunch together when Elliot got me, and being the gentlemen that he is, the Prince offered to walk me down here," Mina explained. "And now it turns out be very fortuitous."

"Your Highness, with all due respect, I think we should talk this over with the King first," I said.

But it was already too late. Elliot had opened the doors, and Kennet entered the room with his usual swagger and walked over to join the Queen.

"What's all this?" Kennet asked, surveying Kasper's and my grave expressions.

"If you're going to accuse a man of something, you must be prepared to let him defend himself." Mina looked at me when she spoke, and her grey eyes were hard as stone.

"Accuse me of what?" Kennet appeared unnerved for a moment—his smile faltering and his eyes darting over to me—but he quickly hid it under his usual arrogance.

I met his gaze and kept my voice even. "I think you were behind everything that happened in Storvatten. You pulled all the strings to frame your brother and get his crown."

Kennet laughed, and I wasn't sure what exactly I'd expected his reaction to be, but he honestly didn't seem upset. His laugh wasn't one of nerves but his usual carefree booming one, like he genuinely found this whole scenario amusing.

"Bryn, you have made a terrible mistake." He scratched his temple and smiled sadly at me. "I didn't pull any strings."

"You're say you're not responsible for what happened in Storvatten?" Mina asked Kennet, but kept her eyes on me.

Kennet shook his head. "No, of course not."

"Now we find ourselves in a terrible predicament," Mina said. "You, Bryn Aven and Kasper Abbot, stand before me accusing an allied Prince of heinous crimes without any evidence to back it up."

"We do—" I began, but the Queen silenced me.

"He denies them all, and as a Prince, I will believe him over the unfounded word of two lowly guards," Mina went on, and I clenched my jaw to keep from yelling at her. "But had I believed you, your claims could have easily led to a war with a peaceful friend."

I lowered my eyes and swallowed hard.

"Ultimately, that would've led to the deaths of many innocent people—both Kanin and Skojare," Mina said. "Do you know what that means, Bryn? You attempted to cause the deaths of your own people and to hurt the King."

"That's not at all what I meant," I insisted desperately. "I was trying to defend the King and the kingdom."

"It's too late." Mina shook her head and attempted to affect a look of sadness, but it fell flat given her cold expression. "The damage is already done. And so you must be punished."

"Punished?" I shook my head, not understanding.

"Yes, both of you, actually." She looked between Kasper and me. "You both attempted to commit treason."

"*Treason?*" I shouted.

"My Queen, there has been a terrible misunderstanding," Kasper said, hurrying to defend himself.

"Elliot, arrest these two and take them to the dungeon until they can stand trial," Queen Mina commanded.

"This wasn't Kasper's idea. It's not his fault," I tried to argue for him.

"Elliot, *now*!" Mina raised her voice, and he hurried to comply.

Members of the Högdragen had a pair of iron shackles on the back of their belts in case they needed to restrain someone, and Elliot pulled them out now. He walked over to his friend, giving Kasper an apologetic look before locking the cuff around his wrist.

Then Elliot moved on to me, meaning to lock the other cuff around my wrist, but I pulled away.

"Your Highness, please, you have to listen to me," I persisted.

"I am the *Queen*." Mina sneered. "How dare you tell me what I have to do."

It was then that I realized my pleas were falling on deaf ears. There was no point in fighting, and I let Elliot arrest me.

FORTY-TWO

castigate

The iron shackle around my wrist felt like it weighed a hundred pounds. Kasper and I walked with our heads down, saying nothing because there was nothing to say. Another guard had joined Elliot, in case we decided to put up a fight, and the four of us walked in silence through the cold corridors of the palace.

I heard hushed whispers as we walked by, but I never looked up to see who was speaking. As defeated as I felt, my mind raced to figure out how to get out of the situation. My father might be able to leverage his position as the Chancellor to get us free, and while I normally hated nepotism, I didn't want Kasper to spend years in prison for a crime he hadn't committed.

Both of us would most certainly lose our careers, but if we were lucky we might not have to forfeit our lives. There was a chance King Evert might not act as harshly as his wife, so hopefully we wouldn't end up in prison for life or exiled.

The highest punishment for treason was execution, but I had to believe it wouldn't come to that.

When we reached the cells located in the dungeon below the palace, we weren't the only ones in there. An old man with a long graying beard had gotten up from his cot to watch our arrival, holding on to the bars and pressing his emaciated, dirty face against them.

This was a long-term prison, which was why it only housed a solitary inmate. There was a jail behind the Högdragen dorms where everyday criminals were kept: thieves and tax evaders, drunks who needed to cool off, even the rare murderer.

The dungeon was for crimes against the kingdom.

The old man in the cell was unrecognizable from who he'd been when he was thrown in the dungeon over three decades ago, but I knew immediately that it was Samuel Peerson. In our textbooks, I'd seen pictures of him from when he'd been arrested in the 1980s. He'd been a young man then, protesting the King's high taxation.

It had been under Karl Strinne's reign, our current King Evert's uncle. Karl had been a much stricter King than his two predecessors, and so even though Samuel had been a Markis—a Kanin of good breeding and the heir to a fortune—King Karl had imprisoned Samuel for publicly disagreeing with him at a meeting, calling Samuel "a traitor" and "an enemy of the kingdom."

And here Samuel remained, wasting away in a prison cell. His skin was pale with years of no sunlight, his eyes bloodshot, and a few of his teeth appeared to be missing.

Even though the Kings who followed Karl were more lax in their rulings, they had never pardoned Samuel Peerson. They wouldn't undo the wrong that had been committed because they refused to undermine a King, even a long-dead one.

If Queen Mina decided that we should spend the rest of our lives in these cells, there was a good chance that King Evert wouldn't overrule her. It would seem like a weakness on his part, as if his wife had been allowed to act without his guidance and he didn't have a handle on the running of his kingdom.

We would die in here, if that's what the Queen wished, and after how she'd acted today, there was no reason to think she wished otherwise.

My eyes were locked on the sad, weepy eyes of Samuel Peerson. I stopped, frozen in my tracks, as I realized that Kasper and I couldn't risk waiting for a trial. Elliot had been leading Kasper along, and the guard that had been charged with me nudged the small of my back.

"Get moving," he barked, and I knew what I had to do.

He was standing directly behind me, so with one quick move I lifted my arm back and slammed the iron cuff into his head. He let out a groan, then fell to the floor unconscious. Kasper and I were still attached by the shackles, so when I moved to the side, he moved with me.

"Hey!" Elliot shouted in surprise and drew his sword on us.

"Elliot, don't do this," I said.

"Please." Kasper pleaded with his friend. "You know we didn't do what the Queen is accusing us of, and if you throw us in these cells, we'll end up just like him."

"They're right, boy," Samuel Peerson said in a hollow, craggy voice.

Elliot looked at the old man with a stricken look on his face, and I knew he had to be making one of the hardest decisions of his life. It was hammered into the Högdragen again and again that they must never disobey the orders of their King or Queen.

Finally, he let out a shaky breath and lowered his sword. He took the keys off his belt and tossed them to Kasper.

"You did the right thing," Kasper assured him as he hurried to unlock his shackle, then handed me the keys so I could take care of mine myself.

"I hope so," Elliot muttered and handed Kasper his sword. "Before you go, will you do me a favor and hit me on the head, so I have an excuse for letting you get away?"

"Okay." Kasper nodded. "And thank you."

Elliot closed his eyes, steeling himself for the blow, and Kasper raised the sword and slammed the bell handle into his head. Elliot cried out in pain and stumbled backward, but he didn't fall unconscious.

"Do you want me to hit you again?" Kasper asked.

"No, no," Elliot said hurriedly. His head had already begun bleeding, and he touched it and winced. "I'll just run and get the guards after you're gone, and tell them I was knocked out."

"Can you give us a ten-minute headstart?" Kasper asked.

Elliot grimaced. "I'll try."

"We have to get out of here," I said, because ten minutes wasn't very long at all.

He nodded, and we turned to make our escape. Before we did, I stopped and tossed the keys to Samuel, who reached his arm out of his cell to catch them.

"There's one key for the shackles, and one for the cell," I told him. "Get out of here as fast as you can."

He'd move slower than us, but since the guards would most likely be far more interested in catching us, Samuel actually had a good chance of making it out.

Kasper reached the top of the steps at the end of the dungeon before I did. They were curved, so I couldn't see the top, and I actually thought he might have left without me. But he was waiting with his back pressed against the wall, peering out around the corner.

"Is anyone coming?" I whispered.

"Two guards went around the corner, so just to be safe we should wait another thirty seconds."

"Once we get past here, we won't be going the same way, so you don't have to wait for me."

He turned back to look at me. "What are you talking about?"

"I'm going to find Kennet. Our only way out of this is getting him to confess his part in this. Otherwise we'll have to spend the rest of our lives on the run."

I wasn't sure how much knocking guards out and escaping a pair of shackles would do to help convince anyone I was innocent, but once I found Kennet and got him alone, I'd do whatever it took to get him to tell the truth.

And if I couldn't get him to admit everything, I would get

him to tell me something that would help me gather more evidence to convince Evert that he was working with Konstantin Black and Viktor Dålig. Evert would take his wife's side in many things, but he would never stomach any aid to his nemesis.

"I'll go with you," Kasper said.

I shook my head. "No, you need to take Tilda and get out of here as fast as you can."

"You think I want to drag Tilda and the baby along with me into a life in exile?" he asked. "I need my name cleared just as much as you do, so I'm going with you. We started this together, we finish this together."

I relented. "Okay."

Kasper leaned forward, craning his neck out into the hall, and it must've been clear, because he dashed out into the hall and I ran after him.

FORTY-THREE

ambuscade

We sat in wait behind the door of the en suite bathroom. I'd left it partially open so I could peer through the narrow crack. When the bedroom creaked open, I held my breath and leaned forward, trying to see the figure who had come in.

In the late 1800s, the Kanin had enjoyed an influx of cash thanks to a few well-placed changelings and the industrial revolution. That allowed Queen Viktoria to undertake a massive remodeling project on the west wing of the palace, including the installation of dumbwaiters in the guest rooms.

Guests of the palace were always dignitaries, and the Queen didn't want them to be forced to trek down the cold halls to the kitchen or wait for servants to bring up inevitably chilly food. (Even in the nineteenth century, we had a problem keeping the massive stone palace warm.)

All Kasper and I had to do was get down to the lower level beneath the west wing, which was separated from the dungeon under the east wing. That required a lot of moving quietly, hiding against walls, and dashing into broom closets and restrooms until guards passed by.

And it all had to be done very quickly. Right now, hardly anyone knew that we'd been arrested, let alone that we'd escaped, so our sneaking around was more of a precaution. But we were in no position to take chances.

Once we made it down to the west wing, I left Kasper to choose the appropriate dumbwaiter because he had more knowledge of the palace. As a Högdragen, he knew most of the ins and outs of the palace, since that had allowed him to better protect it.

Given the cozy relationship between Kennet and our King and Queen, we both surmised that he would most likely be staying in the finest room we had. That fortunately made finding the dumbwaiter a bit easier, because the nicest guest chamber was on the south corner of the palace, in a massive turret.

Once we made it up to the bedroom, I set about checking to see if it was Kennet's room. Thanks to the servants who made the beds and tidied up, it was nearly impossible to tell if the room had been used at all.

The heavy drapes were pulled back from the massive windows that ran along the rounded walls, leaving only sheer curtains to let light in, but I didn't know if that meant anything. Though it was a lush suite, I noticed absently that the French windows were in need of repair—the paint was chipping and the wood appeared warped.

Confirmation that we'd found the right room came from the

massive wardrobe across from the four-poster bed. When I opened it, I found a fur-lined parka and silver suits hanging up, including an all-too-familiar sharkskin one.

Kasper and I decided that our best course of action was to surprise Kennet, especially since we couldn't know if he had a guard or two in tow, so we hid in his bathroom. Kasper stood slightly behind me, leaning against the embossed wallpaper, with Elliot's sword still clutched in his hand.

We'd waited for what felt like eternity, but in reality, it couldn't have been more than ten minutes until the doors finally opened. I caught a glimpse of a shadow—someone moving in the room—but I couldn't tell who the person was, and if it was merely a maid instead of Kennet.

I leaned so close to the door that my nose brushed up against it, and finally he turned enough so I could see his face—it was Kennet. He took off his jacket and tossed it on the bed, and as far as I could tell he was alone. I decided to go for it.

The door didn't make a sound when I opened it, and Kennet stood in front of the window, pushing the voile curtains aside to get a better view of Doldastam.

While we'd been waiting, Kasper and I had decided it would be better if I took the lead with Kennet, since he and I had a bit of a history. But Kasper stayed only a step or two behind me with his sword drawn, so Kennet would know we meant business.

"Kennet," I said.

He whirled around, his eyes startled and wide, but within seconds, a smirk appeared on his face.

FORTY-FOUR

rivalry

Nothing can hold you back, can it?" Kennet asked.

"No thanks to you," I snapped.

"Bryn, that wasn't my idea," he reminded me. "You can't blame me for your Queen being overzealous."

"Yes, yes, I can. You did nothing to defend me."

"What should I have said? 'Yes, it's true what she says. It's all my fault. Lock me up and throw away the key'?"

"That would've been nice," I said dryly.

"Look, I didn't want you locked up, but I didn't exactly have a choice." Kennet held up his hands, trying to appear innocent. "You backed me into a corner."

I shook my head. "You're such a conniving weasel. I can't believe I ever found anything likable about you."

"Hey." He scowled. "I liked you too. And despite everything else that's going on now, I did have fun with you, and I'm sorry that things have gone the way they have."

"Everything you said was a lie," I hissed at him. "Your whole act was to keep me distracted so I wouldn't notice what was really going on with you."

"I'll admit, I was told to keep you occupied so you wouldn't get yourself into any trouble. But that doesn't mean I didn't enjoy my time with you." He tried to flirt with me, but it just felt forced and sleazy. "Some things can be both work *and* pleasure."

"You're so full of shit. You've only ever cared about yourself," I spat at him. "You've told me over and over that you love your brother, and look how you treated him."

His expression hardened. "I do love my brother."

"Spare me your lies, Kennet. We all know what you did."

"You know *nothing* about what I did!" he shouted. "Mikko hated being King. It made him miserable. He never should've been crowned in the first place. But he had to take the job, not because he was the most qualified, not because he was the best one in our family for the position, but simply because he was born first, and Father insisted that Mikko fulfill his obligations."

"So you have him imprisoned for life?" I asked mockingly. "That fixes everything?"

"Once this is all over and I'm officially King, I'll pardon him and set him free. He'll be fine, and he'll be happier in the end." Kennet tried to reason away his sins. "We both will."

"That doesn't change the fact that you tried to kill the woman he loves," I reminded him.

"Is that what Linnea told you?" Kennet rolled his eyes.

"That's some fairy tale fantasy she has. And that's all beside the point, since *I* never laid a hand on her."

"You hired the person who did," I countered.

He sighed. "You make it all sound so evil, but it wasn't. They told me that if I gave them sapphires, they'd help me dethrone my brother in a nonlethal way. Mikko has been so unhappy since he's been King, and I was honestly doing this for him as much as I was for me."

"If that's what you tell yourself, go ahead." I shrugged. "Maybe if you keep on going with that, your brother will pardon you after you confess."

He raised his eyebrows. "Confess? Why on earth would I do that?"

"Because this is over," I told him. "The Queen may be blinded by your lies, but as soon as King Evert hears about your involvement with Konstantin Black, he'll investigate and find out the truth. He's too paranoid to let it go, so you should make it easy on yourself and just admit what you know."

"Konstantin Black?" Kennet laughed. "I never even met the guy before you arrested him."

I shook my head in disbelief. "What are you talking about?"

"I never met him. I'd never even heard of him or this Viktor before you all started going on about them."

I narrowed my eyes. "Then who did you deal with?"

He tilted his head, a bemused smile on his lips. "You still don't get it, do you?"

"What are you talking about?"

"This is bigger than either of us." Kennet stepped closer to me, and from the corner of my eye, I saw Kasper raise his sword. "You think you can come in here and threaten me, and I'll just bow down and do as you say, but you've got *nothing* to threaten me with."

"I think you're grossly underestimating the situation," Kasper growled, and Kennet glanced over at him.

"You and your little sword are nothing compared to what would be done to me if I betrayed my allies," Kennet told him bitterly.

As soon as he said that, my mind flashed back to the dungeon on Storvatten, when Konstantin had still been in his prison cell and Bent Stum had been lying dead with his wrists slit. Konstantin insisted that Bent had been murdered to keep him from spilling the truth, and when I pushed him to tell me by whom, Konstantin told me nearly the exact same thing that Kennet just had.

Whomever they were both working for had them scared as hell.

"You killed Bent Stum," I realized. "So he wouldn't talk and ruin everything for you."

"I did what I had to do," Kennet admitted. "And I'll keep doing what I have to do."

His aquamarine eyes almost always seemed to sparkle, but now as he looked down at me, they seemed much more muted, almost glazed. The smile had gone from his face, replaced by a sad vacancy.

Then, without warning, he raised his arm and punched me in the face. It was so unexpected that I didn't have time to block it. And he was much stronger than I'd anticipated, especially for a Prince. I stumbled back, falling against the bed.

He'd hit me in my left eye, and the trauma to my head was enough to exacerbate my injury from Viktor. My eyesight blurred in both eyes. A white light replaced the vision in my right eye while my left eyelid began to puff up, closing off my sight.

For a few horrible seconds, I could only hear the sound of fighting going on around me—grunting, cursing, and then the clatter of the sword falling to the floor. I wanted to help Kasper, but I couldn't see, and I didn't want to blunder in blindly and make things worse. Kasper wouldn't use deadly force unless absolutely necessary (the sword was meant to be more of a threat) since we needed Kennet alive to clear our names.

Finally, the figures before me came into focus. They were rolling around on the floor, fighting over the sword. I started to move toward it, meaning to grab it, but Kennet got it first and rolled over onto his back, holding the sword pointed out in front of him as Kasper got to his feet.

"This game is done," Kennet said, standing slowly with his eyes and sword locked on Kasper. "You aren't going to let this go, which means that *I* can't let you go."

"It doesn't need to come to this," Kasper said, holding up his hands in a gesture of peace.

Kennet only smirked in reply, and in a moment of desperation, Kasper charged at him. I was sure he meant to get the sword away from Kennet again, but that wasn't what happened.

I was standing right behind Kasper, and I saw the sword come out his back—the sharp metal stained red as it poked out between his shoulder blades. The blood flowered out around it, darkening his white shirt.

Kennet's face paled, and he let go of the sword, allowing Kasper to stagger back. I rushed over, catching him just as he began to fall and lowering him to the floor, but I kept my arm around his shoulders, holding him up so the blade wouldn't move.

FORTY-FIVE

downfall

"It'll be okay," I said thickly, even though I didn't believe it.

Kasper stared at me, his dark eyes uncomprehending. He moved his mouth as if he meant to say something, but nothing came out. And then, as I held him in my arms, Kasper took his last breath and his body went lax.

"It had to be done," Kennet said in a low voice.

When I looked up at him, the only thing I felt was anger—a blinding rage I'd never experienced before. I knew I should try to control it, but just then, I didn't want to.

I jumped and charged at Kennet. He tried to block my attack, but I was faster than him and I hit him in the face, the stomach, the arms—anywhere I could reach. He stepped back, trying to avoid the blows, and he wasn't paying attention to his footing.

His fight with Kasper had left the rug rumpled, and he tripped on it and staggered back. I watched as he fell into the window. The glass didn't shatter, but the locks that held them shut were old, and under his weight the French windows swung open.

Kennet started falling backward, and while I was tempted to let him just fall, I needed him alive. I needed to know who he was working for and what was happening, so Kasper's death wouldn't be entirely in vain.

I ran forward, and I was nearly too late. I leaned out the window, almost throwing myself after him to grab his hand. I gripped it as tightly as I could, holding Kennet as he dangled over five stories above the ground.

"Pull me up!" Kennet yelled, his voice cracking in terror. "I'm sorry for what I did! Just pull me up and I'll do whatever you want!"

"Tell me who you're working for!" I demanded.

"Just pull me up and I'll tell you," he insisted, and his eyes were wild with fear.

The truth was that I was *trying* to pull him, but my grip on him wasn't good enough. I had to use one hand for balance, holding on to the windowsill so I wouldn't tumble out with him. Both of my hands had Kasper's blood on them, leaving them slick, and whenever I tried to lift Kennet, I felt him slipping away.

"Tell me first," I said, trying to pretend like this was my idea and I wasn't losing him.

"Bryn, *please!*" Kennet begged. "I'm sorry! Just help me!"

And I wanted to. As much as I hated Kennet, I wanted him to live so he could pay for what he'd done. But I couldn't hang on.

His hand slipped from my grasp, and he fell to the ground, screaming all the way until he hit the cobblestone courtyard below. I looked away so I didn't have to see the mess he'd become.

I turned back to the room, with the open windows letting in an icy wind behind me. Kasper lay on the floor. I didn't want to just leave him here like this, but I didn't know what I could do.

His eyes were still open, staring up at the ceiling, so I crouched down next to him and closed them gently.

"I'm sorry," I whispered around the lump in my throat.

Kennet had made a lot of noise as he fell, so it wouldn't be long before guards found their way up here to investigate what had happened.

I grabbed a chair and pushed it up against the door, propping it underneath the handle so they'd have a little more fight before they could get in. I went into the bathroom and washed the blood off my hands, trying not to think about where the blood had come from.

The Högdragen would be on the lookout for me, and one thing I'd learned from growing up in Doldastam was that my blond hair made me stand out like a sore thumb. I needed to cover up.

I ran over to the wardrobe and grabbed the parka, then I jumped back into the dumbwaiter and prepared to make my escape.

FORTY-SIX

exile

"Yes, sir. I understand. Of course, sir," Ridley was saying into his cell phone. "I will."

He stood in the living room, his back to me. He still wore the Överste uniform with the silver epaulets on the shoulder. When he hung up the phone, he ran a hand through his hair and let out a heavy sigh.

"Who was that?" I asked.

"Holy crap, Bryn!" Ridley turned around to face me, and his surprise was immediately replaced by relief as he rushed over to me. "What are you doing here?"

"Your back door was unlocked." I motioned to it behind me.

He pushed back the hood of the parka so he could see me more clearly, and he grimaced when he saw my eye, which had to be blackening by now. "Oh, Bryn."

"How bad is it?"

"I'm not sure if you're asking about your eye or the situation," he said. "But the situation is not good. I just got home from work, and the head of the Högdragen called to tell me that you'd been arrested for treason, escaped from prison, and then murdered Kasper Abbott and the Skojare Prince before going on the run again."

"It's not like that." I shook my head. "I never hurt Kasper, and I even told him he shouldn't come with me. Because Tilda—"

My voice caught in my throat as I realized what had just happened. Kasper had become my friend in his own right. He was good and capable, and he was dead. Not to mention what this loss would mean to Tilda. My best friend's husband of less than twenty-four hours and the father of her unborn baby had been killed.

But I couldn't let the full gravity of it hit me, because if I did I would just crumple up and sob.

"And the treason charge is bullshit. I would never do anything to damage this kingdom. I was trying to protect it. It was Kennet. He'd been supporting Konstantin, and I wanted to keep the King safe. And then everything happened so fast, and I got out of there as quick as I could. I took the dumbwaiter to the basement, and then I climbed up a garbage chute to the outside, and I had to sneak around town to get here as fast as I could. But I didn't do those things they say I did. I didn't."

"I know." Ridley put his hand on my face to calm me, since my voice had taken on a frantic pitch, and he looked me in the eyes. "I know you didn't do anything wrong. And you can explain it all to me later, but right now, we need to get you out of here before the Högdragen find you, because they won't believe you."

I nodded, because now everything was too far gone. I'd only been trying to make things right, but I didn't know how I could ever come back from this.

"Stay here," Ridley instructed me. "Lock the door behind me, and don't let anyone in." He started walking toward the door. "And hide, just to be safe."

"Where are you going?" I asked.

"I'm going to get you out of here," he said, like that explained anything, and then he left.

I did as I was told. I locked the doors and then went into his bedroom to hide. The shades were drawn, leaving it nearly dark even though it was still daylight. The afternoon sun was hidden behind an overcast sky, but the extra level of darkness was still comforting.

I leaned against the wall and slowly lowered myself to the floor. And I couldn't think. I tried to figure out my next course of action, but I couldn't. My mind felt numb and blank, and I couldn't process anything that had happened today. It felt like I'd slipped into a big white void that had swallowed me whole, and nothing was real anymore.

"Bryn?" Ridley's panicked voice was in the house, and I hadn't even heard him open the doors. Time no longer seemed to move in any coherent way, and I had no idea if he'd been gone for ten minutes or two hours.

"Bryn?" Ridley repeated, sounding more panicked this time, and he came into the bedroom. "What are you doing? Why didn't you answer me?"

"I don't know," I admitted.

He crouched next to me. "Are you okay?"

"I don't know," I said again. "But I will be."

His eyes searched me in the dark. I didn't know if he believed me or not, but we didn't have time to figure things out right now. "We have to get out of here," he said.

I got up and hurried after him, and that seemed to help. Moving reminded me that I was alive, and there were urgent things I needed to take care of if I wanted to stay that way.

Ridley had gotten an SUV from the King's fleet and parked it in the constricted alley behind his house. I pulled up my hood over my head, and he snuck me out the back door and loaded me into the back of the Land Rover. He covered me in a thick black blanket kept in the back for emergencies, and then he hopped in the driver's seat.

As he drove through town, he said nothing. Underneath the blanket, I couldn't see anything. I just listened to the sound of the car.

It didn't take long before I heard the SUV come to a stop and the window roll down.

"Where are you going?" a man barked, and by the tone of his question, I surmised it was one of the Högdragen guarding the gate.

"I have orders from the King," Ridley replied, sounding just as stern.

"That doesn't tell me where you're going," the Högdragen shot back.

"I am the Överste, Ridley Dresden."

By the sound of the rustling, I guessed that Ridley was pulling out his credentials to show the guard. It was a cross between a passport and an FBI badge, with all the specific information to prove exactly who he was.

"This still doesn't tell me what you're doing, sir," the Högdragen said, but with a bit more respect in his voice now. "Doldastam is on lockdown now."

"I know that," Ridley snapped. "But the King has sent me on a mission to follow up on a lead on Viktor Dålig. Do you want to stop the commander of the army from going after the man who tried to kill the King?"

"No, sir," the Högdragen replied. I heard the muffled sounds of him conversing with another guard but I couldn't understand what they were saying. Then, rather reluctantly, he said, "All right. Go on through."

The gates creaked open loudly, and the SUV started to move. At first, Ridley drove at a reasonable speed, but as soon as we were a safe enough distance away, he sped up, causing the vehicle to bounce around on the worn road.

I pushed the blanket off my head and sat up, looking around at the familiar trees that surrounded us. I wondered dimly if I'd ever see them again, but I had far more important things to worry about.

I climbed up over the seat into the front and sat down next to Ridley.

"How are you doing?" he asked.

"I've been better."

"I got passports and money from the safe." He motioned to a black duffel bag in the backseat.

"Thank you." I looked over at him, and I hoped he understood how much I truly appreciated what he'd done and risked to help me. Ridley reached over, taking my hand in his, and held it on the drive to the train station.

When we pulled into the parking lot, he turned off the car and got out. He grabbed the bag from the back, and I walked around the Land Rover. He took my hand again so we could walk together to the ticket booth, but I stopped.

"What?" Ridley looked back at me.

"You can't go with me. This is where we have to say goodbye."

He shook his head. "What are you talking about?"

"Kennet and Konstantin are just pawns. Somebody else is making the moves, and I need to find out who that it is and make sure they get some semblance of justice. I may never be able to prove my innocence, but I won't stand by and let everything I care about be destroyed."

"That's exactly why I should go with you," Ridley insisted.

"No. I shouldn't have let Kasper go with me, and I won't let you meet his fate," I said.

"Bryn—"

"And more than that," I cut him off, "my parents are still

in Doldastam. I don't know who is behind everything, and they could go after them in retaliation. I need you to go back and make sure they're safe.

"And Tilda," I went on. "She needs someone to help her now. And I need you to tell her that I didn't kill Kasper."

"Bryn, she knows that," he said.

"Tell her anyway, okay?" I persisted. "And tell her I'm sorry. I never meant for him to get hurt." I swallowed back the tears that threatened to form.

Ridley squeezed my hand. "Okay. I'll tell her, and I'll watch out for you parents and Tilda. I won't let anything happen to them while you're gone."

I kissed him then, knowing I might never see him again, that this might be the very last kiss we ever shared, and he set down the duffel bag so he could wrap his arms around me. For a moment, the world fell away around us, and it was only me and him and the way his lips tasted and his arms felt and how desperately I loved him.

He held my face in his hands and looked deep into my eyes. "When this is over, and your parents and Tilda are safe, I will come find you."

The train began to whistle as it pulled into the station, so we didn't have much time. I kissed him again, then grabbed the duffel bag and ran into the station.

FORTY-SEVEN

five days later

The cell phone sat on the counter, the black screen staring up at me, almost taunting me to use it. It'd been five days, and every day had been a battle of will not to call Ridley to find out what was going on.

I didn't know if he'd gotten caught for helping me escape, and I wanted to know how Tilda was doing and if my parents were safe. But the Högdragen were probably monitoring his phone, and even though I'd gotten an untraceable prepaid phone, that could still mean trouble for him.

So I didn't call.

"What are you having?" the waitress on the other side of the cracked vinyl counter asked me, interrupting my staring contest with the phone.

"Um . . ." A badly worn laminated menu sat on the counter next to my phone, and I quickly scanned it to see if anything appealed to me. Most things sounded as if they were cooked in a vat of grease, and my stomach rolled in disgust. That was the price of stopping in dive diners like this, but I didn't know how long I'd be on the run, and these places had the cheapest food—even if all the food was repulsive.

"Just an unsweetened iced tea," I decided.

"Coming right up." She smiled at me as she took the menu. Even though she had the weary expression of someone who was at the end of a ten-hour shift, there was sympathy in her eyes as she looked at me, so I knew I had to look as bad as I felt.

The metal side of the napkin holder worked as an okay mirror, so I tilted it toward me to get a better look. My attempt at dyeing my hair hadn't worked, failing the way it always did since my hair refused to hold any color. The black dye had faded into a sickly grayish-blue, and in another day or two it would be gone entirely.

The black eye Kennet had given me had finally begun to heal. The first few days it had been an awful puffy purple, and now it was fading to a putrid yellow. I tried to cover it up with makeup, but it was still obvious that there was something going on with my eye.

It didn't help that I wasn't sleeping, so there were bags under my eyes, and my skin had an unpleasant pallor. I hadn't been eating well either, since it was hard to find anything that sat well with me on the road. I'd made the mistake of grabbing turkey jerky in desperation last night and ended up throwing it up.

So far, my only plan was to get south and lay low for a little while until I felt like most of the heat was off. I knew Evert wouldn't want to spare many soldiers to go after me, but he would probably send a few. The Skojare would definitely send some of their guards, not that I thought they'd be able to do anything.

But since I was accused of killing a Prince, other Skojare allies might send troops to help find me, like the Trylle or maybe even the Vittra. They lived farther south than we did, which meant I'd have to go even farther to get out of their range until everyone got tired of looking and went home.

I didn't know where I was exactly, but the last sign I'd seen had been for Missouri. I hadn't decided if this was far enough, or if I should keep going. I didn't know where the end of this journey was for me.

The waitress brought back my tea, and I pushed away the napkin holder so I wouldn't have to look at myself anymore. I leaned forward, letting my hair fall over my face as if I could hide myself, and went back to my staring contest with the phone.

I heard the stool next to me creak as someone sat down, which annoyed me since the entire bar was empty. There were plenty of seats for them to sit in without crowding me.

"Need any company?" the guy next to me asked.

"No, I'm good," I said firmly, and tilted my stool away from him a bit.

"A girl alone like you, I really think you could use a friend," he persisted, and it didn't look like he'd get the hint without more force.

"Listen—" I turned to him, preparing to tell him off—but when I saw I was face-to-face with Konstantin Black, the argument died on my lips.

He looked exactly the way he had in the lysa—his hair longer than it had been before, the raven curls framing his face. From the scruff on his cheeks it had to have been a couple days since his last shave, and he wore all black. His smoky gray eyes studied me, and he offered me a hopeful smile.

"So, what do you say, white rabbit?" Konstantin asked. "Friends?"

GLOSSARY

Changeling A child secretly exchanged for another.

Doldastam The capital and largest city of the Kanin, located in northeastern Manitoba, Canada, near the Hudson Bay.

Förening The capital and largest city of the Trylle. A compound in the bluffs along the Mississippi River in Minnesota, United States, where the palace is located.

Hobgoblin An ugly, misshapen troll that stands no more than three feet tall, known only to the Vittra and Omte tribes. They are slow-witted but possess a supernatural strength.

Högdragen An elite guard that protects the Kanin kingdom. They must go through a specialized training process after tracker school, and many prospective guards are unable to complete it because of the difficult requirements in order to graduate. Members of the Högdragen are respected and revered throughout the kingdom, despite the fact that most are born lower class, because of their skill and their unparalleled ability to protect the royal families and the kingdom at large.

Host family The family a changeling is left with. They are chosen based on their ranking in human society, with their wealth being the primary consideration. The higher ranked the member of troll society, the more powerful and affluent the host family their changeling is left with.

Iskyla Small Kanin arctic community in northern Canada.

Kanin One of the more powerful tribes of trolls left. They are considered quiet and peaceful. They are known for their ability to blend in, and like chameleons their skin can change color to help them blend into their surroundings. Like the Trylle, they still practice changeling exchanges, but not nearly as frequently. Only one in ten of their offspring are left as changelings.

Lysa A telekinetic ability related to astral projection that allows one troll to psychically enter another troll's thoughts through a vision, usually a dream.

Mänsklig Often shortened to "mänks." The literal translation for the word "mänsklig" is human, but it has come to describe the human child that is taken when the Trylle offspring is left behind.

Markis A title of male royalty in troll society. Similar to a human duke, it's given to trolls with superior abilities. They have a higher ranking than the average troll, but are beneath the King and Queen. The hierarchy of troll society is as follows:

King/Queen
Prince/Princess
Markis/Marksinna
Högdragen
Troll citizens
Trackers
Humans

Marksinna A title of female royalty in troll society. The female equivalent of the Markis.

Omte Only slightly more populous than the Skojare, the Omte tribe of trolls are known to be rude and somewhat ill tempered. Unlike the other tribes, Omte tend to be less attractive in appearance, and along with the Vittra, they are the only tribes known to have hobgoblins in their population.

Ondarike The capital city of the Vittra. The King and the Queen, along with the majority of the powerful Vittra, live within the palace there. It is located in northern Colorado.

Överste In times of war, the Överste is the officer in charge of commanding the solders. The Överste does not decide any battle plans, but instead receives orders from the King or the Chancellor.

Persuasion A mild form of mind control. The ability to cause another person to act a certain way based on thoughts.

Psychokinesis Blanket term for the production or control of motion, especially in inanimate and remote objects, purportedly by the exercise of psychic powers. This can include mind control, precognition, telekinesis, biological healing, teleportation, and transmutation.

Rektor The Kanin in charge of trackers. The Rektor works with new recruits, helps with placement, and generally works to keep the trackers organized and functioning.

Skojare An aquatic tribe of trolls that is nearly extinct. They require large amounts of fresh water to survive, and one-third of their population possess gills so they are able to breathe underwater. Once plentiful, only about five thousand Skojare are left on the entire planet.

Storvatten The capital city and largest city of the Skojare, located in southern Ontario, Canada, on Lake Superior.

Tonåren In the Skojare society, a time when teenagers seek to explore the human world and escape the isolation of Storvatten. Most teens return home within a few weeks.

Tracker Members of troll society who are specifically trained to track down changelings and bring them home. Trackers have no paranormal abilities, other than an affinity with their particular changeling. They are able to sense danger to their charge and can determine the distance between themselves and their changeling. The lowest members of troll society, other than mänsklig.

Tralla horse A powerful draft horse, larger than a Shire horse or a Clydesdale, originating in Scandinavia and only known to be bred by the Kanin. They are usually used for show, such as in parades or during celebrations.

Trylle Beautiful trolls with powers of psychokinesis whose use of the practice of exchanging changelings is a cornerstone of their society. Like all trolls, they are ill tempered and cunning, and often selfish. Once plentiful, their numbers and abilities are fading, but they are still one of the largest tribes of trolls. They are considered peaceful.

Vittra A more violent faction of trolls whose powers lie in physical strength and longevity, although some mild psychokinesis is not unheard of. They also suffer from frequent infertility. While Vittra are generally beautiful in appearance, more than fifty percent of their offspring are born as hobgoblins. They are one of the only troll tribes to have hobgoblins in their population, along with the Omte.

Biâelse Family Tree

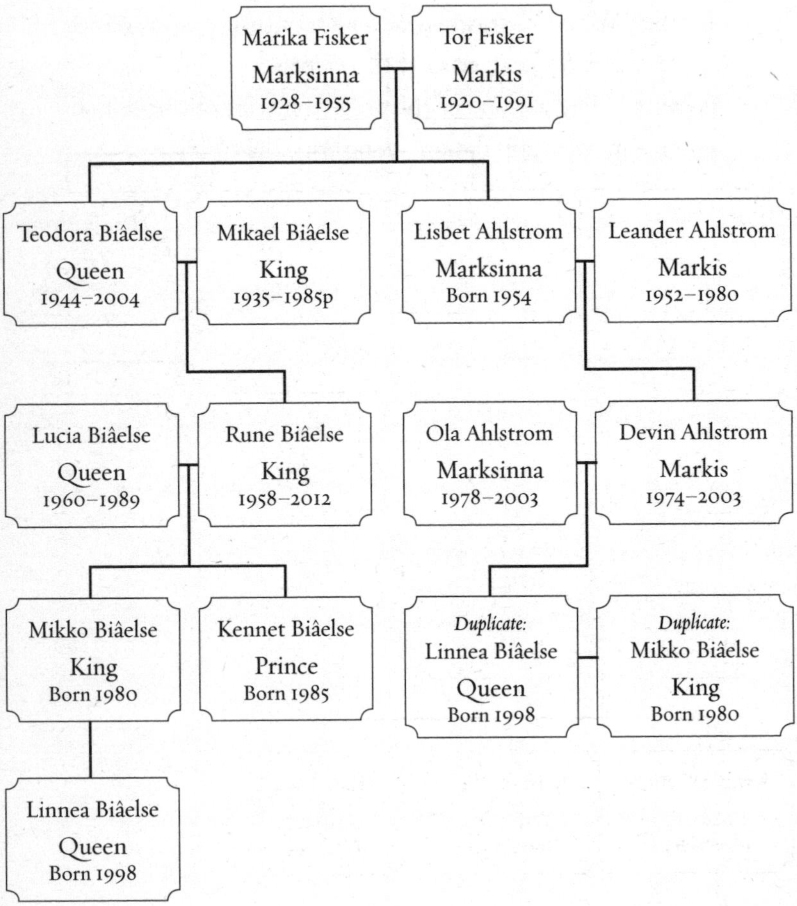
Marika Fisker
Marksinna
1928–1955
Tor Fisker
Markis
1920–1991
Teodora Biâelse
Queen
1944–2004
Mikael Biâelse
King
1935–1985p
Lisbet Ahlstrom
Marksinna
Born 1954
Leander Ahlstrom
Markis
1952–1980
Lucia Biâelse
Queen
1960–1989
Rune Biâelse
King
1958–2012
Ola Ahlstrom
Marksinna
1978–2003
Devin Ahlstrom
Markis
1974–2003
Mikko Biâelse
King
Born 1980
Kennet Biâelse
Prince
Born 1985
Duplicate:
Linnea Biâelse
Queen
Born 1998
Duplicate:
Mikko Biâelse
King
Born 1980
Linnea Biâelse
Queen
Born 1998

Strinne Family Tree

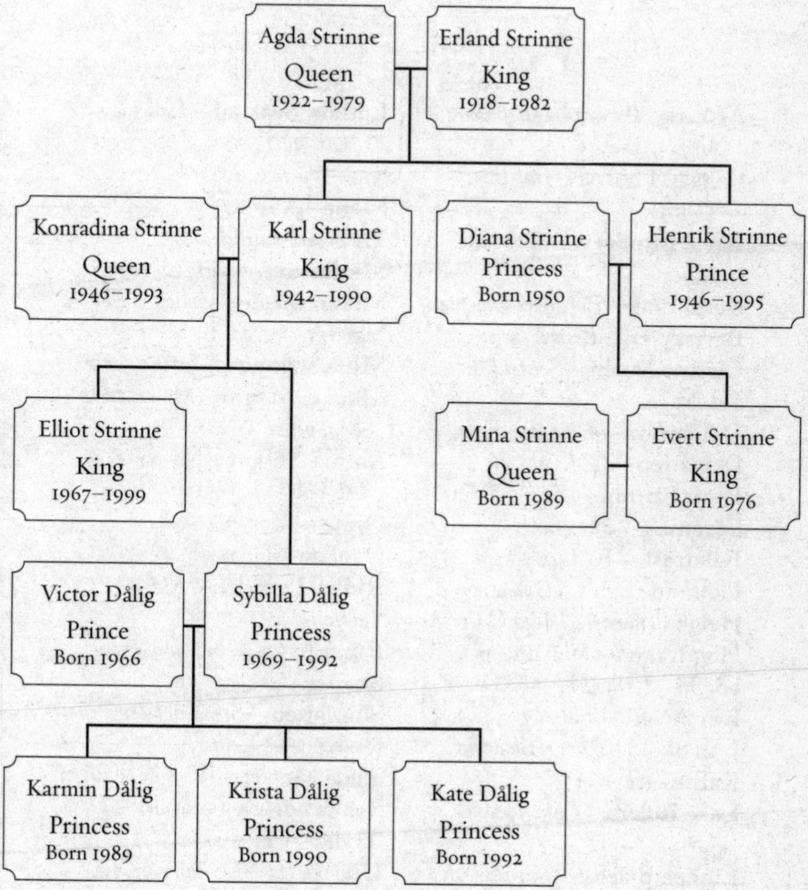
Agda Strinne
Queen
1922–1979
Erland Strinne
King
1918–1982
Konradina Strinne
Queen
1946–1993
Karl Strinne
King
1942–1990
Diana Strinne
Princess
Born 1950
Henrik Strinne
Prince
1946–1995
Elliot Strinne
King
1967–1999
Mina Strinne
Queen
Born 1989
Evert Strinne
King
Born 1976
Victor Dålig
Prince
Born 1966
Sybilla Dålig
Princess
1969–1992
Karmin Dålig
Princess
Born 1989
Krista Dålig
Princess
Born 1990
Kate Dålig
Princess
Born 1992

PRONUNCIATION GUIDE

Älskade Abbott—*Al-skah-duh Ab-bot*
Baltsar Thorne—*Bal-tsar Thorn*
Bayle Lundeen—*Bail Lun-deen*
Bodil Elak—*Boh-deel Eee-luck*
Bryn Aven—*Brin A-ven*
Cyrano Moen—*Sear-uh-no Moe-en*
Doldastam—*Dole-dah-stam*
Eldvatten—*Elld-vah-ten*
Evert Strinne—*Ever-t Strin*
Förening—*Fure-ning*
Fulaträsk—*Fool-uh-trassk*
Gotland rabbit—*Got-land*
Helge Otäck—*Hel-ga Oo-tech*
Högdragen—*Hug-dragon*
Iskyla—*Iss-key-la*
Iver Aven—*Iv-er A-ven*
Juni Sköld—*Joon-y Sh-weld*
Kanin—*cannon*
Lake Isolera—*Lake Ice-oh-lar-uh*
Linnea Biâelse—*Lin-nay-uh Bee–yellsa*
Lisbet Ahlstrom—*Liz-bet All-strum*
Ludlow Svartalf—*Lud-loe Svare-toff*
lysa—*lie-sa*
Måne—*Moe-nay*
Markis—*marquee*
Marksinna—*mark-iss-eena*
Mikko Biâelse—*Mick-o Bee–yellsa*
Mina Strinne—*Mee-na Strin*
Modi & Magni—*Mow-dee & Mahg-nee*
Naima Abbott—*Na-eema Ab-bot*
Omte—*oo-m-tuh*
Överste—*Ur-ve-sh-ter*
Ridley Dresden—*Rid-lee Drez-den*
Runa Aven—*Rue-na A-ven*
Skojare—*sko-yar-uh*
Storvatten—*Store-vot-en*
tonåren—*toe-no-ren*
Tilda Moller—*Till-duh Maul-er*
Tralla horse—*trahl-uh*
Trylle—*trill*
Ulla Tulin—*Oo-lah Two-lin*
Viktor Dålig—*Victor Dough-leg*
Vita—*Vee-tah*
Vittra—*vit-rah*